STONES OF THE SEVEN BOOK 2

DANCE OF DRAGONS

ALLISON ROOK

ACKNOWLEDGMENT

Without a reliable group of brutally honest readers, a book will never live up to its potential. I'm so fortunate to have the best writing friends in the business. Thanks to Nik Everhart, Sam Howard, and Jenni Cornell for invaluable advice, and to the whole Hot Tub Dinosaurs team for supporting this project. Huge thanks to my editor Sara Coombes and my for-matter Kari Holloway, and to the art and design team at Mi-blArt. And as always, thanks to Andrew for all the hours he's wifeless while I escape into magical worlds.

Finally, thanks to you, dear readers, for choosing this book. Let's all keep pushing for the triumph of love in the world.

Find me at AllisonRookRomance.com!

If you enjoyed Dance of Dragons, don't miss Crystal of Memory, Book Three of Stones of the Seven.

CHAPTER 1

The Dragonsworn raided at dusk. Winged beasts cast long, terrifying shadows from the setting sun over the low foothills where Godseye Clan's sheep browsed on the first spring shrubs.

Eryn Drysel, the clan's lore keeper, looked up from the root she was gathering and shouted to her brother's wife.

"Nora, run! Take Filina and go!"

Both women dropped their half-empty baskets. Eryn shoved her five-year-old niece into her mother's arms as the screaming began from the clan's tents down on the plain.

"Go!" she repeated. "I'm right behind you!"

They should have been safe this close to the Forbidden Mountains. Dragon Clan never raided this far north, so close to the domain of the wild dragons. But Eryn picked out at least four bonded dragons descending from the western sky, obedient to their human masters who rode fast horses at the front of the raiding party.

Godseye's hunters had left in the early morning. When they returned, they would find a massacre where their nomadic village had been. Old men, sheepherders, women, and children were no match for the Dragonsworn's clan. Even Godseye's strongest hunters would have fallen to the venomous jaws of the swooping monsters that were landing in the midst of the tents, collapsing the fabric with furious beats of their huge wings.

Eryn stood transfixed, watching the carnage below. The Dragonsworn rode in screaming a war cry, swords cutting down the fleeing people. They would take everything of value, murder as many as they chose, take some away in chains, and leave the wretched survivors to rebuild with the scraps they left behind.

"Eryn, come on!"

Nora's voice cut through her fugue.

Run. Hide.

The last of winter's snow still clung to the shady hillside as they scrambled upward, searching for somewhere to secret themselves. Eryn's sheepskin boots slipped on loose rocks, her woolen cloak flapping behind her as she followed Nora and Filina, no longer daring to look back. Her heart pounded in her ears, breath coming in ragged gasps. The scrubby bushes offered nowhere to hide. If the dragonsworn searched these hills, they would be found and killed; or worse.

The hill became steeper, dropping off to Eryn's right in a sheer, rocky cliff down to a distant creek below. Up ahead, she glimpsed a shadow in the rocks. A cave entrance? Or at least enough of an overhang to protect them from the dragon eyes that flew above them?

Eryn risked a glance back.

No dragons were searching the hills yet. They all appeared to have landed and were fighting beside their masters.

Killing my people. Taking our livelihoods.

Bile burned her throat. Hatred for the dragons and the cruel men who controlled them seared through her chest, heaving under her thick, beaded tunic. She turned back up the hill to see Nora and Filina far ahead of her. They had almost made it to the shadowed overhang.

Beneath Eryn's foot, the slippery shale gave way. She choked back a scream, grasping at thorny bushes, just showing the first buds of spring. The thorns tore off in her grasp and she pitched down the steep ravine, tumbling and sliding off the edge of the hillside.

Sharp rocks slowed her fall, cutting her skin as she slid between them but offering no purchase. She rolled like a pebble in a creek, down and down, finally sliding to a halt in the shadow of the hillside.

For long moments, she lay there on the stony ground, lungs empty, eyes squinted shut against the pain.

Breathe. Breathe. You can breathe.

Every intake of air was agony, ribs screaming as she struggled not to cry out. She opened her eyes, blinking sandy gravel from her lids. With torn, bleeding hands she touched her face, feeling down her neck and arms. No bones protruded from her scratched and battered skin. Everything hurt, but Baltenn had smiled upon her. She was alive. And though she could clearly hear the Dragonsworn rampaging through her clan from just around the edge of the cliff she'd tumbled down, she couldn't see them. So they couldn't see her.

Get up. Hide.

Only the faintest glow from the setting sun reached this ravine. In the dim purple light, she rolled onto her belly, grunting in pain. *Left knee. Right knee. Push up.* She struggled to all fours and rocked upright, kneeling on the hard ground. Just ahead of her, the little creek gurgled with sweet, clean water. She and Nora had filled their water jugs from this very creek that morning, waving farewell and good hunting to Eryn's brother, who had taken Nora as his wife and made them sisters. Nora had smiled at her man, happy as always that she'd been wed to a kind hunter who was good to her and cared about their daughter.

Stand. Move before they come searching.

They might not come. It had been a hard winter, winds sweeping along the plains, driving Eryn's people to these hills where they pitched their shelters and burned the scrub trees against the bitter snow. The dragonsworn would not find much food to pillage, but they would slaughter enough sheep for a feast and drink until morning. By the time Godseye's hunters returned, Dragon Clan would be gone, returned to the rest of their hated people with everything they could carry. If Eryn could evade them tonight, she would be safe. She could help her people rebuild with whatever was left.

She wobbled to her feet, head aching and ribs burning. Pain flared in her right ankle, but it held her weight. Blood flowed from a thousand cuts on her arms and hands. *Follow the creek away from the village and find somewhere to curl up out of sight.*

Three shuffling steps were halted by a blast of hot air from behind her.

Eryn froze.

The smell of blood and acid blew past her again in a warm whoosh that made her loose golden hair flutter around her battered face.

She slowly turned.

A dragon reared up behind her, black as midnight. Great obsidian wings fanned the air, and sapphire eyes bored into her gaze, paralyzing her feet in the rocky dirt.

Run.

Every instinct shrieked for her to flee, but the dragon's stare was hypnotic. Her feet tangled as she tried to turn, and she collapsed to her knees onto the rocks, eyes still locked with the dragon's.

Venom dripped from the beast's open jaws, acid poison splattering onto Eryn's bare arm. It burned like a brand into her cut skin, and she inhaled a shuddering moan, unable to even scream for the pain.

Every nerve fired in her body. Every muscle tensed.

A shouted voice reached her ears, but the words meant nothing. Above her, the dragon lowered onto its front legs, the great black wings folding over its long back.

Dear Lord Baltenn, let it eat me quickly, Eryn prayed, unable to move beyond the shivering trembles that grew in her limbs with every second.

In a single venomous breath, the dragon turned away. With a thunderclap, its wings spread and it launched into the sky.

Eryn flopped sideways onto the ground, and the darkening night went black.

CHAPTER 2

Dane Rowe looked up from the feasting, the hot grease from roasted lamb moistening his lips. Into his mind came a sharp pull of images and feelings.

Need. Come. A scent reached Dane's brain, not through his own nostrils, but through the powerful sense of Ilst, his blood-bonded dragon. *Human female. Blood. Danger.*

Most of his communication with Ilst came as images and feelings, not words. But in the year and three seasons since Ilst had hatched and bonded to him, he'd become as familiar with her senses as with his own. As she matured, she was learning to put actual words into his head. Someday they would speak in complete sentences, unheard by anyone else. But for now, it was mostly single words punctuated with smells and emotions.

She was out in the darkness somewhere, beyond the glow of the celebratory fires where the Dragon Clan enjoyed the spoils of their easy victory. The thought came again. *Need.* And the smell of blood.

Dane sighed and wiped his mouth on the back of his sleeve. He and twenty of his fellow warriors had swept through the village at sunset. They had earned this feast. Clan Chief Krunnan had curtailed the killings and pillage at a reasonable level. He never let the more bloodthirsty of his warriors slaughter an entire village. *If we kill them all, they can't re-

build. Then who will we kill next year? The old man said it with a bellowing laugh, and Dane saw the wisdom in the practice. Tonight they feasted on lamb, mutton, and root stew, grudgingly prepared by the Dragon Clan's warrior women. When the surviving villagers crept out of hiding and returned to the remains of their tents, they would find enough of their flocks and possessions to ensure their survival.

"Hatchling, enjoying the feast?"

Dane bristled at the nickname. In his twenty-four summers, he'd become as strong as any clansman, as broad of chest and powerful in battle. But he'd only had Ilst for a year. To the older dragonsworn, he was barely worth his place at the fire.

He nodded at Brinir. The bearded giant was only a few summers older than Dane, but his leather armor was splashed with blood from the villagers he'd cut down that evening. The clan chief's rules were needed, or men like Brinir would kill every man and child that fled these tents. And the women would wish they'd died with their men.

Need. Now.

It was no use ignoring Ilst. When she got her talons into something, she never, ever let it go. She was always there in his mind, as he was in hers, but if she wanted his attention, the cream-colored dragon would stomp all over his thoughts until she got her way.

He stood up, unfolding from the thick blanket he was sitting on. The warmth of the fire fell away as he strode into the darkness, following the pull of his dragon's call. He chewed the last of the lamb meat from the shank as he walked, dropping the bone onto the scrubby grass. His eyes adjusted to the dark night, only a sliver of moon illuminating the low hills.

Cold wind buffeted his cheeks, and he pulled up the hood of his cloak. The chill in his spine came not only from the night air, but from the danger of their position. While nothing on the ground could threaten Dragon Clan, they were too close to the Forbidden Mountains. A blood-bonded dragon was soul mate to its warrior. Wild dragons hated both warrior and dragon alike. Dragon Clan counted on the winds to keep them safe, blowing from the north all winter and through the first of spring. The wild dragons in the north would not smell them here, too close to the edge of their domain. When the winds changed, no bonded dragon would be safe here, except for the week of the sacrifice. It was a knife's edge they danced every year.

Lost in thought, Dane splashed a foot into a shallow creek, still half-choked with ice. He jumped back before the chilly water could soak through his boots. Kneeling at the edge, he paused to plunge his hands into the icy flow, splashing his face to wash away the stickiness of the feast.

Now.

Dane chuckled. *What's so important out here?* Ilst could feel his thoughts, still more images than words—same as he felt hers, so when he had something important to say, he usually spoke aloud. Out here, in enemy territory, he kept silent. The hunters of the little tent village they'd pillaged could return at any time. They would never dare attack while the clan was in residence. But one warrior alone might prove too tempting a target. They would never know until it was too late that a dragonsworn warrior was never alone.

The creek led up a small rise, and into a steep-sided ravine. Thin moonlight barely lit the rough, rocky ground, and Dane chose each step carefully. Rounding a curve, he smiled as a pale shape reflected the starlight.

Ilst.

Even after a year as her bonded warrior, the sight of her still took his breath. Her smooth-scaled body was the color of warmed cream, darkening to bark-brown on her face, legs, tail, spikes, and wingtips. Full grown, she stood as tall at the shoulder as Dane's height, the length of four horses from her nose to the tip of her long, muscular tail, with a wingspan almost as wide as the clan chief's tent. Her wings were folded over her back now, long neck bent over something on the ground that had her full attention.

"What is it, beloved?"

A thrill of pleasure poured off Ilst at the term of endearment. Dane would never call her such a thing in the hearing of the other warriors. Brinir would never let him rest if he heard "the hatchling" speak such to his dragon. Brinir's own beast was a foul thing, clay red with a blocky head that shared his master's cruel carelessness. Nothing like the glory of elegant Ilst.

Dane peered around his dragon.

A woman lay on the ground, still as death.

"She's gone, Ilst," Dane said. "You can eat her if you want." As if she needed his permission.

Impatience and irritation from Ilst, and the distinct feeling that Dane was an idiot.

"What, you're not hungry? Eat too many skinny winter sheep?"

Ilst nudged the woman with her nose.

Still soft, Dane noted. Not stiff yet.

The woman was scratched and battered. Her arms, ghost-white in the moonlight, had deep cuts crusted with blood. Golden hair had pulled loose from its braid and framed her face where she lay on the rocks. Sweet Lord Baltenn, she was beautiful. What a shame.

Dane knelt next to her and pushed down the cowl of her cloak to reveal her throat. Her skin was cold as the rocks she lay on, but as he held his fingers to her neck, he realized Ilst was right. She was alive. But if he left her here, she'd be frozen to death by morning, no matter what damage she had sustained.

He gathered her into his arms and followed Ilst out of the little canyon. The woman barely stirred, but a tiny moan escaped her lips. He carried her carefully, mindful that her injuries might yet prove fatal.

When he reached the light of the fires, the other warriors were already fighting over the spoils.

Eight bound captives knelt at sword point near the fire. All were women, and all but one were already claimed. Dane hung back, holding the unconscious woman in his arms.

"This one's mine," Brinir roared at Tornnen, facing off against the short, wide dragonsworn warrior. The woman between them cowered.

"You already have three eindon back at camp," Tornnen growled. "I'm taking this one. You can have her when I'm finished."

Brinir barked a laugh. "She won't be good for anything when you're finished. I claimed her, and I'll have her."

The other seven women already wore neck chains with the rune of their owner stamped on a flat bronze runelock disk that hung from the iron links. This last woman was not yet chained, but both Brinir and Tornnen had disks to spare, prizes won for prowess in battle and in tournaments. Dane's own belt pouch held an unused runelock, but he'd missed the claiming of eindon from this raid. Just like every other raid since he'd become a warrior and earned the right. No woman or girl had ever seemed worth the responsibility of taking as his property. No dragonsworn warrior lacked for willing company among the clan's women. He didn't need to own a female to enjoy a woman's touch.

In minutes, the fight was over. Brinir jerked the woman to her feet and attached the bronze disk with his rune on it to a chain he clamped around her neck, then shoved her back to the ground. Tornnen grumbled, wiping blood from his swollen nose.

Another break might only make him less ugly. The thought was Dane's, but he felt Ilst's humor in his mind.

"What have you got, Hatchling? A dead woman?" Brinir roared laughter. "That seems just about your speed." He looked around the fire. "Who's got iron links for Dane's corpse eindon?"

Dane ignored him and laid the woman near the fire. In the flickering light, she was stunning, even scratched and swollen as she was. Her eyelids fluttered.

"Let's see what you got there." Brinir towered over them. "Quite a beauty, your dead girl," he said. "Sure you don't want to claim her? Warm her up by the fire and have her before she gets too stiff for you to spread her legs?" Again, he belched a huge guffaw at his own joke.

Dane bent over the girl, hiding her face from Brinir. In his shadow, her lips twitched.

"I'll claim her," Dane said. "Bring me the iron."

All the warriors, dragonsworn and horsemen alike, laughed at his joke.

Someone tossed him a short chain of heavy links. He made a show of wrapping them around her neck and pulling a bronze disk from his pouch. The laughter grew as he joined the iron chain in his fingers. Once sealed with the runelock, an eindon was the property of their owner until they died or were released. In all his life, Dane had only seen a handful released. Their lives were short, brutal, and full of misery at the hands of their owners. They were always either strong young men who were worked to death, or comely women who had to be guarded lest they take their own lives to escape their torment.

"He's really going to do it!" Tornnen shoved Brinir out of the way. "Dane, why are you wasting a disk on a corpse?"

With a twist of bronze in his fingers, Dane joined the ends of the iron chain around the woman's neck.

She gasped and sat bolt upright, huge blue eyes blinking in the firelight.

"Baltenn's balls, she's not dead," Brinir muttered.

Dane smiled at the woman. She looked at him, hands raising to touch the chain around her neck.

With a moaning grunt, she punched Dane straight in the face.

CHAPTER 3

Eryn crouched at the edge of the tent. Until tonight, it had belonged to one of her brother's friends, a hard man who had three wives and was eyeing Eryn as a fourth until she pledged herself as Godseye Clan's caldera, keeper of lore and wisdom. She would rather live alone and chaste than be claimed as bride, no better than a prize sheep, used for breeding and service to the "rams." Men like her brother, kind to their wives and children, were rare. Her heart gave a squeeze within her painful ribs. *Nora. Filina.* She offered a silent prayer to Baltenn that her sister-in-law and niece had escaped the massacre.

"Here, my eindon, you must be hungry."

Across the fire, the man stood, face veiled by smoke.

Eryn's fingers traced the iron links around her neck, and the rune-stamped bronze that clasped the chain. *Eindon.* That's what she was now. No more the esteemed student of Godseye's lore. Eindon was an ancient word from a long-lost language, but on the dragon raiders' lips, it sounded wholly appropriate. It meant, "owned." Owned. The man across the fire had claimed her as a spoil of war. She belonged to him now until he released her, or she died.

And it was hardly a war. They came when Godseye's hunters were away from their camp. Those men would return to destruction, huddled survivors, decimated flocks. The meat held out by the man—her owner now—was surely from her clan's sheep, already weak from a hard winter.

The man stepped around the fire. Golden light illuminated his face from below. Wide, clean-shaven jaw. Deep set blue eyes under a mane of unruly blonde hair, darker than Eryn's own. He had taken off his fur overcloak to reveal a dark brown shirt open at the neck. Unbidden, her eyes trailed down his body. Broad shoulders and thick arms. Narrow waist, and strong legs in dark leather pants and tall black boots. When she returned her gaze to his face, he was staring into her eyes, unblinking in the smoky tent.

He held out the meat again. "You're injured, and you have to eat to heal. Our herbwoman is far away in our camp, so you have to be strong until we get to her."

Eryn had resolved not to speak to her captor, but the words blurted out of her.

"I am my clan's caldera. If you haven't destroyed all my herbs and seeds when you killed my people, I don't need your barbarian herbwoman."

The words were agony, each breath a shooting pain from the left side of her ribcage. Her ribs were broken, or at least badly bruised for certain, but she noticed that her bloody hands had been cleaned. The wounds still burned like acid, and her head was full of the scent of wet fur—not an actual smell, but a memory—a dream. A nightmare. She glanced around the tent again. Her life would be a nightmare from here on.

Despite her resolve, her stomach betrayed her, growling at the scent of meat. The barbarian man was holding out the cooked mutton with his fingers, shining with grease.

Don't take it. He's feeding you like a pet.

She could starve herself until she was too weak to move. Waste away and die. But Eryn didn't want to die. Not here. Not in chains. She would escape, or die with a sword in her ribs, thrust from behind as she ran from captivity. And for that, she had to be stronger. The Dragon Clan was a bunch of ignorant barbarians. Eryn was caldera-in-training. She would outwit this oaf and find her freedom, no matter what it took.

She snatched the meat from his hands, their fingers brushing as she pulled the hot, oily bites from his grip. Moving sent a shock of pain down her ribcage and she winced again, shoving the mutton into her mouth.

"Be careful," he said, squatting in front of her. "You're hurt. Move slowly until you heal."

The fire was at his side now, illuminating his deep blue eyes. He looked honestly concerned.

The way you'd worry if one of your lambs was injured. Eventually you'd eat that lamb anyway.

"I'm fine," she muttered around the last bite of meat.

He pulled an oil-treated skin from his belt and offered her a drink.

She grudgingly accepted, but instead of the bitter beer she expected, got a sip of clear, fresh water. It cooled her burning throat, washing away the last of the nightmare that clouded her mind.

The walls of the tent felt suddenly close as the man crouched in front of her. He smelled of leather and sweat, and another scent that rocked her back for a moment, zapping into her brain like a lightning strike on a mountaintop.

Dragon.

"There was a dragon," she began, stopping when a stupid, childish grin lit his features.

"Ilst," he replied, with a look in his eyes of a cool breeze in the summer. "She's my dragon. I'm her dragonsworn warrior. She's the most beautiful dragon that was ever hatched. You're going to love her so much."

She remembered the great obsidian beast, iridescent in the starlight, looming over her at the bottom of the gorge. Eryn was no expert on dragons, but it shocked her to hear that the black monster was female. She would have sworn it was male.

"She's pale, like dark cream," the barbarian man was saying, lost in his own mind, eyes looking right through Eryn. "But her nose and her ears, and all four feet taper to dark brown. The edges of her wings are the color of mahogany bark." He refocused on Eryn's face. "Her wings are almost the color of your hair, gold in the firelight. Most females are just brown, but she's special. And she found you. She's the smartest of all the dragons, and she saved your life."

He spoke like a child on their name-day party, as if a dragon were a new toy or sweet.

Or like a lover in the first throes of infatuation. Before it turned to obsession, possession.

But his words sunk in, and she shook her head. The dragon she remembered was black, reflecting dim rainbows off his scales under the moon.

You dreamed it. You rolled down the hill and hit your head, and dreamed of a dragon because dragons were killing your people. Of course it was true. She wouldn't be alive if the black dragon had been real.

"Why?" The word slipped out before she could stop it.

"Why what?" The barbarian man was still smiling, still obviously dreaming of his filthy, murderous dragon.

"Why did your dragon save my life?"

The man sat back on his heels, wrapping the waterskin's spout with cord and tying it to his belt. "I have no idea. She called to me out in the wasteland, and I found her standing over you. I thought you were dead, but when I picked you up, I realized you were just badly injured. When I carried you back, all the other warriors thought you were dead as well. They thought I was crazy for claiming a dead body." He gestured to the rune locked around her neck. "But then you woke up, and…" he trailed off, hand rising to his nose.

Eryn saw a tiny spot of dried blood just under his left nostril.

"I woke up and punched you in the face," she finished for him.

"Yes. Why did you do that?"

Ignorant barbarian. Could he honestly be this stupid? Because you raided my village. Because you slaughtered our flocks, killed our people, destroyed our homes. Because your beloved ugly dragon beat tents to the ground with her wings and joined the rest of her disgusting kind in eating my clanspeople.

She said none of that. Eventually he seemed to sort it out.

"We are Dragon Clan." He lifted his chin when he said it. "It's right that we take what we want from the lesser clans. Only we know the secret of Baltenn, how to claim a dragon egg and make the bond that makes us who we are. Only the strongest warriors survive the test. You're eindon, but you're mine. You belong to a dragonsworn warrior, part of the greatest clan in all of Den Woth. It was the luckiest day of your life when Ilst found you. Your children will be Dragon Clan, and our sons will be dragonsworn like me."

Eryn's mouth hung open, eyes locked with the fervent barbarian. *He honestly believes that. He thinks I'm lucky to be a slave to a clan of ignorant killers. He thinks I should be thrilled that my children—*her thoughts slammed to a halt. *Our children. Our sons.* The man had no question that Eryn would bear his children. *Because I'm his property. His breeding stock.* The very thing she'd sworn to avoid, pledging her life to serve her clan as caldera, to eschew the company of men and the gift of children. She'd never regretted that decision, pledged on a cold night when a man lay dead at her feet four winters earlier.

And now I'm exactly what I would have been. Property of a man. A place for him to plant his seed. An ewe to carry his lambs. And I'm supposed to be overjoyed.

He interrupted her train of thought.

"I don't even know what your name is."

She narrowed her eyes. "Does it matter? Do eindon have names? Does a broodmare need a name?"

He stood up, head brushing the top of the soot-stained tent. "Of course eindon have names." There was another pile of furs on the far side of the fire, and he plopped down onto the pile, grinning at Eryn. "Dragons have names, and we name all our horses. Doesn't your former clan name their horses?"

Sweet Baltenn. He's as thick as a ram's horn. "Some of my murdered clanspeople named their horses."

He ignored the barb, sitting up straight on the pile of furs. "I am Dane Rowe, son of Calnan Rowe, sworn to dragon Ilst. You are my eindon. You are mine, and all you do is done in my name. You wear my rune as a sign of my possession, and my responsibility."

Possession. She knew the word well.

This is your life now. Keep the ignorant barbarian happy.

"My name is Eryn." She didn't give her father's name, the surname she shared with her sister-in-law, Nora, and her niece, Filina. When her brother returned from the hunt, she prayed he might find them hiding in the hills.

"Eryn," the barbarian said. *Dane. His name is Dane.* "Well, Eryn, you should sleep a few hours. We ride out before sunrise." He stretched out on the furs and closed his eyes.

She could kill him where he lay. Wait for him to fall asleep and slit his throat. The fool hadn't even taken her knife, tucked into her belt. In the dark of night, she could try to slip away into the mountains and hide until the wretched dragon men rode away in the morning.

She slipped the knife from her belt and pushed up to her knees, wincing at the flare of pain from her ribs. Silently she shuffled forward, pulling her left foot under her. A jolt of agony shot up her right leg when she tried to steady it beneath her, and she fell back onto her bedding, choking back a cry.

Her ankle was swollen nearly twice its size, already turning dark. Gritting her teeth, she wiggled the toes and moved her foot up and down, just a few inches. Hot pain coursed through her, but nothing ground or clicked. A bad sprain, not a break. She hoped.

With a whimper and a grunt, she settled back on the fur. This barbarian man, Dane Rowe, would live through the night. No running to the hills for her until this ankle healed. She tore strips of cloth from the blanket at her feet and bound her ankle tightly so it wouldn't swell any further. A few weeks, maybe.

And then she would kill this killer, and escape.

CHAPTER 4

The fire had burned down to embers when Dane awoke. From outside the tent came the sounds of his clan stirring, and in his head Ilst's prodding urged him to stretch and sit up.

Sky pink. Go.

Warmth suffused Dane's chest. Those were some of the clearest words Ilst had ever spoken into his head. Their bond grew stronger every day, and his pride in her swelled. The woman, his first eindon, hadn't looked suitably impressed when he'd told her how lucky she was to be part of Dragon Clan last night. "But she hasn't seen you in daylight," he murmured, knowing Ilst would feel his words through their bond. "She'll understand."

Eryn. She was already sitting up across the fire circle, checking a bandage around her right ankle.

"Oh, is it broken?" Dane jumped to his feet and hurried over to her. *You didn't notice. Didn't check her for wounds beyond her cut up arms and hands.* He chastised himself. She was his responsibility now. Everything she said or did would carry his name, and the name of Ilst as well. "Can you walk?"

She glared at him. "Does it matter?"

Her hostility set him back. Didn't she understand? He'd rescued her from death, and more than that, from a long, soul-crushing life as part of a lesser clan. Whatever man would have claimed her from her own clan would never be dragonsworn. Her children would never have known the wind of flight through a dragon's bond, looking up at her from below as her shadow passed over him, protecting his people and their herds from above. Surely every woman from every lesser clan dreamed of joining Dragon Clan.

And Dane would treat her kindly. With a start, he realized what she must fear.

"I'm not like some of my clan," he blurted out. "I won't beat you or hurt you. I'm a good man."

Her eyes stared a thousand swords into his soul.

"Yes, I can tell from my people's blood on your cloak that you're a prize."

With a start, Dane looked down to where his cloak lay on the woven rugs that made the tent's floor. Was it bloody? The thick fur wasn't clean, necessarily, but it wasn't soaked in blood. *And that's not the point, is it?*

"We only kill those who fight back," he muttered, but Eryn had already turned away.

He watched her pulling on the cloak she'd been wearing when he found her, covering up the long, loose pants and beaded tunic that were wrinkled and filthy.

Dane's weapons lay where he'd left them, and out of the corner of his eye, he saw Eryn watching him belt on the scabbard and knives. Ilst's voice murmured in his head. *Woman angry. Danger.*

"She's no danger."

Eryn eyed him, sitting on her bedding, cloak wrapped around her shoulders. "Who's no danger?"

"Ilst says you're dangerous. Angry and dangerous."

She wrinkled her nose, and Dane's stomach flipped. With the dim light of pre-dawn coming through the smoke hole in the tent's roof, she was even more stunning than under the starlight.

"Dragons can't talk."

He grinned. "Dragons can't make words you hear out loud," he agreed. "But Ilst and I are bloodbound. She talks right into my mind, and only I can hear her."

She didn't look impressed. "Right." She opened her mouth to say more, but a horn sounded through the camp.

"Time to saddle up. It's a long way home."

Dane pulled the resisting woman to her feet, hearing the clink of the chain around her neck. His rune shone in the glow of the embers, and a flush of pride raced through him. The most beautiful woman in Dragon Clan was his.

Care. An image of knives and blood flashed into Dane's mind from Ilst's. Eryn wore a knife at her belt, but she wasn't reaching for it.

No, she didn't understand her luck. But he'd show her. In no time at all, she'd weep with gratitude for her great fortune. And he hadn't lied when he said he wouldn't beat her. He'd grown up seeing the men around him wasting their eindon, thrashing the men until they couldn't work, and abusing the women until they sometimes took their own lives. But his own mother was eindon, and his father never had to beat her. She was gentle and kind to Dane until she died of a fever six winters past. Eryn would see.

She protested, but he slung his arm under her shoulders, supporting her slight frame as she hobbled out under the tent flap. All around them the camp was alive with his fellow warriors. They emerged from the tents they had commandeered for the night, some of them pulling their new eindon women behind them. Those women were bound, hands tied in front of them, with ropes around their necks, being led like cattle. Dane straightened up, supporting Eryn. She wasn't bound. She didn't need to be. *She can't even walk on her own.* He batted the thought away. Even if she weren't injured, Eryn wouldn't run.

In his mind, Ilst laughed.

"Wait," Eryn said, and Dane stopped.

She pointed to a small tent on the edge of the camp. "That's my tent, and my things are in it. I'm caldera."

"You've said. I don't know what that is."

She rolled her eyes. "I'm lorekeeper, teacher, and healer to my clan. I have herbs and medicines in there. I want to keep them."

"Your former clan," he reminded her. "And we have an herbwoman back with the herds. That's where we're heading today." He smiled. "But we should absolutely take your things. She'll be glad of the supplies when we get home."

They made a detour to the small tent, where he quickly packed up the things she wanted. By the time they left the tent, he was laden with packs containing seeds, dried plants, and Baltenn knew what else, along with a clean tunic and pants for Eryn.

When they arrived at the picket where the rest of the warriors were already saddling their horses, they were greeted with cheers and whistles.

"Got her so she can't even walk!" Brinir shouted. "Bet you're exhausted. Maybe we don't call you 'Hatchling' anymore. Good work!"

Heat burned Dane's face, and Eryn stiffened in his arms. He wanted to tell the other dragonsworn that he was wrong. Eryn was injured, and he didn't want to cause her pain. He could wait until she was healed to claim her under a blanket. But all the other dragonsworn and warriors joined in congratulating him on his supposed conquest. He could see the envy in their eyes. Eryn's beauty far outshone the women they had claimed, including the eindon from raids of the past. He said nothing.

"She's not that pretty."

The muttered words made Dane pause, moving down the line of horses.

Rina Gorinar sat atop her dun mare, looking down at Dane and Eryn. She was Brinir's woman now, not eindon, but clan-born, and a warrior in her own right. Her hair hung in a long braid tossed over one shoulder, and narrow eyes peered down a long, straight nose. She laid a hand on the hilt of her sword and spat on the ground at Eryn's feet.

The insult to his eindon was an insult to him. But he expected no less from Rina.

"She's not your concern," he said, ignoring the challenge in her posture.

He shouldn't walk by. Though Rina was only a warrior, her man was Brinir, a dragonsworn years before Dane bonded with Ilst. She claimed Brinir's status as his wife, and Dane should answer with respect. But the horn sounded again. Time to go. He hustled Eryn away, feeling Rina's stare at their backs.

Dane commandeered a packhorse, attaching his own packs and Eryn's to the saddle before tacking up his own horse, a brown stallion with patches of white. The beast could easily carry his weight and Eryn's for the long ride west. They would meet up with the rest of Dragon Clan, moving their cattle herds for spring grazing in the central plains, guarded by those dragonsworn who hadn't come on this distant raid. Dane's father and his dragon would be with the clan, along with Dane's siblings, awaiting his return.

The sun was not yet visible over the foothills in the east when they joined the line of horses heading away from the decimated camp. Fires still smoldered; tents lay in shambles. Stray sheep bleated from the hillsides as they rode away. There would be plenty of survivors coming down out of the hills where they'd run to hide in the fury of the raid.

"Your former clan will be fine," he said to Eryn, who sat on a pad behind his saddle. "I'm sure lots of your people will be coming down to clean up when we leave."

"And what will they find?" Eryn said into his shoulder. "Tents destroyed. Flocks scattered and decimated. And their healer gone." She sighed. "I shouldn't have taken all the healing powders. I should have left them for my people."

"Dragon Clan are your people now," he reminded her.

Wrong. Idiot. Ilst's thoughts rammed into his brain. From the strength of the images, he knew she was close, and craned his neck to peer into the pink morning sky.

"There!" He pointed to her familiar form, circling high above them. "There's Ilst. Isn't she the most beautiful thing?"

Ilst dove from the sky, wheeling to show off her flight skills. Several other dragons circled nearby, but none were as lovely as her.

Hands grabbed his waist, Eryn clutching him tight as Ilst flapped her great wings, swooping past Dane, flipping her tail in greeting.

"Don't be scared," he said to Eryn. "Ilst is my dragon. She would never hurt any Dragon Clan, and you're hers as much as mine now."

"I'm not scared." Eryn loosened her grip and leaned back away from him, letting a chill wind blow between them. "And I will never, ever be yours."

CHAPTER 5

Eryn shivered in the cold wind. The man who sat in front of her on the saddle would be warm. If she wrapped her arms around him and snuggled into the fur cloak on his back, the chill that ached in her ribs would abate. It would warm the links of the chain around her neck, like ice in a winter stream.

Never.

Every word out of his mouth revealed him for the barbarian he was. He honestly seemed to think she should be grateful that he'd taken her as a slave. So convinced of his clan's superiority, he was obviously far too thick to ever consider that life as a Dragon Clan eindon was a nightmare from which she had yet to wake up. That his empty promise not to beat her made a puffball of difference in her loathing of him.

She saw the way he beamed when his fellow dragon trash thought she was limping for a different reason. True, he hadn't taken her by force. Yet. Maybe he wanted her healed so she could put up a better fight. Some men thrived on that. Likely, he was just too tired from all the killing and pillaging, or too drunk on sour beer to do what men always tried to do, sooner or later. There was no doubt in her mind that tonight he would force her legs apart and start trying to plant his seed inside her.

Our sons will be dragonsworn. He'd said it last night. And he honestly thought she should be thrilled.

We will have no sons. No daughters. I'll slit his throat and be long gone before his line takes root in my body.

The sky lightened to pink as the line of riders spread out, winding through the foothills toward the plains in the west. High above, dragons circled.

One detached itself from the group and dove down toward them. Eryn stifled a shriek as it pulled up short, throwing out its wings, buffeting them with wind before flying off again. Even from behind him, she could feel the grin on Dane's face.

That was his dragon, his other slave. Ilst, he called her. Cream and brown, she looked like half of the other dragons that swooped around the line of riders, showing off. Eryn fought the urge to be impressed. It was hard not to be. There were maybe six or eight of them flying lazily around the barbarian clan, and as the morning wore on, she began to sort out which dragon seemed to belong to which man.

At the front of their line, a tall, strong-looking man rode on a dark brown horse. The dragon that stayed near him flashed in the sun before soaring down the line, surveying the riders as it flew.

Obsidian scales reflected the sun that peeked over the mountains behind them, casting a rainbow sheen as the dragon banked right in front of Dane's horse. By far the largest, the great beast was magnificent in its power.

The dragon's eye bored into Eryn's for an instant before it winged away, straight up into the sky.

"What dragon was that?" She asked the question before she could stop herself.

"That's Ardos," Dane answered. "Bloodbound to Chief Krunnan. Glorious, isn't he? Ilst thinks so, anyway."

"Are they a pair? Do they have…eggs together?" *Why do you care? They're all just mindless beasts, owned by these men just like you are.*

"Oh, no," Dane said. "Bloodbound dragons don't breed. All our eggs come from the wild dragons in the east mountains."

Despite herself, she was intrigued.

"You steal wild dragon eggs?"

"Of course not. It's a ritual; what makes our clan special. Baltenn's gift. They know their part." He made a sharp intake of breath. "I guess you'll see in a few weeks."

He stopped talking then, and she didn't ask any further.

As the morning wore on, her ankle throbbed where it hung over the horse's side. As tightly as she had wrapped it, she could feel it swelling in the bandage. It held her weight, and with a bit of time, she would have managed to fashion a crutch so she could walk on her own. But she hadn't had time. And the man, Dane, seemed to revel in dragging her along, parading her in front of his leering friends.

They rode down through the hills, pausing to let their horses drink from the cold stream flowing down toward the great H'rol River that rushed toward the sea, far to the south. It dumped into the harbor just above the narrow strait of land that divided Den Woth from Concadia to the east. The dragons drank from the other side, and Eryn tried to recognize individuals.

"The females are all the brown ones?"

Dane helped her off the horse and supported her as she stretched her legs. He helped her over to a large stone, where she sat and rewrapped her ankle even tighter while he refilled their waterskins.

"Not just brown," he answered, tying up the filled skins and fishing in his pack. "Ilst is cream. Tornnen's Urrgar is much darker. But the other colors are all males."

The black dragon, Ardos, walked behind the rest of them, surprisingly graceful on the ground with his wings tucked against his sides. Spikes traveled the lengths of all of their backs, from hand-length barbs on top of their heads, to arm's-length in the center of their spines, all the way down their long, sinuous tails. Ilst's were chocolate brown, like her nose and legs. Other dragons were shades of green and blue, and one the color of old, dried blood.

"Which is that? The red one?"

Dane's face clouded. "That's Brinir's Chern." The tone of Dane's voice told Eryn what she needed to know about Brinir. Not a friend. She looked back over the group of men and women, and saw a huge, bearded man. An eindon woman knelt next to him, both eyes blackened, and her face swollen such that it took Eryn a long moment to recognize her as one of Godseye Clan's herdsman's daughters. She couldn't recall the girl's name, but Eryn's heart wept for the girl. She knelt at the big man's feet, battered face staring at the ground. Broken already. Eryn shivered. Dane had said she should be happy to be his eindon, and not one of the other dragonsworn's. For a tiny fraction of a second, she was.

He offered her a hard bread roll and a squishy wedge of sheep milk cheese, warm from its place in the pouch under his cloak. It tasted like home, and her throat closed around it. She forced it down with a drink of cold water.

"Wait here."

He left her on the stone, feeling the warmth of the sun on her shoulders for a short while. She caught stares and glares from the clanspeople sizing her up, and she straightened her shoulders under their scrutiny, throwing her long, pale hair over her shoulder. Some of the men wore brass runes on their sword belts like Dane's, and she realized those men must be the dragonsworn. Each rune was a single letter, and if Dane's and the bearded beast Brinir's were an indication, each was the first letter of their name.

Shocking they can even remember that. Ignorant slobs.

Dane returned carrying a short, stout branch. With a quick knife flourish, he whittled one end round and smooth, and handed it to her. "There. Can you walk with that?"

She tested it, feeling the soft wood, smoothed by his knife under her hand. It held her weight, supported her to limp along the rough ground.

Eryn forced out a "thank you," and he grinned.

They remounted and continued the journey. The trail led them through a narrow pass, near the bottom of the foothills where the endless plain stretched on to the west.

Eryn peered around Dane's bulk, looking ahead down the path.

With a thick, wet grunt, the warrior in front of them slid off the side of his horse. Erin craned to see an arrow sticking out of the man's neck. It bore fletching of gold and green. Godseye colors. Her clan hunters were retaliating.

Shouts rang out amongst the clan. "Ambush! Attack!"

Dane twisted in the saddle, and for a moment she thought he'd been hit. Her stomach did a strange flip that she didn't want to consider.

"Get under that overhang," he said, grabbing her by the shoulders and shoving her over onto the packhorse. "Stay underneath until it's safe."

She cried out as her bruised ribs clanged against the packsaddle. She flung her leg over and grabbed the lead rope Dane tossed her. He shot away on his stallion as dragons roared overhead.

Chapter 6

Dane spent a moment watching Eryn bolt for cover in the shade of the hills on the packhorse. Then, with a deep war cry, he raised his sword and charged.

He looked up into the pines with double sight. Through Ilst's eyes, he saw the same scene as she wheeled overhead, searching for a target. *There.* Movement, and a tiny glint of light against the sheen of a polished bow. He pulled up, wheeling to the left.

An arrow whizzed past him, missing his chest by inches. His voice mirrored Ilst's roar of challenge as he charged up the hill.

He zeroed in on a man, hidden behind a scrubby bush, arrow poised to shoot. Dane turned to the right, drawing the man's aim, and his attention.

From above, Ilst was death. Dane watched through her eyes as she dove, reaching out with her front talons. She snatched the man as he drew back the bow to fire at Dane, pulling him off his feet. His weight pulled her down, wingtips touching the ground as she hauled him up. A dragon couldn't carry a man into the sky, but she lifted him up, hauling him a few feet into the air, her wicked talons puncturing his chest before hurling him to roll in a bloody heap down the hill.

Dane's chest warmed with pride.

"You are a queen among dragons!"

She preened, beating the air to rise back into the hill.

Arrows flew from both sides of the narrow path. Dane charged up the side of the hill. With Ilst's sight, he spotted the men hiding in the hills, firing on Dragon Clan's warriors. Dane's stallion leaped a small ravine, and Dane lowered his sword. The enemy spun to face him, bow drawn, but his arrow flew wide. The man's head flew through the air, loosed by a sweep of Dane's curved sword as he charged past.

An arrow thunked into his saddle, burying itself into the hard leather.

"Ilst, to me!" He didn't need to shout. She was there in his head, in his eyes, in his heart.

The man whose arrow came so close gave a gurgling cry as Ilst's talons punctured his shoulder, flinging him off balance. The bow fell from his hands as he rolled down the hill, right under the hooves of Dane's horse.

Shouts echoed across the hills as one by one, the attackers met their end. Dragons tore limbs from living men, crunching bones with slurps of acid drool.

In less than ten minutes, it was over. No more arrows flew from the trees. Swords were wiped and sheathed, and weapons quickly looted from the bodies. Down on the trail that wound between the hills, the dragons were already at work, rounding up the newly acquired eindon who had used the distraction to attempt to flee. The great, winged beasts herded packhorses and humans back from the trail and sniffed out their hiding places in the hills. By the time Dane descended to the main group, all of the captives were accounted for.

One of them was dead, a young woman with a gold and green fletched arrow sticking out of her chest. Brinir cut his rune from the girl's neck, kicking her already bruised and swollen face where she lay in a pool of blood.

But the cowardly ambush attackers had done their damage. Five Dragon Clan warriors were killed outright, expertly-shot arrows through necks and eyes. Two more lay on the ground, pouring blood onto the early spring grass.

Dane rode past them to the group of eindon. Eryn's face shone with sweat, and the packhorse she sat on heaved with flaring nostrils.

She tried to escape. She ran, and the dragons herded her back. The horse is winded because she tried to leave. From Ilst's mind, he got an image of Eryn on the packhorse from above, then wheeling in front of her, as horse and fleeing rider were chased back to the group.

Anger warred with humiliation in his heart. The fact that some of the new eindon looked like they had run—some with new bruises and covered in dirt—didn't matter. Eryn tried to run. His first eindon, this woman who filled him with pride and earned him the envy of all the other dragonsworn, had tried to leave him.

He approached, looking her over for wounds. When his gaze reached her face, he realized she was doing the same to him. He took the packhorse's lead rope from her hands and led it away from the rest of the group. Eryn sat tall in the packsaddle. Good. No wounds, no dirt. No one would know she tried to escape.

"You're not injured?" he asked, and she shook her head, lips pressed together.

He sighed. "You ran. I can tell from the horse that you tried to leave."

She didn't answer, just looked at him with that same expression she had given him last night. Like she couldn't believe the depths of his stupidity.

He lowered his voice. "Why? Why would you run? I told you I wouldn't beat you like the others do. You're Dragon Clan now. Why would you ever try to leave?"

Finally she spoke. "I don't even know how to explain it to you in words you'll understand. I guess it will just have to be a mystery."

Dane sat back in his saddle, staring at her face. Her clear blue eyes were wide, blinking under long lashes. Her lips were curved into the tiniest smile around the edges, as if she knew a joke she wasn't sharing.

He thought he understood women. The young women of Dragon Clan seemed to find him desirable. And since he returned from the Dragonfang Pass with Ilst's egg two years ago, he'd never lacked for female company. Just like men, women wanted power and status. And a woman's way to status was through the man who claimed her. Any woman in the clan would die of joy to bind herself to a dragonsworn. Eindon would never have their own status in the clan, but through her sons, Eryn would eventually claim a measure of respect that no one outside the clan could ever hope to achieve. Dragon Clan eindon, those who survived and adapted to their lives, were still better than any other clan in Den Woth. Why would she ever try to return to her decimated former people when they clearly couldn't hope to stand against the power of the dragon?

A shout from a warrior interrupted his thoughts.

"Chief Krunnan! Someone come and bring a horse!"

Eryn didn't resist as Dane tugged her packhorse next to his and pulled her onto his horse. Her bruised ribs stole her breath for a long moment, but she didn't cry out.

We never had a chance.

Godseye hunters were masters of the bow. With the element of surprise, they had taken down five of the filthy barbarians, badly injured two others, and at least given minor injury to several more. But with the dragons from above, the archers in the forest were quickly cut down. Was her brother among the dead? She would never know. They were left to rot where they fell.

It was all over too quickly. When Dane threw her onto the pack horse, she'd bolted back up the path. Surely the barbarians would be busy long enough for her to find a place to ditch the horse and hide. But in no time at all, Dane's dragon blocked her path, hissing at her, poison drool dripping from bloody fangs. Her little horse wheeled and charged back to the pack, and nothing she could do would turn it.

Fine. She wasn't ready yet anyway. Not until her ankle was healed and she could fend for herself.

Now she settled in behind him as he galloped over to where several of his people stood around a man propped up against a large rock on the trail. The man's long gray beard was matted with bloody vomit, but his eyes were focused.

One of the barbarians was tugging at an arrow sticking out of the old man's belly.

Before she could think, she was off the packhorse, hobbling with the stick Dane had given her.

"Stop! You can't just pull it out!"

The barbarian turned to glare at her.

"Eindon do not speak to dragonsworn." He turned to Dane, who was right behind her, putting his arm under her shoulders. "Hatchling, control your woman. Or I'll do it for you."

Hatchling?

Eryn had no time to muse why anyone would call the muscular warrior at her back such a derogatory name.

"You can't just rip out a gut shot," she tried again. "You have no idea what that arrow has cut through."

Eryn did. The bloody vomit on the man's chin was a dead giveaway. The arrow had clearly penetrated somewhere into his intestines. He was bleeding into his belly, and if the arrow were just pulled, the toxic digestive slime would pour out inside the man. His death would be slow and agonizing.

Good.

This man was clearly their leader. Who better to die to avenge Eryn's people?

Still, her training loosened her tongue. "You have to cut down to it, sew up the wounds inside as you go…" But the red-bearded giant ignored her. His hands wrapped around the arrow, and he braced his other against the old man's chest. With a single effort, he ripped the arrow free. The wide, triangular point brought a fetid smell from inside the man's gut. The chief roared in agony, panting on the ground.

Dane hustled Eryn away from the scene. When they were out of earshot, he turned on her, face boiling with rage.

"What in Baltenn's name did you think you were doing? You have no place to shame a warrior like that. Brinir would be well in his rights to demand your tongue for questioning him."

Heat fired up Eryn's neck.

"Oh, and who am I to question the medicine skills of a barbarian? Your clan chief is going to die. Pulling that arrow out let all the poison in his guts leak out into his belly. After three or four days of tremendous suffering, he's going to die, and there's nothing anyone can do about it. That insufferable oaf killed your chief just now. And I have no idea why I tried to stop him."

Dane's expression softened, but his eyes were still aflame. "You're an herbwoman. We brought your medicines." He gestured to where the horses stood. "You can redeem my honor by saving the chief."

Idiot. I just told him there's no saving him.

"Were you not listening to me? I just told you it's over. Nothing in the world will save that man. You smelled it. Haven't you ever smelled a wound like that before? You can't possibly be this stupid."

The anger returned to Dane's jaw. "I am far from stupid. And yes, every man here knows that smell means death. But you seem to think you're so much smarter than all of us, so I thought maybe you'd use your superior knowledge to help your clan chief."

"He's not my clan chief."

The big, bearded man stalked over to Dane and Eryn. *Brinir. This one is Brinir, and his dragon is the ugly red monster.*

"The arrow went through his gut. Chief Krunnan is going to die." He turned to Eryn. "And I'm going to cut the tongue out of this pretty little bitch's head. If she doesn't choke to death on her own blood, you can still use her just fine."

"Wait," Dane said, stepping between them. "She's an herbwoman. We have her supplies. Maybe she can save him."

No, Dane. Don't say that.

"Nothing can save him," she said, backing away from Brinir. "You shouldn't have pulled the arrow out. I might have been able to help him, but now it's too late."

Brinir pulled his knife from his belt and pushed Dane aside.

"The best I can do," Eryn continued, trying to keep the tremor from her voice, "is try to control his pain until he dies. It could take days, and it will be very, very painful."

Brinir's small, hooded eyes bored into Eryn's. "Can you keep him alive until we get back to our camp? Our herbwoman can save him when we get there."

No she can't. But then he can die on her, and not on me.

"I'll do my best."

He lowered his knife. "You better. If he dies before we reach the herds, you die with him."

CHAPTER 7

Dane rode next to the cart that carried his chief and his eindon. Eryn sat next to the tough old man, clearly doing her best to keep him comfortable and conscious. On the other side, Ardos, the chief's black dragon, paced, craning his long neck over the side to blow hot breath onto his master. Eryn flinched away from his huge head, huddling against the edge until he blinked at her and withdrew, allowing her to tend to the chief.

Eryn's methods fascinated Dane, and he peppered her with questions as she worked.

"Why do you make him lie on his stomach like a dog?"

She looked up from her lap, where she pawed through her pack of medicines. "The wound is very infected. The arrow went through his intestine, and the contents spilled into his belly. He's strong, and the bleeding hasn't killed him, but the infection will." She found the bottle she was looking for, holding it up to the light. Thick, amber liquid was crystallized around the stopper. "So I keep the original wound open so the poison can drain out, and I keep him on his belly because liquids flow down, not up."

He'd never seen this done before. Over his years as a young warrior, even before Ilst made him dragonsworn, he'd been in many raids. Seen many men with swords or arrows, or, on one occasion, the horn of a terrified bull through the gut. They always died, sometimes in hours, sometimes in days. But Chief Krunnan was strong. A chief had to be the strongest among them, and Krunnan had ruled without challenge for years, since his son Brinir was just a boy. Many men were stronger now, and if a challenge were made, it wouldn't go well for Krunnan. It was a sign of the clan's respect that no one had taken his title.

That would change the moment he died. Dane turned away from the thought. Blood might spill that day. But maybe Eryn could prevent it.

In the cart, she helped the chief roll over onto his back.

Dane watched as she pulled back the fur rugs that covered him, lifting his shirt to reveal a bandage over his abdomen, wet with dark yellow liquid. She pulled the wrapping down to expose a small, ragged hole on the right side of his abdomen.

Such a small wound. How could it possibly take out Chief Krunnan?

Eryn's delicate fingers gripped a small, blunt piece of metal.

"This is going to hurt," she told the chief.

The old man nodded, face pale but eyes open to the cloudy sky above. Ardos arched his neck over the cart, glaring at Eryn. The chief took a sharp breath and held it, cheeks turning red and teeth gritted as Eryn pushed the blunt piece of metal into the wound. Ardos hissed, eyes narrowed. Fluid bubbled out of the hole when she withdrew the probe and Chief Krunnan grunted out his breath.

"Why did you do that?" Dane asked.

Eryn sighed, turning that look on him again…like he was a pesky child asking his mother a million questions. "I have to keep the hole open to drain, or the infection gets trapped inside."

She pulled the stopper on the crystallized bottle and smelled the contents. From its mouth, she dribbled thick, amber liquid straight into the hole. Then she pulled the bandage around so a clean part was just beneath the wound before tugging it up to cover the open hole. A low growl from Ardos accompanied the chief's low moan of pain.

From her pack, Eryn pulled a small pouch and withdrew a small brown twig. She dropped it into a pottery bowl and ground it with the heel of the metal probe. Without looking at Dane, she said, "This is white dewcup root. It's good for infection, though it's certainly up against a difficult foe." A little water from her waterskin made the powder into a weak brown liquid, which she held to the chief's lips as he drank. She followed this with a long drink of water, which made the chief cough and sputter, groaning at the pain.

"That's good," she murmured. "You're still strong enough to cough. Now roll back over and try not to die."

Dane blanched. If the chief were stronger, he'd have backhanded anyone who spoke to him like that. It worried Dane more than anything else that the old man just scowled and obeyed. Eryn arranged the furs under his head and shoulders and covered him back up. Dane kept an eye on Ardos, expecting the great dragon to bite Eryn's head off for her insolence, but Ardos merely rumbled deep in his throat and walked on, guarding his master from the ground.

They rode through most of the night, pausing a few hours to rest the horses. No tents were erected, and Eryn stayed in the cart with the chief. Some of the warriors propped a pole up at the front of the cart and draped a tent canvas over the top to protect the chief from a light, cold drizzle that began after midnight. They brought stones heated in the fire to warm the little makeshift shelter, and Dane kept their waterskins full. Ilst kept watch for danger from above, landing at night to doze next to Dane on the ground near the cart.

***

In the darkest part of night, the chief awoke.

"Eindon?"

Eryn took a moment to realize he was addressing her. "I'm here."

The man rolled onto his side, and Eryn gave him a few sips of water. His eyes were remarkably clear in the light of their tiny lantern.

"I'm going to die, aren't I?"

Eryn shivered. *If he dies, I die with him.* "You're strong," she soothed. "If anyone can survive a wound like this, it's you." She laid her wrist on his forearm. He wasn't burning with fever. "You're doing very well. We're going to get you home."

He grunted and gave her a small smile. "You're kind to care for me like this. Most new eindon are far less tractable."

I would happily watch you die if our fates weren't tied together. She sighed at the thought. *Would I really?* She was a healer, an herbwoman. And even the head of a clan of monsters deserved a chance. He'd been gentle in his words so far.

"Which of my dragonsworn has claimed you?"

Eryn held up the lock around her neck. "His name is Dane."

Chief Krunnan nodded. "Dane is a good man. Arrogant but not a brute like my son. He'll treat you kindly. You must be angry, being taken from your own people, but we aren't all the monsters you fear we are. You can have a good life with us. Especially with a young man like Dane."

The talk exhausted him, and Eryn helped him roll back onto his stomach. She gave him another packet of pain killing herbs to chew and thought about his words until dawn broke over the land.

***

The low hills rippled down to a wide, flat prairie. Short spring grass covered the endless stretch of land. A cloudy, drizzling night gave way to pink morning, and by afternoon the air had warmed enough for Dane to shed his heavy cloak, face turned to the sun. The days would get longer and longer until high summer, when the nights only lasted a few hours.

Wildflowers Dane had never noticed before poked through the grasses, and Eryn asked him to gather the stems for some medicine concoction. It was a task for eindon, who were ordered to comply, pulling the thick, thorny stems from the ground. As the cart rolled along, Eryn cut the roots and flowers away, littering the ground in her wake. She cut the stems into pieces, spreading them over the back of the cart to dry in the sun.

Ilst and the other dragons feasted on the herds of shaggy deer that grazed the plains and made plenty of kills to supply the little raiding party, now a caravan of pillaged goods, with meat. Dane smiled at Ilst's delight, diving from the heights, the herd scattering in terror before her, choosing her prey from the thundering mass of bodies. She snapped her wings open at the bottom of her dive, reaching out with her hind claws to snatch a deer, crushing its chest in her grasp. Some of her kills were dropped at the feet of Ardos, who tore at the meat and snapped it down as Eryn watched in open-mouthed horror.

After two and a half days of hard travel, they reached the edge of Dragon Clan's own herds. Huge cattle grazed in the sun, calves gamboling around their mothers' hooves. Herdsmen nodded respect to the warrior party, and from above echoed greeting calls from those dragons who stayed with the rest of the clan and the herds, welcoming the party home.

Tents came into view, and Dane grinned. *Home.* Wherever the grazing took them, far across the plains as the season changed, the sharp peaks of the hundreds of tents was Dragon Clan's home. They ruled the plains from the ocean in the west to the craggy hills in the south, from the narrow strip of land that connected Den Woth to Concadia in the east, to the Grayfang Mountains in the north, home to the wild dragons.

A crowd gathered around them as they rolled into camp, down the wide pathway trodden flat by people and horses that led to the largest tent in the center, at the edge of a large, cleared circle of ground. Chief Krunnan's woman rushed out of their tent, flanked by their three young daughters. She leaped into the cart, shoving Eryn aside. Ardos grumbled as she ripped the blankets from the chief, pulling down the bandage to reveal the open hole.

"Who is this eindon? She rounded on Eryn. "What ignorant clan are you from? You haven't even stitched his wound! Look how it oozes!"

The chief sat up with a grunt. His cheeks had a hint of color. "Woman, I'm alive with a gut wound…"

His wife cut him off. "It'll go putrid. What fool doesn't know how to close a wound so it doesn't go putrid?" She clapped her hands, and four eindon men bearing the chief's rune rushed out and climbed into the cart. They used the blanket he lay on to carry the chief into his tent.

Eryn closed her bag of medicines and stood in the cart, holding the edge to support herself. Her eyes were fire. "If your healer closes that wound now, the chief will die. It doesn't smell putrid because my medicines are working."

The crowd gaped at her.

Dane hopped into the cart and helped her down, swinging her in his arms to the ground. "Ragna is our herbalist and the chief's first wife, mother of many of his children. You did well to keep him alive. Now she will heal him."

"Now she will kill him if she seals up the infection inside of him. It's too soon. Without the honey in the wound and the root, he'll die. It needs to stay open until it drains clear. It's only Baltenn's will that he's lived this long."

Across the cleared circle in the middle of the camp, Ardos grumbled.

"Eryn, listen to me," Dane said, holding Eryn by the shoulders. "You did very well. You helped him stay alive all this way. It's not your place to question our herbalist. You need to learn your place here." He pulled her bag from the back of the cart and handed it to a young boy. "Take this to my tent, and help your brother get the rest of our things from our packhorse." The boy scurried away, a look of awe on his face. Dane smiled. Out in the raiding party, he was the youngest of the dragonsworn. Here, he was one of eighteen men bloodbonded to a dragon.

At home with his clan, he was royalty.

Chapter 8

Eryn unpacked her few possessions in the tent of her barbarian captor. She leaned the cane against the thick tent wall, kneeling to inventory her herbs. Dane had left her alone, making the rounds among his friends, who were largely left behind here at the camp.

All the clans of Den Woth were nomadic. Across the border in Concadia, there were grand cities, with towers and castles, and permanent homes where people stayed their whole lives on one tiny patch of ground, never leaving the walls of their town to follow the changing seasons. If the raid hadn't happened, she would have crossed the border this summer, traveling with Nora to the hidden city of Tiezahal to study. Nora had studied there before she married Eryn's brother, Falnar, and had their daughter, back when she was preparing to become the caldera for Godseye Clan. But a caldera didn't marry, and when Falnar asked her to leave the position and become his woman, she accepted. Eryn jumped at the chance to take on the role.

It was an easy choice. Caldera was the only woman immune to a man's claim on her. Women in Godseye could not turn down a marriage claim, and Eryn shuddered at the thought of who might have claimed her. Until then, Falnar had kept her safe, but it was far too close. Eryn never wanted to feel a man's hands on her again, and now there was no Falnar to protect her from this man whose rune was locked around her neck.

She knelt on the rug-covered floor, laying out bottles and pouches. This tent was larger than any Godseye tent. Six poles supported the sides and a center pole held the top up so that Dane would be able to stand upright without hitting his head. A wooden chest that probably held his clothing, and a rack of weapons stood along one wall. Her eyes were drawn to a bed of thick furs and blankets across the cozy room. She'd been lucky so far. The first night, when Dane had claimed her, he'd respected her injuries and kept his hands off of her. Since then, she'd dozed in the cart, tending to her patient. How many times along the endless, bumpy road had she thought about dosing the old man with too much poppy or hemlock? The chief of this barbarian clan had ordered the raid that ransacked her clan's nomadic home. But if he died, she would die right behind him. The big man, Brinir—she shuddered at the glint in his eyes when he'd made the threat—he would have happily killed her, and he wouldn't have made it quick. It took all of her skill to bring the clan chief home. Another day or two, and he might have been out of danger. Now his wife had taken over his care. The man was strong. It was possible that even if she closed the wound, he might be healed enough to survive. Eryn doubted it. The drainage was still too thick, the infection too deep. If she sealed those toxins inside him, even his strength wouldn't be enough. And that was fine, wasn't it? Only her caldera pride wanted the man to survive. If his wife managed to kill him now, good riddance. She'd done what she was supposed to do.

But now she had no patient, no cart. The sun was long since down. She expected feasting and drinking to celebrate the successful raid, but the camp was relatively quiet, no doubt because their leader was in peril. Children squealed outside, men laughed at a bonfire in the clearing in the middle of the camp, but here in Dane's tent, she was finally alone. Not for long. When he was full of meat and beer, he'd return, and his patience would certainly be gone.

It could be worse. It could be Brinir. She'd seen his eindon here, and they all had the sagging shoulders and dead eyes of true slaves. They looked even more afraid of Brinir's hard-faced woman, Rina.

She shook her head. Yes, it could be worse. But it would be so much better…if they had never come at all.

"Dane?" A tiny voice made Eryn spin around.

Standing under the opened tent flap was a small girl. She couldn't be more than six or seven. Nora's age. Eryn's heart gave a squeeze, and she made a quick, silent prayer that her niece had found safety.

The girl's eyes widened, and she took a step back, peering under the flap.

"Hello," Eryn said. The girl even looked a little like Nora. Blond and pink-cheeked.

"Who are you? Why are you in Dane's tent?"

Eryn flushed. "I'm…" she sighed. *Might as well say it.* "I'm his eindon. My name is Eryn."

The girl smiled. "I'm Suki. Dane's my brother, and he's the strongest dragonsworn in the clan. And Ilst is the best dragon." She paused, looking at Eryn. "So you must be the best eindon."

Indeed. Highest of the low.

Eryn shrugged. "I don't know if I'm the best, but—" She cut off as a pair of arms grabbed the girl from behind. Without thinking, she bolted for the tent flap, throwing herself at the dark shadow who was swinging the little girl around. She flailed at the arms holding the girl until she realized the shrieks coming from the child were joyous, not frightened.

"Dane! You're finally home!"

Eryn stepped back, wincing on her ankle.

"And who's the best little sister ever?" Dane said, laughing into the child's hair. "Were you a good girl while I was gone?"

The girl flipped around in his arms, hugging him close. Eryn faded back into the tent, hobbling back to her sack of herbs and medications.

In a few moments, the tent flap opened and Dane ducked inside. The little fire in the center of the tent made his eyes glitter. Or maybe that was just the beer.

"How is the chief?" she asked before he could speak.

Dane smiled. "Ragna says he is doing well. You did good work, Eryn. When he is well, I'm sure I'll get a runelock for your skill."

She stared at him.

"A runelock," he said, pointing to the bronze disk around her neck that clasped the chain and the others he wore dangling from his belt. "It's a gift from the chief, a recognition of a worthy deed. Dragonsworn earn them, and it's a sign of our status. It's how we claim eindon, as well."

She scowled. "And my medicine will earn one for you?"

He grinned. "Almost certainly. You bring honor to my name, even if you don't know how to hold your tongue."

She turned back to her herbs. "Then I should have let him die."

"Eryn, that's an awful thing to say." Dane crouched next to her. The smell of beer on his breath was sweet, not sour, and his leather boots brought the warm scent of horse. "I had a lot of time to think on the journey, and I understand now. You're upset because of the people we killed in the raid. I understand that. But in time, you'll forget them. This is your home now, and with your skills, you'll be honored among eindon."

She turned to face him. His hair was loose, in golden waves hanging around his neck. His shirt was tight across his broad shoulders.

"And what does that make me? Compared to the lowest clansperson?"

He blinked. "Well, lower than one born to the clan, of course. But our children will be clan-born."

There it was. *Our children.*

The thought lit a warmth in his eyes.

"You're healing well." His gaze took in her body, kneeling on the floor.

"It still hurts when I breathe."

He smiled. "Leave your herbs for now. Come and let's make a Dragon Clan baby." He laid a hand across her shoulders to help her up, as he had many times on the journey here. But this time the touch held a promise.

Eryn's heart pounded, her mouth dry. *You knew this would happen. You're his slave. His property. He's going to take you. And if you fight, he'll hurt you.* She was frozen, kneeling on the floor. He hadn't hurt her yet, hadn't struck her even when she'd lashed out, dishonoring him in front of his fellow warriors. He'd been kind to her. But he'd killed, pillaged, destroyed. However gentle he acted, the man was a barbarian.

"Eryn, come with me." His voice was more insistent now, his arm around her back tighter.

Just close your eyes and think of something else. Let him mount you like a ram in the mountains. It won't take long, and then it will be over. For tonight, anyway.

She stood and let him lead her over to the pile of furs. *Take your mind somewhere else.* An image flashed into her mind, of the last time a man tried to touch her this way. She still had a tiny scar on her lip from the back of his hand. She remembered the rage in his eyes. The shock when she fought back. That time, Falnar had been there to save her virtue and her soul. But Falnar wasn't here now. She would not fight back. There was no point.

Dane turned her to face him, standing next to his bedding. "You're so beautiful," he murmured. "I'm so lucky Ilst found you."

He brushed the hair back from her cheek and she squeezed her eyes shut. *Killer.* The words of the dying chief came back to her. *Kind,* he'd called Dane. He, too, had mentioned her luck at being Dane's eindon.

His hands caressed the iron links and the brass runelock that marked her as his property. "You're mine forever, Eryn." She stiffened, muscles hard as stone as he ran his hands over her shoulders, cupping the back of her head. The heat of his face warmed hers, and the touch of his lips against hers stirred a warmth that made her shiver in terror. Her lips were a hard line, and he moved a hand around to cup her chin. "You can relax. I know you're still hurt. I'll be gentle."

And he was. His lips sought hers again, soft against her stony face.

He pulled away. "You don't have to be scared," he said. "I know what I'm doing. I know how to make a woman happy."

She opened her eyes. He was smiling, the firelight making his eyes shine. Those soft lips... *He's a killer. A handsome killer. Which doesn't matter at all.*

He moved in again, arms dropping around her back to pull her against him. His chest was warm, arms strong around her. She was iron in his embrace.

"Eryn, what's wrong? Don't you want me?"

He looked like a kicked lamb, shocked and sad and betrayed.

"It doesn't matter what I want. I'm a slave. Just do what you have to do and be done."

Dane stepped back, dropping his hands. "I..." He stared at her. "All the women here say I'm handsome. They're happy to share my tent. Why would you say something like that?"

Could the man honestly not understand? A dragonsworn, high in status, master of his fate…he honestly looked baffled that she wasn't delighted to drop her clothing for him.

"Is it your first time? I know how to make it not hurt. I can bring you so much pleasure. I know all the places that a woman needs to be…"

"Enough!" she blurted, shutting her eyes again. "Just do it and get finished and let me be. You own me and I cannot fight you off. You'll have what you want no matter what I do, so please just stop pretending you care what I want and just get this over with."

The kicked-lamb look got even sadder.

"Eryn, I don't want that. Why would I want a woman who doesn't want me? I'm not a bull in the field. I just…" He shook his head. "I don't understand your clan. I don't understand you."

He grabbed his cloak and left the tent.

CHAPTER 9

Dane wound his way between the tents toward the plain beyond. The dwellings got smaller, rougher, as he left the prestigious center of the camp out toward the lower status—the herders, the slaughterers, the cooks, and finally to those with no skill, only the strength of their backs. These last held eindon that were no longer wanted by their owners, mostly damaged beyond repair. Some of the lowest status took them in and fed them, though they were useless to the clan and were killed if they slowed the group down when it was time to move east as the summer wore on.

Ilst waited for him past the last lean-to shelters, between the clan and their herds grazing and dozing in the spring grass beyond. Dragons were day-hunters, and they had all feasted on specifically culled cattle upon their return. Only the fittest of the herds were permitted to breed, and Dragon Clan cattle were prized all over Den Woth for their meat, their leather, and their thick, wooly hides of winter. They would start to shed out soon, and the long hairs made scratchy, warm fabric that sold well to the traveling traders that came from the east.

"Ilst, I don't understand women." Dane picked up a small bag of tools next to a small bonfire, and Ilst cozied up to be pampered. He used a blunt pick to clean out the beds of her claws, and she held her huge talons up one by one for him to attend her. "Eryn is so beautiful, so smart. I was sure the chief would never make it back here, but she's amazing. I think she might know more than Ragna, even. How could someone from a lesser clan be better than our herbwoman?"

A deep sigh rumbled from Ilst's throat as Dane moved on to the back talons. Blood was caked under the nail bed, and she grunted as he took a bucket of warm water and a wire brush to scrub it out.

"But she..." he trailed off. Ilst knew. Though he tended to speak to her aloud, she was always in his head and his heart, just as he was in hers. She was there when he kissed Eryn's lips. It was like kissing a granite stone, or a clay doll. Hard and unyielding.

"She must be afraid I'll hurt her, but I wouldn't. If she had any idea how she makes me feel, she'd understand that. I want her to be happy. I want her to want me like I want her and she just...doesn't. I don't know what to do."

Foolish. Childish. Selfish. The feelings wafted from Ilst as Dane finished her last claw and reached for a thick, cowhide towel to wipe down her scales.

"I'm not selfish. I'm never selfish in bed."

Ilst's chuckle vibrated through his head.

"What do you know, anyway? Bloodbound dragons don't breed. You couldn't possibly understand." He rubbed the thick scales on her face, and she leaned into him, letting him polish each scale to a soft shine in the firelight. Her small ears got a good rub before he moved to the spikes down her back, cream fading to chocolate at the tips. As he worked, her pleasure in the grooming warmed him. Ilst understood him. No human could ever hold his heart the way Ilst did. She was his blood, his beloved since the moment she hatched. While a woman could please his body, only Ilst could warm his soul.

"She's looking good, Dane."

The voice behind him made him whirl around, towel in hand. Ilst's rumbles of pleasure turned to a deeper, more menacing growl.

Rina stood behind him, dressed in warrior leather. She was tall and strong, with muscles to rival any young man. Long, light brown hair was pulled back from her face, revealing high cheekbones and chilly eyes that never wrinkled when she smiled. She moved in closer, so he could smell the smoke from the bonfire on her, the beer on her breath, and the blood still on her leather pants.

"Thanks. Ilst always looks good." Dane turned back to his dragon, who had stretched out her neck into a long, sideways curve, tail stiff. Ilst's distaste for Rina was evident in her posture, but only a dragonsworn would understand the threat of that neck. Rina couldn't possibly read a dragon's body language. A woman could never bind a dragon.

"You left the feasting early. Anxious to get home to your new property?"

Dane bristled at the term. Yes, eindon were property. They were also responsibility. His own mother had been eindon, and she was a good, kind woman. His father treated her gently, and she knew her duty. She had died birthing his little sister, Suki.

"Anxious to tend to Ilst," he responded, hoping she'd take the hint.

Rina smiled up at the scowling dragon. "She's growing into quite a beauty. Everyone says so."

Despite himself, Dane warmed at the praise. "She is, isn't she?" He resumed his polishing, but Ilst was not mollified, black eyes penetrating the woman behind him.

"It's still so chilly out here," Rina said, moving closer to Dane. "Dragons are so warm."

"Maybe you should cuddle up to Chern." As if Brinir's ugly beast would ever snuggle with a human.

"Maybe I feel like cuddling up with something a little softer," Rina replied. She was right behind him now, hands reaching around to rest on his waist. Dane went as rigid as Ilst when Rina's hands moved up to stroke his chest.

He pulled away and moved back to Ilst's tail, now raised in an even more aggressive stance.

"Ilst is feeling agitated. Best you should go on now," Dane warned.

A childish pout creased Rina's hard features. "I'm feeling agitated, too. Don't you remember how much fun it was when we got agitated together?"

He did remember. Rina had only been Brinir's wife for a week before the raid when Dane claimed Eryn. Before that she was free, and enjoyed that freedom with any young warrior that caught her eye. Dane was one of them and he knew Rina would have preferred Dane as her husband. She was never what Dane wanted in a wife, even before Eryn came into his life. But under the blankets, Rina was a wildcat. He still had a couple of small scars on his back from her nails. The thought should have excited him but looking at her only made him aware of how much more beautiful Eryn was. How much he'd rather have her hands on his chest.

"Go back to Brinir, Rina. He'll be looking for you."

She kicked the bucket of water, spilling it into the dirt. "He's got plenty of eindon. He doesn't want my kind of fun tonight." Her eyes roamed Dane up and down. " I won't tell him. He won't miss me for an hour, and it's so cold out here. Let's go back and show your new eindon how it's done. Young, stupid thing like her…she should watch how a real woman pleases a man."

The thought made Dane's stomach drop into his boots. *Eryn would…* He paused. Eryn might be relieved. She clearly didn't want Dane. Maybe she'd be just as happy if Dane found release elsewhere. Or maybe if she saw what he had to offer a woman, she might… *no*. Dane wanted Eryn to want him. And there was no part for Rina in that.

"Sorry, Rina," he said. "Our time is over. Go home to Brinir and show him why he married you. Ilst is all I need tonight."

The pale dragon curled her neck around him, putting herself between her dragonsworn and the warrior that was riling his blood. She hissed at Rina, and the woman backed away.

"Fine, suit yourself," she muttered. "But you'll come back when you're bored of that lifeless lamb. When you want a warrior, not a slave, you know where I'll be." She huffed away into the darkness.

From around his body, Ilst's neck relaxed. She resumed her happy rumble as Rina's footsteps faded away.

Dane relaxed as well. He recognized that any other man would have willingly taken up Rina's advance tonight. At one time, her body under his had been all he wanted. But where her cheeks were hard, Eryn's were soft. Where Rina had muscle, Eryn had strength. Rina wanted Dane, but Dane realized that all he wanted was Eryn. And not as dragonsworn with eindon, a forced compliance. She might learn to pretend to want him, or he could beat her into submission and take her whenever he wanted to. But that wasn't what made his heart stir, and Ilst rumbled with pleasure. He didn't want Eryn until she wanted him. He had no idea how to make that happen. But whatever it took, he would find a way into her willing arms.

CHAPTER 10

Eryn woke to a high-pitched wail that shot ice down her spine. She bolted upright, throwing off the warm furs of her bed, looking wide-eyed around the tent. Early morning light spilled in around the cracks and across the cold coals in the middle of the tent. Dane was already on his feet, throwing off his own blanket.

"What is it? Attack?" Her voice trembled at the thought of more bloodshed.

Dane's face was pale. "Not attack. It's Ardos. It's the death keen."

An image flitted through Eryn's mind. Ardos. The huge black dragon that had watched her like an eagle every step of the way as Eryn used every trick she knew to keep the clan chief alive. Ardos was the chief's dragon, and a stronger, more powerful creature she couldn't imagine.

"The dragon? He's dying?"

Dane belted on his sword and took a swig from the flask at his waist. "No. Chief Krunnan. And not dying. He's dead."

The shivers from the keening turned to frozen shards in her blood. *If he dies you die.* The bearded barbarian had said it in the cart on the way.

"He was getting better when we got here," she stammered. "I told the woman not to close the wound…"

The warmth of Dane's hand on her arm silenced her. "It's not your fault, Eryn. No one survives a wound like that. It was the grace of Baltenn himself that you brought him home to die with his clan." His face was a storm of worry. "You did as you were asked. No one can blame you for this." He looked as uncertain as Eryn felt.

She threw on her hooded cloak, cinching it around her neck–covering the hated slave chain–grabbed her cane, and followed him through the tent flap. A stream of people thronged into the central clearing where the great black dragon sat in the middle of the ground, head pointed at the sky, wailing the chilling death call.

"Wait here."

Dane left her alone, gathering with the other dragonsworn just outside the chief's tent. She melted into her hood, watching the clan's reaction to the keening dragon. No one approached it. Babies wailed in their mothers' arms, children clung to their fathers, women held each other. Except for the babies, no tears were shed. Only the dragon seemed to feel grief. The rest were worried, anxious.

Eryn's own heart was in turmoil. The chief was dead. The man who ordered the raid that decimated her own clan, killed her people, would kill no more. *Good.* But even as she thought it, some of the dragon's anguish poked at the edges of her mind. The chief had been brave, never crying out when she'd reopened the wound to keep it draining, never questioning her orders. *He'd still be alive if that woman had listened to me.* The clan chief was as strong as any man she'd ever known, and his people had obviously prospered under his leadership. And his dragon—she would swear the beast had loved him.

It had no choice. Dragons are slaves here, just like you. If it came to love its master, it's only because it knew no better. But still, the keening tore into her heart. Ardos's grief poured in through her ears and into her throat, which tightened up even as hot tears threatened her eyes.

She knuckled them away with anger and astonishment. The more Dragon Clan dead, the happier she would be. If every person around her crumpled to the ground this very instant, she would dance with joy. *Would you, though? Every person?*

Her eyes flickered back to the group of dragonsworn, finding Dane's broad shoulders as he stood with his back to her. Did his dragon love him like Ardos clearly loved the chief? She shook the thought away.

A rough hand grabbed her arm, and her hood was flung back.

"The eindon's to blame! She killed him with her potions!"

Eryn looked into the hard face of the warrior woman who had glared at her the whole way here. Rina dragged her over to where the men were gathered around the mouth of the tent and pushed her to her knees. "This eindon killed our chief. She poisoned him as he lay injured."

Eryn sputtered, face going cold, but Dane's hand on her shoulder was firm.

"She did no such thing. Our chief was awake and talking when he was brought home. He was getting better. She kept him alive when no one else could have. You all saw his wound. No man lives with a gut wound like that."

Muttering all around. Eryn risked a glance up. Rina glared down at her. At Rina's shoulder, the bearded Brinir's face held no expression. Dane stood over her, eyes like iron, staring a hot challenge at Rina.

An older man raised his hands. "Be calm, son. Now is not the time for war among us." Streaks of gray in the man's hair caught the morning light, and eyes like Dane's turned down to Eryn. "I saw the chief upon his return. He did not look poisoned. He looked like he might survive."

"He would have if I'd continued his care." The words slipped out of Eryn's mouth before she could stop them.

The older man gave the hint of a smile and glanced at Dane. "You chose a spirited little hawk, didn't you, son?" He addressed the rest of the group. "Dragon Clan takes the best from every clan in Den Woth." He looked back at Eryn. "If she has hastened the death of our chief, Baltenn surely knows, and will choose her upon his stone. If Baltenn wills her to live, we will take her knowledge for our own." His shoulders sagged. "For today, we will honor our chief and prepare him to fly to his fathers. We can do no more."

There was grumbling around the group, but no one protested as Dane helped Eryn stand, pulling her under his arm. She shivered at the glares of the men and the narrowed eyes of Rina.

With a start, she realized the keening had stopped. In the center of the clearing, Ardos crouched, muscles taut. He launched himself into the air, obsidian wings shining with iridescent rainbows in the morning sun. The wind from his flight cooled Eryn's hot face as the dragonsworn dispersed, leaving her huddled against Dane's side.

"What happens to a dragon when its warrior dies?" she murmured.

Dane sighed. "When the funeral is complete and Chief Krunnan's soul rises to join his father and his father's father in the immortal clan of Baltenn himself, Ardos will leave. There is no place in the clan for a dragon with no warrior."

A deep sadness shadowed Eryn's heart for a moment before she shook it away. *Who cares what happens to a dragon? At least it's finally free.* Her fingers traced Dane's rune etched into the brass lock at her throat. *At least the dragon is free.*

CHAPTER 11

Dane stood in the clearing where all the clan's drag-onsworn ringed Chief Krunnan's body. He had never been part of the innermost circle before. The last time a man of sufficient rank to merit the full funeral cer-emony had died, Dane had not been dragonsworn, merely part of the crowd that surrounded their circle now, all silent under the crescent moon. The sky above was filled with drag-ons, all bloodbound to the clan. Ardos flew among them for the last time. His warrior was dead, their bond broken. When the ceremony was complete, he would fly off into the night, never to return.

Each dragonsworn held a torch aloft. In the flickering firelight, the shaman stood at the head of Chief Krunnan's pyre. Laid out in his armor atop wood stacked waist high, the chief's body was painted with symbols understood only by the shaman and the great god Baltenn himself, who would receive the chief into his immortal clan when the ceremony was complete. Strong-scented herbs surrounded the corpse, and in the center of the chief's chest lay a single obsidian scale, plucked from Ardos's hide by the shaman. The scale would tell Baltenn that the chief was no mere warrior, but dragonsworn, exalted to the highest rank among the god's own clan.

The shaman chanted low. He wore the bleached skull of a bull on his head, and his ceremonial costume was made of carved bone beads strung together, crossed strands over his chest, around his waist, and dangling from both arms. When he moved, the tones were the music of the dead.

Dane held his torch as the shaman clicked and jangled around the body, stomping his bare feet on the cold ground. The chanting grew louder, words Dane didn't know—the language of the gods. He caught the names of Krunnan and Baltenn, and of Mordall, the god of death. In other lands, they worshiped other gods, but Dane only knew these two. Mordall took the spirits of the common clanspeople, who did not merit a dragonsworn funeral. But Mordall would step aside and allow Baltenn to claim his own. This Dane knew for certain, and he shivered at the thought that when he died, he would receive this eternal honor, and fly with his god forever. Warmth flowed from him to Ilst, circling above. Her bonding to him had changed not only his life, but his eternity.

Dragons need no gods.

It was the clearest thought Ilst had ever sent him, and the torch wavered in his hand. He had never considered what happened to a dragon when it died. Surely Ilst would join him in Baltenn's clan? Or if she died before him, he would find her there? The thought turned his stomach. Eternity without Ilst? Though she had been bonded to him for only two years, she was as much a part of him as his arm or his beating heart.

The shaman completed his circuit around the body. The two dragonsworn at the foot of the pyre separated to make room between them. Ragna, the chief's woman, stepped into the circle. She wore a heavy cloak of mourning, dark cloth covering her from head to toe. From within the cloak, she produced a small ceramic bowl. The shaman took it from her, and turned back to the body, collecting the herbs from around the chief. He placed the stems and dried petals in the bowl, still chanting, and used one of the stems to take fire from a torch and light the bowl's contents. The herbs flared up with green flame, illuminating his skull-covered face with unearthly light.

While the herbs burned, Ragna pulled a small knife from her cloak. She threw back the hood and knelt in front of the pyre, at the chief's feet. Her chanting joined the shaman's, and she raised the knife to her face. Blood flowed as she cut three vertical lines beneath each eye, a finger-length each down her cheeks. The six lines looked like bloody tear tracks, dripping off her jaw.

The shaman dipped his fingers into the clay bowl and pulled out a small wad of ash. Still chanting, he rubbed the ash into the bleeding slices on Ragna's face. Her cheeks would forever show the black tattooed tears of mordanii, the mourning mark. No man would touch her, and when she died, she would join the chief in Baltenn's clan, Krunnan's woman forever.

When the bowl was empty and Ragna's face smeared with blood and ash, she stood and stepped back from the pyre. The shaman finished his chanting and took his place at the chief's head.

With one motion, Dane and the other dragonsworn stepped forward, lowering their torches to light the pyre. It crackled softly until the oil-soaked logs under the body caught with a whoosh. Dane and the others stepped back, holding their torches aloft again, faces hot as the funeral pyre burned.

A shadow cut through the column of smoke as Ardos dove from the starlit heavens. His wings fanned the blaze, filling the circle with smoke as he flapped twice over the pyre, roaring his anguish to the smiling moon above. Then he was gone, and the smoke rose straight up again, taking Chief Krunnan's spirit to Baltenn's immortal command.

***

The pyre burned for hours. Dane's eyes watered from the smoke as he stood in the guard of honor circling the blaze. From all around them, the rest of the clan drifted away, back to their tents, their women, their children. When the fire finally died, the dragonsworn would gather the ashes into small cloth packets, which they would give to their dragons at dawn. The chief's cremated remains would be scattered into the winds from the dragons' flight as the sun cast its first shadows across the plain. Dane felt a flush of pride that Ilst would be among them.

He thought of Eryn, who would have returned to his tent by now. She must be dazzled by this ceremony. Surely her people had nothing to compare to the majesty of a dragonsworn's funeral, or the promise of eternity in Baltenn's clan.

Dane smiled. *Perhaps she'll join me there one day.* Eindon were not worthy to wear the mordanii tattoos, but in time, Eryn might earn her freedom. Dane's own mother had before she died. Only the clan chief could grant an eindon their freedom and welcome them as a full member of the Dragon Clan, but it was not impossible. His mother had died years before, but Dane's father mourned her as a wife, not an eindon. If Chief Krunnan had lived, he might have freed Eryn for the service of saving his life. The thought gave Dane's heart a squeeze. What would she have done then? Run back to her old clan? Stayed here with Dragon Clan but not as his property? Would another man take her and claim her as his own? She chafed under the chain and his rune; he knew that. But he would never hurt her. The rest of the clan would make no such promises. She was only safe with him.

He had to show her that, make her understand. One day she would choose to stay, even if she were freed. One day she would wear the mordanii for him, when Dane's body lay on a pyre and Ilst mourned him from the sky.

One day, she'd be his by choice, and not by chain.

CHAPTER 12

Eryn stood at the back of the crowd ringing the funeral pyre. Surrounded by other eindon and the lowest of the clanspeople, she couldn't see anything and had to strain to hear the chanting from their shaman.

She knew some words of the language he spoke. When she began her training as caldera, she'd started learning the old tongue. It was a difficult language to learn, as some of the sounds had no written counterpart. Not that anyone here probably knew how to write. Nora taught her all she could once it became clear that Nora was marrying Eryn's brother, and not becoming caldera herself. They had little to work with. Their former caldera had died the winter before, and neither Nora nor Eryn had made the journey to Tiezahal, the foreign city where they would study a whole summer with the wise women there, learning secrets and lore, medicine and tradition. The city was hidden in the southern mountains on the landbridge that connected Den Woth to Concadia, and its library was legendary. Eryn would have gone there this summer to study, and Nora had told her everything she knew about the wonders of the city of stone.

But now, of course, none of that would happen. She was the property of a barbarian, a dragon-slaver, part of a herding clan that was so feared and reviled they weren't even allowed to cross the border into the city at all.

She listened to the chanting. It was all about Baltenn, one of the lesser gods. Mordall, god of death, was hardly mentioned at all, and the other five gods were completely absent. The shaman seemed to be imploring Baltenn to take the dead chief up into some kind of clan-in-the sky, presumably to wreak havoc there as well. The chief's woman, Ragna, joined the chant, pledging herself to serve her dead man forever. Did she even know what she was saying? Eryn couldn't see what was happening, but the crowd around her whispered something about face tattoos, the mark of a dragonsworn's widow. It hardly mattered to Eryn. The woman had caused her husband's death. He'd been getting better under Eryn's care, but the mighty Dragon woman wouldn't listen to a slave. Now they'd pick a new barbarian king, and everything would go on as usual.

She'd already sorted out most of the hierarchy. The dragonslavers were the top of the heap, followed by the warriors who didn't have dragons. Eryn had no idea how they enslaved dragons, or decided who got one, but it made no difference to her. Then came the men who worked with the cattle, Clan Dragon's prized herd. Then their artisans, such as they were. Finally came the women, then the elderly and infirm, and the eindon on the bottom. Some of the eindon worked with the cattle, others in various jobs around the tent city. A few were missing a foot, hobbling around on crutches. The ones who'd tried to escape. They could still tan cowhide or clean the long, shaggy hair that was sheared off the hides and woven into coarse, scratchy cloth. They could still cook or clean for the clan. But they certainly couldn't run again.

Eryn glanced behind her. Everyone was focused on the funeral. Could she use the darkness and distraction to escape? A hive of tents lay between her and the open fields where the cattle grazed. Would anyone be watching out there? Could she possibly do it?

But where would she run? There were no mountains here. Nowhere to hide. This wide plain was days' walk from any land she knew, any foothills that would conceal her. And on her ankle, she wouldn't move anywhere nearly fast enough.

Above her, a dragon roared. She watched, transfixed, as the huge black dragon that had belonged to the chief dove down toward the fire. He pulled up at the last moment, fanning the blaze with his wings, before circling up through the tower of smoke. With a final roar, he disappeared into the night. His grief sounded real and felt hollow in her chest. Whatever the clan did to bind the dragons, this one's anguish was palpable. In his way, he had loved his barbarian master.

You're free now. No more a slave. How she envied the dragon, sailing off to a new life of freedom.

They were all above the crowd, circling, some kind of honor guard watching over the funeral from the sky. Watching everyone. She could almost feel their eyes on her as she took an experimental step backwards, away from the crowd.

Perhaps if she stole a horse? With enough head start, could she outrun pursuit? She would need a horse. Her ankle was much improved from her poultices and tight wrapping, but she was nowhere near ready to run.

The answer came from above, as a waft of dragonstench blew down, ruffling her hair. She looked up into the dark eyes of Dane's dragon. *Ilst.* She wheeled over Eryn's head, glaring down at her.

No, not even with a horse. *He uses the dragon to watch me from the sky.* She would never make it, and the attempt would cost her a foot.

Not now, then. Perhaps some time in the future a chance would arise. She would be ready.

The crowd began to disperse, people heading to their own tents. Dane had told her he was part of the guard that would watch the body burn all night. Their tent would be hers alone until morning. She followed the crowd picking her way past cookfires and carts, past crying toddlers kept up way too late, past old women and tired men, to Dane's tent. It was just on the outside of the clearing where the pyre burned, and the scent of burning herbs, woodfire, and a darker, meatier scent filled the air. Their tent flap was closed with a thick cowhide hung in the doorway. She turned to look back at the funeral. The blazing pyre was ringed with men, maybe fifteen or twenty of them, all holding torches and watching as their leader burned. Ragna was there, wearing a long dark cloak. She was turned away from Eryn, hood shadowing the new tattoos on the older woman's face. Dane had told Eryn all about the funeral ceremony for a lost chief. The marks on Ragna's cheeks made her untouchable to any man, bonded as she was to a dead one.

Did eindon get marked like that? Dane seemed to have no other woman, certainly no wife. If he died before he chose a wife, would Eryn stand at the foot of his pyre with ash on her face, carved into the tracts of tears she wouldn't cry?

She wouldn't be free then. But she would be slave to a dead man, untouchable by others. Perhaps her life might be as she planned it, alone, with no man's hands upon her skin, free to practice her herbcraft and learn the barbarians' lore, whatever it was?

Assuming he had no wife when he died. Assuming an eindon could become untouchable. If Dane had a wife, then what? She didn't know what happened to eindon when their owner died. Would she be given to someone else? Surely not freed. If your master's death made you free, there would be a lot more dead dragonsworn, victims of unfortunate accidents that had nothing at all to do with their newly freed eindon. No, even Dragon Clan wasn't that stupid.

But Dane wasn't dying. She watched him, holding his torch, flames dancing across his face. Unlike the bearded, grizzled men around him, he honestly looked sad. He kept glancing up to the sky where his dragon circled with the others. At one point he looked over the pyre, catching Eryn's eye. He gave her a tiny nod, and the ghost of a smile, before turning his gaze back to the burning chief.

In the cold, still night air, an instant of warmth heated Eryn's belly. She brushed it away, turning her back to the pyre and the men with torches.

Some way, somehow, she'd find a way to fly away from here, free like the obsidian dragon. She'd leave Dane, with his strong chest and gentle eyes, his watching dragon and warm tent behind, and she would never, ever look back.

Chapter 13

After the long night standing vigil over the pyre, after collecting the ashes and distributing them among the dragons to be scattered over the plains from the sky, Dane returned to his tent and collapsed into his bed. Eryn was there and had cooked a meal that he ate before falling into a deep sleep.

When he awoke, Eryn was still there, with another meal prepared. It smelled odd, with spices he didn't recognize, and more vegetables than he generally preferred, but it all melded together into a surprisingly delicious red stew that she poured over cooked diced roots. He ate it all under her watchful eye.

"That was really good," he said, belting on his weapons. "You're a great cook."

She didn't answer, just rinsed the bowl in a bucket of water.

"I have to go to the opening, to witness the transfer. We'll have a new chief by sundown."

Eryn just looked at him, her face clearly stating that she couldn't possibly care less who the chief was.

"It might be my father," he continued, throwing on his fur cloak. Or it could be Brinir."

At that name, Eryn's eyes snapped to his.

Ah, so you do *care.*

"Brinir is his son, so there's a chance he might have chosen him. But Brinir is young, just a few years dragonsworn. Some of the older men might have a hard time following someone so inexperienced. There would definitely be a challenge. Brinir would fight anyone who didn't accept him, and that could be a disaster. When dragonsworn fight, their dragons become enemies as well. We have few enough as it is. Losing Ardos was a huge blow." He laced his boots and straightened up. "But we'll have another very soon." His eyes clouded. "While I'm gone, you should pack your things, and mine as well. We'll be leaving in the morning for Baltenn's stone and the Grayfang mountains. Go to the butcher and the foodmaster to get our travel food. We'll be gone for two weeks. They'll know what you need."

By the time he reached the chief's tent, the sun had nearly set. Ragna had cleared all of her things out and removed Krunnan's personal items. The armor, weapons, and pennant of Dragon Clan Chief were piled in the corner, waiting for the next chief to assume his position. All of the other dragonsworn had assembled and stood waiting for him, along with the shaman who had removed the strings of bones and now wore his normal brown robe. He still wore the buffalo skull, peering out through the eyeholes.

In the center of the floor sat a carved wooden box. Square, a hand's width on each side, it bore Krunnan's rune on all four sides. The top was blank with a hole in the center. On one side, a slit in the top would allow a small scrap of paper to be slid into the box. If another scrap was slid in later, it would lay on top of the first.

Many in Dragon Clan had little use for writing, but all men knew their own runes and the runes of others. Chief Krunnan would have chosen his own successor by writing the man's rune and slipping the paper inside the box. If he had changed his mind over the course of his leadership, he had only to write a new rune and slip it in. That new rune would be on top. In this way, the box contained a record of the chief's choices through his time as chief. If the man whose rune was on top was unable to become chief—perhaps if a battle claimed both of their lives so the chief had no time to choose a new successor—the next name underneath would assume the role. As long as there was no challenge to the succession, there would be no fighting today.

As Krunnan's son, Brinir had the honor of driving the spike. He took a long, smooth iron nail and set it into the small hole in the box. With one blow of his great hammer, he crushed the box, driving the nail through the papers and straight down onto the bottom of the box, pinning the papers against the wood.

He stepped back, and the shaman pulled the box from the ground, grunting with the effort. Brinir's nail had driven it hard into the ground.

There were three papers impaled against the wood.

Please, lord Baltenn. Not Brinir. He's not ready. He's selfish and impulsive. He'll get people killed. And he didn't like Dane.

And Dane didn't like the way Brinir looked at Eryn. Not one bit.

If Brinir was chief, Dane had no doubt who would be sent on the most dangerous raids, leaving his eindon alone in the camp. No doubt if Dane fell in battle, Brinir would replace the rune on Eryn's neck with his own. Eindon didn't live long as Brinir's property. Most managed to kill themselves in a matter of months. Dane thought Rina probably had something to do with that as well.

The shaman held the paper up for all to see.

Thank you, Baltenn. Thank you for guiding our former chief.

"I hold here the will of Chief Krunnan, his dying wish for Clan Dragon. Calnan Rowe is named Clan Chief."

Dane's father let out a huge sigh. Dane did, too.

There was some grumbling from Brinir and his friend Tornnen, but a quick glance around the assembled men showed everyone else in assent. No one would support Brinir's challenge. Today there would be no fight. Dane's father was clan chief until his death.

By tomorrow the woodcutters would prepare a new wooden cube, and Chief Calnan would slide in a rune, his first choice to take over when he died.

Let that be many years from now, Dane silently prayed. His father was the best choice. Even tempered, battle-hardened, and wise, he would continue the prosperity that Chief Krunnan had begun.

They lined up to swear fealty to him. One by one they stood before him and declared their loyalty. Chief Calnan placed a hand on each man's shoulder in turn, accepting their oath.

When it was Dane's turn, he stood in front of his father, huge smiles on both of their faces. "I pledge you the strength of my arm, the power of my dragon, and the courage of my heart. For the clan, for our chief, and for our people, I will follow your command."

Calnan placed a hand on his son's shoulder. "For the clan, for our dragons, and for our people, I hear your words and accept your pledge."

Tonight, they would feast.

And tomorrow, the six youngest dragonsworn, including Dane, would each choose one of their eindon to take on the long journey to the Grayfang mountains. Dane had only Eryn, so she would have to be his offering. At least one of those eindon would not come home. And from that sacrifice, a new dragon would be bound to a young warrior. Such was the way of Dragon Clan, the yearly sacrifice to keep their numbers strong.

Please, lord Baltenn, he prayed again. *Please don't choose Eryn.*

CHAPTER 14

Eryn asked once where they were going. On the first morning of the journey, she rode her horse close to Dane's.

"Where is the Stone of Baltenn? And why are we going there?"

He wouldn't meet her eyes. "The Stone of Baltenn guards the only pass through the Grayfang mountains. Wild dragons live in those mountains. When the fourth moon rises full, Baltenn will judge the warriors who hope to become dragonsworn." He nodded behind them at five men who rode in the middle of the pack. Ranging from perhaps seventeen to almost thirty, all were muscular, with hard eyes. "They will submit to the Dance of Dragons, and those who survive will have the chance to bloodbond with an egg, which the dragons will give us."

That sounds fishy. "Wild dragons just give you eggs? Why would they do that?"

He edged his horse a few steps away. "It's an ancient pact between our clan and the dragons."

That's no answer.

"Why wouldn't they survive the Dance, whatever that is?"

He shrugged. "The Dance sends their spirits to Baltenn to be judged. He doesn't always send them back."

It hadn't escaped her attention that each dragonsworn had an eindon with him. "Dane, why am I here?"

He smiled, a hollow, ghostly smile. "You're here because you're mine. Why would I want to leave you behind?"

His words sounded sincere, but Eryn caught the flicker of his eyes. There was something he wasn't telling her.

Behind her in the saddle, her pack shifted. She'd brought all of her herbs in case she was needed for some injury or illness along the way. If it happened to some of the drag-onsworn, like Brinir, she might "accidentally" choose the wrong herbs. Who would know? But she might also be killed if anyone suspected.

The other eindon women rode with their horses teth-ered to their owners'. She'd seen them around the camp; most of them, anyway. One of the women was missing a foot, and another was missing both of her eyes. No bandage covered the holes, and the empty sockets were horrifying. Eryn was glad the poor woman couldn't see her own reflec-tion in water. What had merited such a punishment? The lack of other scars on her face showed it was certainly deliberate. Did she look at another man? Steal something? But that would likely cost her a hand. Eryn shivered. *Barbarians.* Would Dane do that to her if he thought she looked at the wrong thing?

No. He's not like them.

As soon as the thought drifted into her head, she batted it away. Of course he was like them. The fact that he wasn't a rapist and hadn't forced himself on her didn't make him any less barbarian. He was being kind because he wanted her in his bed, and apparently he didn't want a woman who fought back or lay like a statue. *He'll be waiting a long time.*

There was no one here to protect her except him. She'd seen how the other men looked at her. The chain around her neck made her an eindon slave. Dane's rune made her his. But in a strange way, what made her eindon also kept her safe.

She belonged to Dane, and even the other dragonsworn seemed to respect that.

If anything happens to Dane, I'll use the right herbs.

She hadn't asked yet, but couldn't shake the thought.

"Dane, if a dragonsworn dies, what happens to their eindon?"

He rode back over to her. "They're given to any dragonsworn that want them, that have runes enough to claim them."

"Did the old chief have any?"

He snorted. "Of course. He had around ten. I thought about claiming one of the younger men to help with Ilst's care, but honestly I prefer caring for her myself. And we don't need anyone else to worry about." He looked into her eyes. "Eindon are a responsibility. You're mine to care for, and I'm responsible for what you do. You're fed and housed because of my status, and my work for the clan."

She asked the other question. "Are eindon ever freed?"

His face fell. "On occasion. A dragonsworn can free an eindon, but it almost never happens. Sometimes one who has borne him many children and been a good mother might be freed. When my mother was dying, my father freed her so she could be honored in death as Dragon Clan."

What an honor. And what timing. Dying, useless for more children, so he frees her when it costs him nothing.

"She raised me to respect our eindon." He looked around at some of the other men.

Tornnen was pulling the rope for his eindon's horse. She was the blind one. He eased the horse up next to his, and when it was close, he reached out and smacked the woman on the cheek. She flinched away. Never saw it coming. Tornnen and the nearby dragonsworn laughed.

Brinir called out, "Hope Baltenn wants a blind one. Be nice to get rid of that burden."

Tornnen shrugged. "She still serves her purpose." The others laughed again.

Dane looked at Eryn. "You have Ilst to thank that you're mine."

She peered straight back. "I have Ilst to thank for finding me at all. If she hadn't, you would have left and I would still be with my clan. What's left of it."

Dane had no answer for that.

CHAPTER 15

The journey took five days of hard riding. It was colder in the northern plains, wind whipping down across the whole of Den Woth to batter against the high mountains that became visible in the distance. Dane showed Eryn how to erect their travel tent at night, and she used the provisions on the horse cart to make their meals. He tried to engage her in conversation as they rode, but she always kept just barely too much distance between their horses. At night, the dragonsworn drank and threw carved bone dice, betting coins and weapons and the use of their eindon on the results. Dane drank with them but didn't play their game. If he lost Eryn, even for a night, she would never forgive him.

And she was worth waiting for. She was softening to him; he was sure of it. She still fingered the chain around her neck when they spoke, and probably wasn't aware she was doing it. It bothered her. And why shouldn't it? Her own clan was inferior and had allowed her to be captured. She was incredibly lucky that Dane had found her and not a brute like Brinir. His eindon on this trip was missing a foot from an early escape attempt. He hoped she would be chosen, or maybe the blinded woman. That had been gruesome. Tornnen had done it in front of everyone, all the while looking to Brinir for approval. Rina had held the woman's head down, sitting on her long hair where she lay on the ground, bound hand and foot. Tornnen had done the job carefully, first the right eye, then the left. Ragna packed herbs into the empty holes and they left her there all night in the cold. Dane shivered at the memory. No, he would not let Eryn fall into anyone else's hands, and thanked Baltenn for his eindon mother, who showed him that eindon were just people who couldn't help the clan they'd been born to. He hoped Eryn might befriend some of the eindon they'd brought on the journey, to see how lucky she was to be his, but the other women chosen to come were mostly beyond conversation, just dull-eyed husks who probably hoped they wouldn't return.

On the evening of the fifth day, they reached the pass. The Grayfang mountains had no foothills leading up to them. They rose straight from the plains like jagged teeth, pushing above the clouds. A single pass opened to the flatlands, right into the sheer cliffs up a twisting path of switchbacks. They herded the horses into a small outcropping of rocks at the base of the path. The well-trained beasts would graze until their return, and the dragons would protect them.

They had to leave their dragons behind. The wild dragons who lived in the lands beyond the pass hated the bloodbound. Ilst didn't know why, or if she did, she couldn't tell him. Before they began the climb, he checked her all over, teeth and claw.

"You have to stay here with the others," he told her, whispering as he wiped every scale. "We'll get you a new member of the flock—hopefully two or three this year. But you have to wait out here. I'll be back in three days." Displeasure rolled through his mind. Ilst was highly upset to be parted from him.

Care. Do not trust dragons.

He chuckled. "Only you, Ilst. I only trust you."

The dragons took to the air, circling near the cliffs. Kalg, the senior dragon present, would join the clan at Baltenn's stone for the ceremony tonight, but the rest would not venture up the pass. There was plenty for them to hunt on the plains, though nothing as nourishing as the great herds they had left back home. By the time they left the mountains, dragon eggs safely nestled on the cart, the rest of the clan would have moved the herds east, toward the dragonsworn. Four days' journey back instead of five. The nomadic tribe would circle the whole plain over the course of the year, ending up back where they had left them, where the best winter grazing kept the herd healthy through the cold months.

Feeling Ilst's heartbreaking sadness, he left her and joined the rest of the group, heading up the switchback trail. After an hour of climbing, the trail dove straight toward the center of the mountain, passing between tall cliffs that opened out wide at the top to the darkening sky. In the middle of a large clearing full of scrubby brush, Baltenn's stone sat. A huge round slab of granite etched with the runes of Baltenn in the center, it lay flat on a square base.

The shaman spent an hour sweeping off the Stone, brushing out dirt and pollen from every tiny crack. This was where Baltenn would choose which of the young men they'd brought were worthy of bloodbonding to an egg. And the great god would also choose which eindon would serve as the ancient sacrifice, the bargain between Dragon Clan and the wild dragons that allowed the humans to claim new eggs.

High cliffs channeled the wind straight up through the pass. There was no room in the clearing for tents, only bedrolls of warm fur. Dane smiled a bit, watching Eryn lay out their sleeping furs. She left some distance between them, but if the night grew chilly enough, she might snuggle in for warmth.

The sun set and the moon rose, shining white, cold light through the pass. A shadow passed over the moon as Kalg winged her way up from the plains below. The space between the cliffs took maneuvering for her to land, and she fanned them with icy wing-beats, kicking up dirt with her claws. Her dragonsworn, Kienno, laid a hand on her neck as she snorted, hot breath steaming in the night.

"Arise, warriors, and seek your destiny upon the Stone of Baltenn." The shaman's voice carried over the dragon's scuffling. Both man and beast knew their parts.

Five young hopefuls had accompanied the dragonsworn and eindon on the journey, each hoping to return with an egg of their own. Dane remembered his own ceremony just two years ago, when he'd earned the egg that hatched Ilst, most perfect of all dragons. He could almost smell the excitement and fear rolling off the young men who would do the Dance of Dragons tonight.

The shaman approached the Stone. "Lord Baltenn, we send you our strongest warriors. If you find them worthy of your highest honor, return them to us and let their names be held high among the Dragon Clan. If they be found wanting, consume their spirits and leave their empty shells as a gift to the dragons who give us our name."

The first young warrior removed his clothing and climbed up onto the Stone. He lay there naked, eyes fixed on the full moon. Dane remembered his own ceremony, the ice cold of the Stone on his own back, the chilly wind rushing through the pass. He remembered the shadow of the dragon that fell over his shivering form and the searing pain of the dragon's fang as it punctured his left bicep. His world had gone black then, but he knew that, like this young man now, he had done the Dance of Dragons as the venom took hold, limbs jerking, eyes rolled back in his head.

Dane looked over to where Eryn stood with the other eindon, pressed up against the cliff wall, watching this for the first time. His chest puffed with pride. *She sees what I went through—what I survived.* In the distance, he felt Ilst's amused chuckle.

The young man on the Stone jerked and thrashed, knocking his head against the granite. He would have a terrible headache if he awakened from the poison. When he finally stilled, Dane and the other dragonsworn pulled his limp body from the Stone and laid him to the side. In a few hours, he would either wake up exalted, or not at all.

The next warrior took his place on the Stone and submitted to the bite. By the time all five had done the Dance, the moon had traveled across the sky, out of sight behind the cliff wall. Kalg launched herself into the sky in a shower of dirt and sand, returning to the rest of the flock that waited on the outside of the pass.

They left the naked men lying in a row, covered in furs against the cold night air. No one ever spoke of the journey the spirit took in those hours of stillness. Dane wondered if it was because, like him, they didn't remember. He had only the vaguest image, more nightmare than memory, of a huge shaggy form and his own silent screams. Did other men kneel at the feet of Lord Baltenn, god of dragons and beasts? Did the god talk with him? Had he spoken with Lord Baltenn, and the memory of the lord's face was too perfect to remember? Dane had no answers.

The shaman cleaned off the Stone in preparation for tomorrow's choosing ceremony, and they all retired to their bedrolls to await the god's decision.

CHAPTER 16

Eryn lay awake, listening to the snores of the drag-onsworn around her and the still, eerie quiet of the men who had been bitten. Dane assured her that at least one would survive the poison and awaken by morning.

"At least one is always chosen," he murmured from his bedroll next to hers. She'd laid them out next to a small rock outcropping that blocked a little of the wind.

"Do they ever all survive it?" *Always the caldera, even in this clan which has no lorekeeper because none of them can probably read more than their own names.* The ceremony was barbaric, as she expected. She'd seen the scar on Dane's bicep but never con-sidered asking where it came from. *He did that. Laid there naked on that rock and let a venomous dragon bite him.* She couldn't help but be intrigued. No one in her clan had had any idea how Dragon Clan bonded their dragons. Did surviving the venom somehow make them smell familiar to a dragon hatchling? She knew there were more ceremonies to come, and al-though she scoffed at the idea that Baltenn himself had any-thing to do with who lived and who died, she couldn't pre-tend not to be fascinated with the ritual. And the thought of him lying naked on the stone...*No.* She ignored the tiny flare of warmth that image ignited between her thighs.

"I've never heard of them all surviving," Dane answered. "But maybe if only one warrior came, he'd have a better chance?"

"And no one has kept any records? Of who gets bitten, who survives, how many?" She couldn't believe that even the shaman was as backwards as the rest of them.

"Not that I know of."

They lay in silence for a while. Mice scuttled around the clearing, hoping for a bit of food left unwrapped. Bats flew overhead, calling their tiny, high-pitched cries into the night. Beyond this pass was unknown to her, but she could almost feel the presence of the wild dragons on the far side of the mountain range. Her people called it the Forbidden Valley, and no one had ever recorded anything about what lay through the pass.

"How many wild dragons are there?"

She felt Dane shift behind her. "We'll see maybe thirty or forty tomorrow night. They'll all come for..." he trailed off.

He'd been evasive about this journey since they left the rest of the clan. His eyes didn't meet hers when she asked, but the few words she'd coaxed out of the other eindon women were ominous. Not all of the warriors would survive this night. And not all of the eindon would be coming home.

Home. As if the clan of barbarians could ever be her home.

She asked the one question she dreaded the answer to. "Dane, can you protect me from whatever else is going to happen up here?"

He paused a long time before answering. "This is Lord Baltenn's sacred clearing. Upon his Stone the choices are made. From any threat on the ground or the sky, I will protect you until my death, but his will cannot be denied. If he chooses you tomorrow, I cannot change his decision."

She heard the quaver in his voice. The brash, cocky idiot was afraid. Scared of the god? Or scared of the god's will?

"Eryn, if you're cold, you can move over next to me. You're safe, and it's warmer with two."

An instant of jealousy flashed through Eryn's mind. *Who has he shared a bedroll with?* She pressed her cold lips together. *Who cares?* But despite the rock edge, the wind bit hard.

"Just to sleep? To keep warm?" She felt stupid asking.

"Just to sleep."

The cold air froze her hands as she wiggled out of her bedroll and dragged it a few feet over to where Dane lay. He held his fur blanket open, and she dove under it, facing away from him and curling up into a ball. His chest was warm against her back, breath hot in her ear. Furs covered them both in a cocoon of comfort. She pulled the blanket up over her head and snuggled back against him.

Just to keep warm.

He wrapped an arm over hers, pulling her in close, but true to his word, his hands didn't wander. He smelled of horse and dragon, and against her will, she relaxed.

In a short time, his breathing deepened and evened out. She lay awake, wrapped in his comforting heat, imagining what horror might await her when the sun rose in the morning.

Her ankle was improving every day, and it no longer hurt to breathe. She wished she knew what the next few days would bring. Perhaps there would be an opportunity to escape in the Forbidden Valley. The bonded dragons were all on the outside of the mountain range. No eyes would be watching her from the sky, or at least, no eyes that would betray her to a warrior. Dane had told her that he shared thoughts with Ilst, and he seemed to mean it literally, though she couldn't imagine such a thing. But she had no doubt that if she tried to leave the clan, either warriors or a dragon would find her outside these mountains. Maybe they would be so distracted by whatever was coming that there would be a moment she could slip away. Her people were shepherds, and the tough mountain sheep they bred were at home in the hills. Eryn was raised in the mountains, though nothing as intimidating as this. Dragon Clan were people of the plains. Surely, she could hide in the mountains.

Her mind drifted back to the night she was captured. To her sister-in-law, Nora, and her niece, Filina. They must have found a place to hide, before Eryn had tumbled down the hill where Dane found her unconscious. But no one had been searching for them. Dane and the rest would certainly search for her. For how long? They wouldn't stay here forever, away from their precious dragons. Without their great flying beasts, they were just warriors. If she could slip away here, and survive in the Forbidden Valley until they left, she might be free.

Her fingers rubbed the rune around her neck, cold metal against her skin. *He thinks I'm his. No better than a dragon slave. He'll find a new one when I'm gone.*

With her head lying pillowed on his arm, his soft breathing on the back of her neck, she closed her eyes and slept, and dreamed of strong arms wrapping her body in pleasure.

Chapter 17

Dane awoke before dawn, warm softness in his arms. Eryn lay sleeping against him, her back pressed into his belly, cheek lying against the scar on his bicep where he'd been bitten in the ceremony two years earlier. He remembered waking up the next morning, head on fire, arm pounding with pain. But he would do it again any day.

Far out on the plain below, Ilst was asleep. Her mind was fuzzy to him when she slept. When they were both awake, he could always feel her presence. His father had been dragonsworn for years—since before Dane was born—and had helped Dane in the early days of Ilst's hatching—when their bond was wild and uncontrolled. He'd felt her every emotion and physical sensation, which was mostly hunger as she grew and grew. They learned to separate their thoughts from the tangled mess of the first days, and to communicate through feelings and later, words. When they were both awake, he could reach out to her as long as she was close enough, and tune into her mind as if it were his own. He'd watched through her eyes as she soared over the prairie, strengthening her wings and learning to hunt. Felt her claws as his own, snatching a cow from the herd, talons snapping its neck. Dragons weren't much larger in body than the cattle of Dragon Clan's herd, so they couldn't carry prey of that size into the air. But the satisfaction of the kill on the ground, the taste of blood in her mouth, and the pride of defending her meal against the other dragons…his heart pounded with pride.

Within the hour, the young warriors who were destined to be dragonsworn would awaken. He knew them all and had played with them as children, learning to shoot a bow and wield a sword. Some of them would not wake up. They would already be stiff when pulled from the furs, rejected by Baltenn. Death by dragon bite was not a gentle way to die, though certainly honorable for a warrior. But it was worth the gamble to gain a dragon of their own.

Eryn stirred against him. He felt her stiffen when she realized she lay snuggled in his embrace, and he held still, breathing softly. His arm was asleep where she'd lain on it all night, but he didn't budge.

I'm not so bad.

She'd see it in time. She'd want him like he wanted her.

Assuming she wasn't chosen today. Assuming she made the journey home with him.

He was torn, wanting the young warriors to survive their choosing, but not wanting so many to wake up that the odds of Eryn being chosen increased.

Each new dragonsworn needed an egg. The ancient bargain with the wild dragons called for sacrifice. They would happily accept the bodies of the dead hopefuls, but an egg required a living woman, a gift on the mountain. For each egg they gained, an eindon must be given. So, for each warrior who woke up, an eindon would die tomorrow at dawn. Wild dragons demanded their due.

Eryn's voice was soft. "Are the men alive?"

His heart swelled. She was so kind. Her first thought upon waking was for the men she claimed to despise.

Unless she knew. Maybe she was just calculating her odds.

"I don't know yet. But it's almost time to get up and see."

She relaxed against him for a moment, and he luxuriated in their shared warmth. *It could be like this every morning.* The thought heated him all the way through.

Not yet. He pulled away from her, not wanting her to feel the heat of his desire for her through his pants. She'd be out of the bedroll like an arrow from a bow if she felt that.

But with his movement, the spell was broken. She scuttled away, letting the cold air rush in as she sat up from their blankets. *Soon, maybe.* He focused on Ilst, waiting for his body to relax. *Soon.*

The camp stirred all around. He threw off the blanket and sat up, pulling the waterskin from behind him and taking a long drink. Eryn was already rolling up her blankets and didn't meet his eyes.

He left his blankets for her to pick up and hurried over to the furs covering the hopefuls. The shaman was already there.

Two. Of the five young men who were bitten, only two stirred. The other three lay still, eyes open, tears frozen on their faces. Three mouths were open and stiff, tongues swollen and protruding through dark lips.

He joined the shaman in pulling the two living young men from the furs, wrapping their punctured arms, and helping them into clothing. They were confused, elated for themselves but anguished for their friends who were not so fortunate. Dane shared their feelings.

Two new dragonsworn. Two eggs. Two eindon out of the six that were brought along for the purpose. Eryn had a one out of three chance of being chosen.

Please, Lord Baltenn. Please don't take her. She's special.

Ilst purred in his mind. Eryn hadn't shown any interest in Dane's dragon, but Ilst approved of her anyway. She'd never purred about any other woman he'd brought to his bed.

They pulled the bodies of the three dead to the edge of the path. When they left the open clearing where the Stone stood, they would take the bodies on up the pass and into the valley beyond, a gift for the dragons. There was no shame in being gifted to a dragon, eaten by the greatest of Baltenn's creations. It was a fitting end for a young warrior and an honor for an eindon. Just not Eryn.

The sky was gray above as they ate a cold meal of dried beef. Dane and the dragonsworn would pass the morning drinking and gambling, celebrating the new additions to their ranks. When the sun peaked in the sky, the eindon choosing would begin.

Chapter 18

Eryn stood behind Dane, her hands gripping the edges of her cloak, worrying the fur between her fingers. They gathered at Baltenn's Stone, a big flat slab of rock with runes carved into it—just the name of Baltenn, as she expected from this clan of illiterates. The six dragonsworn who had come on this journey knelt around the stone, each with his eindon behind him. Upon the table sat a metal rune in front of each man, the same runelocks they used when claiming new eindon with chains.

The wind had stopped. The wide clearing in the mountain pass felt silent and ominous. No mice scuttled in the underbrush; no birds wheeled overhead. Eryn felt totally alone, though she pressed up against Dane's back, peering around his side.

He had been so warm this morning. She awoke before he did and laid still under the furs, listening to his soft snores. His arm was draped over her shoulder, her back pressed into his chest. Outside, the night had been full of the calls of insects and the flapping wings of bats on the hunt. But under the furs, there was only his heartbeat against her spine, his pulse matching hers. Her instinct was to pull away, to run in the dark of night. Instead, she lay still until his breathing changed and she felt him stir to wakefulness. For the tiniest moment, she had felt safe in his arms. But there was no safety here. As she stared at the hard faces of the men around the stone, and the worn, defeated eyes of the women who slumped behind them, she knew that for all his act of patience and gentleness, Dane was no different from the rest of his barbarian friends. How could he be? Cruelty and dominance were all this clan knew.

Two of the other eindon had been through this before. Although the women weren't close, Eryn had prized the information out of them while the stone was set for this choosing.

A woman's life for a dragon egg. They needed two, one for each man who had survived the dance. Two women out of the six here.

From their brief huddle, Eryn knew that Trinda, the girl who had been blinded by Tornnen, hoped to be chosen. She was so desperate to escape the man's brutality that death seemed the only answer. Calla, Brinir's eindon who had lost a foot as punishment for an escape attempt, seemed ambivalent. The other three were likewise resigned to their fate. Live as a slave, or die tomorrow…it hardly mattered to them. Whatever lives they had lived before the chains were wrapped around their necks—those lives were gone. They had long since abandoned hope of returning to them.

The shaman moved into the circle of men, standing at the edge of the round, flat stone.

"Lord Baltenn has provided, and his will shall choose those most worthy of answering his call. The people of the dragon shall fulfill the ancient contract, and the dragonsworn will forever praise his name."

His hands were cupped, and from between his fingers, Eryn saw skittering movement. He leaned across the table, centering his hands in the middle of the stone, and opened them. A mouse dropped onto the granite surface, black eyes blinking in the morning light.

"Lord Baltenn," the shaman intoned, "let this, the least of your beasts, reveal the dragonsworn who is most worthy of the great honor his sacrifice will bring."

His sacrifice. Eryn's pulse pounded in her temples. *That's all we are. Property to be sacrificed. A gift to be given.* She glanced at the eyeless woman behind Tornnen. *Or used-up refuse to be thrown away.*

The mouse sat still in the center of the stone for a long moment. Eventually it would move, skittering away. Whichever rune it touched on its way to escape, that dragonsworn would be eliminated from contention, their eindon safe.

Heart in her throat, Eryn watched, hands rising unbidden to grip Dane's shoulders from behind.

The mouse twitched, every man's eyes upon it. With a lurch, it skittered across the stone, running across one of the runes in its path. The rune's owner, a dark-eyed, bearded man, grabbed the mouse and handed it back to the shaman. With a chuckle, the dragonsworn picked up his rune and shoved his eindon back. "Guess I'm stuck with you a while longer." Eryn couldn't tell if the woman's eyes filled with relief or despair.

Dragonsworn shifted, moving their runes back to even spacing around the circle in the absence of the first to be eliminated.

Five left. Three will be safe, and two… Eryn gripped Dane's shoulders harder. *Please, please, please, not us.*

The shaman dropped the mouse again, and Dane leaned forward under Eryn's grip.

Come on, little mouse. Come this way, she silently willed it.

And for a moment, it did. The little creature crawled right toward Dane for a moment before stopping and zipping off at an angle.

It crawled straight over Brinir's rune.

The big man nodded, picking up his rune. Calla, his ein-don hobbled away, limping on the thick, padded bandage where her ankle ended, the foot chopped off long ago.

Four left.

The next to be released was the oldest of the drag-onsworn, a quiet man who shrugged, standing up and speaking to his eindon. "Six years I've offered you, and six years Lord Baltenn hasn't wanted you. Maybe I should just let you go."

For a moment, something like hope lifted the woman's features, but then the man laughed, and her face fell back to the ground. They shuffled back to let the remaining three move into position, evenly spaced around the stone.

Three of us left. Two will die tomorrow.

Torrnen was to their left and a young dragonsworn named Lurin to their right. Lurin's eindon, a woman not much older than Eryn, had a nose that had been broken, and was missing all of her front teeth. Her name was Silva, and she might have been beautiful before she was chained and obviously beaten. Now she stood behind Lurin, arms hanging limp at her side. She stared off into the distance, not even looking as the shaman prepared to drop the mouse one final time.

Dane gripped the edge of the stone table. Lurin and Torrnen shared a chuckle, looking across the stone at him. "Worried you might lose your pretty little pet, Dane?" Torrnen asked. "She doesn't look like she wants to leave you, but if we lose ours, you'll share her on the way back, won't you? I promise not to cut anything out of her as long as she behaves."

Dane just grunted, and the shaman dropped the mouse in the middle of the table.

Eryn stared at it, praying silently. She could almost hear its tiny heartbeat, fluttering in terror. Her nails dug into Dane's shoulders, but he didn't move.

Please come here, she begged the mouse. *Please come to our rune.*

The mouse hesitated. It took three steps toward Torn-nen.

"No!" Eryn tried to stifle her cry.

Dane reached up and laid his hand over hers. She gripped his fingers, eyes never leaving the mouse.

Please come to us. Please.

She threw her soul into the silent prayer, squeezing Dane's hand.

With a tiny squeak, the mouse dashed across the table, crossing Dane's rune and dropping off the edge of the table into his lap.

Chapter 19

Dane grabbed the mouse in one hand and his rune in the other. Cupping the mouse gently, he wrapped his arms around Eryn. For a brief second, their eyes locked, and he smiled.

"Lord Baltenn is letting me keep you."

Her face hardened, and she pulled away from him.

"Wouldn't want a god to take what's yours."

Dane's jaw tightened. *I don't understand her. She should be happy, shouldn't she?* While it was a great honor to be traded to the dragons in exchange for an egg, surely she didn't want to die, did she? Maybe her clan was even more pious than Dragon Clan. Maybe she did want to be the sacrifice and give her life to the god of dragons.

"Did your clan offer their lives to Lord Baltenn? We can sacrifice a calf when we return to the herds if it makes you feel better."

He didn't think it was possible for her expression to harden any more, but she was like the stone of granite behind him.

"My clan did not make human sacrifice. I have no desire to be given to a dragon."

In his head, he could almost see Ilst rolling her eyes. The dragon was too far away to speak into his head, but through their bond he could feel her mirth. Ilst liked Eryn, probably because Dane did, despite her strange ways. Ilst would be happy when they returned down the cliff together.

But first, there was the sacrifice.

Everyone packed up, and the three dead warriors were wrapped with rope to make it easier to pull them up and down the steepest part of the journey. The dragonsworn would take turns hauling them to the Valley of Dragons.

They picked up their personal belongings, Eryn shouldering her bag of herbs and medications. No one had needed medical care on the journey, but she was prepared. His heart swelled with pride again. Not only was she the most beautiful eindon in the clan, but she was smart enough to be her clan's herbwoman. They had another name for it, though, and he tried to engage her in conversation as they followed the switchback trail higher into the cliff.

"What did your clan call you?" He gestured to the pack on her back.

She stared into him. "Eryn."

"No, no. I know your name." Her look cut him to ribbons. *She thinks you're an idiot.* Far away, Ilst laughed and agreed. "I mean what you are. Not just an herbwoman, right?"

Her hands adjusted the pack on her shoulders. "Caldera," she said. "Keeper of lore, master of medicine, holder of ancient wisdom." She paused. "That's what I would have become, had I not been captured and made a slave."

Ah. She was still angry about that. Dane had no idea how to convince her that her luck had changed for the better when she became Dragon Clan. Even an eindon was better than any lesser clan. But he'd tried explaining that, and it didn't seem to get through.

"How close were you to finishing your training, or whatever it was?"

She sighed. "I would have traveled this summer to Tiezahal and studied under the Tieza, a great teacher, holder of wisdom. Her library holds all the knowledge of the clans of Den Woth, and the learning of all Concadia as well." A side-eye glance and a twitch of her lips was replaced in an instant with her mask of ice again. "A library is a place where there are books. And books are lots of pieces of parchment all put together, and they all have writing on them." She took a breath. "And writing is— "

His face flushed. "I know what writing is. Believe it or not, I can read more than just a single rune."

She cocked an eyebrow at him. "How many? Two? Three? Can you read four runes all at once, or do you have to take a break in between?"

Dane glanced around to make sure none of the other dragonsworn were listening to their exchange. He should beat her for talking to him like that. Brinir would cut out her tongue if she were his. He shuddered at the thought of Brinir's hands on her. Then he thought about his own hands on her. Not for a beating. She wouldn't respond to that. His eindon mother's spirit, which awaited his father's death to re-unite them, would haunt him if he struck Eryn in anger. But Baltenn's balls, she was a challenge.

The trail narrowed, and they skittered up the loose stone pathway, cliff walls close on each side.

He tried a different tack. Maybe she had really wanted to go to Tiezahal. Dragon Clan didn't trade directly with Concadia, but through the Rooted Clan who lived near the border, they were able to trade for any goods they wanted from the heathen land to the east.

"If you're upset about that trip, we could go there our-selves. If you want to see all the books there, I'm sure—"

"We can't go to Tiezahal." Her voice was flat. "Do you not even know that? Dragon Clan isn't welcome in Concadia.

Something about a group of barbarians with human-eating dragons just isn't welcome in a civilized city."

She stumbled over a stone, dropping to her knees, but shrugged Dane's hands away when he tried to help her up.

"And how will they keep us out?" Dane pulled himself up a steep, rocky rise and reached a hand back to Eryn. After a moment eyeing the path, she let him help her. The trail flattened out, winding between huge stones. This was the summit of the climb. From here, they would descend to their campsite for the night, near the opening of the path to the valley of dragons.

"My brother's wife has been there," she said quietly. "She went when she was my age, before she married my brother and had my niece. She said there are guards at the border. No dragons allowed in. We would have to leave your precious dragon behind to enter, and pretend we were from some other clan."

There was something in her tone. Softness. Sadness.

"Well," Dane said, "I'm sure she can train someone new. And you can learn from our herbwoman."

She gave him a look that clearly told him what she thought about Dragon Clan's herbwoman. Until he met Eryn, he would have defended Ragna's superiority to anyone. But the chief had died in her care, after Eryn brought him safely home. Surely no clan could have better knowledge than Dragon Clan's. But he didn't know a thing about the city she named. His world was the vast plain of Den Woth, ringed by mountains and the distant sea. He wasn't lying when he said he could read. But for the first time in his life, he wondered what else he'd always taken for granted. What other things he simply didn't know.

The trail curved and descended. Here in the narrow pass, they couldn't track the sun across the sky, but as the shadows deepened, they reached a small valley, already green as spring warmed the ground. They would camp here tonight, and at dawn, make the final descent into the land of the wild dragons.

CHAPTER 20

They had no tents, but the wind didn't rush through this little valley like it had high on the trail. It was warmer here, with the first signs of spring carpeting the ground in soft grass and early wildflowers. The valley was small, no more than a few hundred paces wide, but a small copse of trees surrounded a little brook that brought icy runoff down the mountain. In the fading light, Eryn filled her waterskin, taking a moment to splash her face and rinse out her dusty mouth in the cold, fresh water.

"Here. There's fresh water."

Eryn turned to see Silva leading Trinda, the blinded eindon, over to the stream. Tomorrow morning, both of the women would be given to the wild dragons. Eryn shuddered, watching them kneel at the stream to cup water in their hands. Neither looked afraid. If Eryn had been chosen, she would be eyeing the path, looking for any way to escape her fate. But these women were broken, defeated. Live as slave to a brute, or die in the jaws of a dragon… Who could say what choice she would make?

Dane's laughter echoed across the little valley, and she turned to look at him. He was standing with one of the young men who had survived the venomous dragon bite, who was slated to receive a dragon egg with however this ghastly trade was accomplished. The younger man's eyes were alight, and Dane inclined his head, clearly sharing some knowledge he thought was important. He glanced her way, and she quickly turned her gaze back to the two eindon.

What could she possibly do? They were clearly resigned to their fate. How could she help them? *You can't. This is the way of the clan.* The thought almost seemed to come from outside her own head. The clan. The barbarians who didn't even know they weren't allowed outside their own lands.

The shaman approached Trinda and Silva. "Come, honored eindon. We must prepare you for your glorious fate." He led them across the valley and into the copse of trees. Eryn watched them go, heart wrenching for their "glorious fate."

She felt a presence behind her.

"So, eindon, Dane's kept you all to himself so far. But I think it's time we became acquainted."

Eryn didn't have to look. Brinir. Hard, callous hands grabbed her arms from behind, pulling her up and spinning her around. Her bruised ribs flared with pain, and she gasped, pulling her face away from the bearded man.

"You are a pretty thing, aren't you?" One hand gripped her bicep, hard enough to leave a bruise. With the other, he reached up to cup her chin, forcing her to face him. "Doesn't look like he's had to beat you at all, yet. Compliant, then. But I like a little fight."

His breath was sour in her face, and the heat in his eyes seared straight through her. Without thinking, she cried out.

"Dane! Help me!"

Brinir laughed, spraying spit into her face. "Aw, crying for your boy? Dane won't miss you for an hour or so. Come on, girl. I'll show you what a real man can do with a woman."

He dragged her back toward the trees, squeezing until she thought her upper arm would break. She braced her feet in the grass, but Brinir was twice her weight. She might as well have been fighting a dragon.

In an instant, the pressure on her arm was gone. She stumbled to her knees as Brinir was whipped around, letting her go.

"Hands off my eindon."

She had never been happier to hear Dane's voice.

She looked up to see the two men face to face. Brinir rubbed his shoulder where Dane must have punched him to make him let her go.

"You haven't shared her at all. It's high time we had a turn."

Even in the fading light, the rage on Dane's face lit him from within. "I don't intend to share her. No one gets a turn unless I say. You know the laws. Hands off."

They stared at each other for a long moment. There was no chief here to make Brinir obey whatever law allowed Dane to keep her for himself. If the rest of the dragonsworn allowed it, Dane was one against many.

After a long, tense glare, Brinir stepped back, laughing. He clapped Dane on the shoulder. "Seems you're not ready to share your good fortune with your brother dragonsworn." He glanced down at Eryn. "When you tire of her, I'm first in line. If you want to swap, the one I brought is very well trained. Not much of a runner, but she knows what she's for."

Dane's lips were a hard, straight line. "I'll bear that in mind." He pushed past Brinir and helped Eryn up, half-carrying her away from the trees and over to where he'd spread their bedroll.

There was no chance she was sleeping anywhere but wrapped in his protective arms tonight.

***

Eryn awoke to snoring through the camp. She had dreamed of Nora and Falina. They were running through a field of flowers, and her niece stopped to pick one. It was deep, twilight blue, and she reached for the petals.

"No, Filina, not that one," Eryn said. "Don't touch those petals. That's evening groundrose. If you get the dust in your mouth, you'll be sick in the morning."

Filina stared at her in the dream. She raised the flower to her lips. "It's all right, aunt Eryn. I can't get sick. I'm a dragon."

As Eryn watched in horror, Filina's face lengthened, fangs growing from her scaly lips, dripping with venom. Before the hideous transformation was complete, Eryn bolted into wakefulness, chest heaving and sweat on her forehead.

Behind her in the bedroll, Dane grunted and rolled over. His arm left her shoulder, and he lay on his back. In moments, he was snoring softly, his rumble added to those of the men bedded down around them.

Mind on fire, Eryn peered into the moonlit valley. Last night's fire had burned to embers, and a soft glow of matching orange flickered through the trees where the shaman had taken Trinda and Silva, the sacrifices.

You'll be sick in the morning.

The dream words floated back to her in the night.

She eased her way out of the bedding, listening to Dane's breathing. Satisfied that he still slumbered, she grabbed her bag of medicines, shivering in the night air. She didn't dare stop to put on her boots, and in a few steps her thick socks were soaked with cold dew.

Outside the copse of trees, she paused. If the shaman was still there, she would turn back. But as she peered through the trunks, she saw two forms sitting at the fire. She crept close.

"Trinda? Silva?" she whispered.

The two women looked up from the fire, Trinda's empty eyes hollow in the orange light.

"Who's there? Eryn?"

Careful not to make a sound, Eryn crept through the trees. She knelt next to the doomed women.

"I cannot take you away from here or save your lives. But I was my clan's caldera. I have herbs that can help."

Trinda smiled. Eryn had never seen the expression on her face before. "We don't need saving. Lord Baltenn chose to deliver us from our suffering. We go willingly to the dragons."

Silva didn't look quite so sure. "Lord Baltenn has spoken. We cannot question. But… how can you help us?"

Eryn opened her bag. "I have seeds. I'll make you each a packet. When the dragons come, chew it quickly. You will feel no pain, no fear. You'll be asleep before their teeth can touch you."

Trinda's long hair waved as she nodded. "That is appreciated. We must die. But we don't have to suffer."

You don't. But someone should.

"And there is another herb," Eryn continued. "A flower. I am not Dragon Clan. I am Godseye. And when our loved ones go to Baltenn's embrace, we anoint them with this flower. It's called…" she hesitated for a moment. "It's called purelily, and it cleanses us of all evil so we can meet our god with clean hearts. Would you allow me to do this now, to prepare you to meet him tomorrow?"

The two women nodded, holding hands. "We are not Dragon Clan either. And we would be honored to receive that blessing."

Eryn considered the roots, dried petals, seeds, and pollens in her kit. The white poppy seeds were the easy choice, but the other? *Don't kill them. They don't know any better.* She set the root aside and selected the evening groundrose instead. *Just enough so that Trinda and Silva aren't soon forgotten.* She pulled the two small pouches out of her bag, along with a small bowl and mixing paddle. First, she made the packets of white poppy seeds, filling each with enough seeds to kill a horse.

She had spoken true—if the women chewed them in time, they would be long past feeling anything when the dragons ate them.

The second pouch she tipped into the bowl, adding a few drops from a tiny bottle. She mixed the dust into a thick paste, careful not to get any on her clothing.

"Your hair," she said. "Let me anoint your hair."

Both women had long, dark hair, lank and greasy. Eryn mixed the evening groundrose paste into the strands, braiding the hair into plaits wrapped around their heads and tucked to form a sticky crown.

"You mustn't touch your hair tonight," she warned them. "Keep it pure for Lord Baltenn."

The smiles and thanks turned Eryn's stomach. But perhaps it didn't matter. If they believed they were pure for the god, no one would tell them otherwise. No one but her would ever know.

She left them and paused to wash her hands in the stream, tiptoeing back to Dane's bed. He rolled back over to wrap her in his arms when she crawled in next to him, and she lay awake until dawn, shivering in his warmth.

Chapter 21

They left the camp before dawn, padding single file down the narrow pass. The oldest of the dragonsworn led them, followed by the two sacrifices, then the two young men who would gain the precious eggs in exchange for the sacrifice. Dane and Eryn brought up the rear of the procession. She seemed edgy this morning, quiet and distracted. He reminded himself that this was all new to her, and she must be overwhelmed. No outsider knew the clan's secrets; how they acquired the eggs, and how they bonded the dragon inside to its warrior.

He glanced behind him as they descended the rocky path. It was his turn to drag a dead warrior, and he grunted as the body bounced along behind him. "You know, most of Dragon Clan doesn't even know the secrets you've seen. Only dragonsworn and their eindon, and the shamans know the secrets. It's prized knowledge."

The war on her face was priceless. Knowledge that no one else knew? For someone who was so proud of her learning, that must be like sweet cane syrup. The fact that it came from this clan that she obviously thought were a bunch of illiterate barbarians? Dane grinned as Eryn wrestled with the thought.

"Has anyone ever written it down? The ritual, the sacrifice?"

Dane shrugged. "Maybe the shamans have. Probably not, though. When you write something down, it's available to anyone. Secrets aren't secret if everyone can read them."

Ahead, the path opened up. Dane scooted forward, walking the last few steps backward so he could see Eryn's reaction to the valley.

She stopped just a step onto the wide plateau, the pink of dawn warming her features.

"Sweet seasons. It's magnificent." She seemed unaware that she had spoken, mouth open as she gazed out across the wide valley that opened up before them. Dane turned to take it in for himself.

It truly was magnificent. The Greyfang mountains bordered this land, keeping it walled away from the flat prairies of Den Woth. The path they traveled spilled them out onto a wide plateau above the floor of the valley that stretched into the distance, where snow-capped peaks led into unmapped dragon lands. Spring had warmed the land here, and wildflowers carpeted the valley as far as the dawn's light stretched. Herds of deer flowed like water across the valley, flowers waving as they leaped through the fields. The hillsides glowed in golden petals, blending into purple and blue that dominated the flatland below.

"Mountain maid, springlily, so much riverseal…" Eryn's eyes sparkled as she named the flowers, hands clutching her herb bag.

"I knew you'd be amazed," Dane murmured.

"Can I harvest here?" she asked, stepping over to the edge of the plateau? "Some of these plants I've never seen before. Can I take what I want?"

"I don't see why not. We won't be here very long, but I don't think anyone will mind if you take what you can reach from the path. The dragons won't care."

She suddenly seemed to remember why they were here. "Wild dragons. This is their land." She nodded to herself. "Will we see them?"

He chuckled. "Any minute now."

And as if on cue, they came, winging in from the distant hills. Dane felt Eryn's hand in his, clutching his fingers as the dragons soared through the sky. The huge males were solid color, iridescent blues and greens, a few that were gold, and one silver whose scales reflected the spreading pink dawn. The females were rainbows, each one's scales and spikes reflecting every color as they wheeled in the sky.

"How are they so beautiful?"

Dane knew the comment wasn't meant for him. He just breathed in the sweet scent of the valley, sharing in Eryn's wonder.

The dragons eyed the party of humans, back-winging to observe them from the air, kicking up dirt and flower petals that rained on the group. One by one, they flew to another wide, flat plateau a short way around the cliffs, scuffling for position around a wide, flat stone in the middle.

The three dead warrior hopefuls were unwrapped and disrobed, left lying on the flat jut of rock, a gift for the dragons, but not the sacrifice they demanded.

Dane and Eryn followed the rest of their group, edging across a narrow path along the edge of the cliff they had emerged through. Eryn grabbed every plant she could reach, tucking them into her pack.

"Watch your footing. It's a long way down."

Up ahead, Calla was struggling. The pad she wore on the stump of her ankle where her foot had been taken gave her no grip on the uneven path. Her dragonsworn, Brinir, didn't look back, but when they reached a wide patch, Dane reached for the girl. She flinched away from him, and his heart twisted. *This is what Eryn thinks we are.* He looked at the line of dragonsworn. *Because most of them are.*

"Let me help you. We all have to gather with the drag-ons."

He crouched down and Eryn helped the woman climb onto his back. He gripped her skinny legs. She weighed nothing. Didn't Brinir even feed her? He probably thought she'd be chosen for the sacrifice, so why waste the food?

Dane carried Calla with Eryn right behind, across the path around the cliff.

"Look! It's a nest!"

Dane followed Eryn's pointing finger. In a protected crevasse above them was a neat bowl of woven branches and leaves. Eryn dropped her pack on the path and scrambled up as far as she could, grabbing roots and rock to peer over the side of the nest.

"Eryn, no! You can't take an egg. It's an exchange!"

Wind buffeted them from behind. They both looked up as a rainbow female landed on the edge of the cavern. She lowered her neck, hissing at Eryn, acid venom dripping from her fangs.

"I'm not taking anything. It's just so beautiful."

Eryn didn't even seem frightened. She climbed down, face alight. "It's amazing. Bigger than I expected, and just one egg."

She's fearless. She just stared down a dragon in its own nest.

The dragon sniffed all around her egg, using her nose to cover it in leaves and dirt. With a final hiss, she launched into the air, flying over to where the other dozen dragons waited for the humans to arrive.

Dane's heart pounded as they assembled on the edge of the plateau. A dozen unbonded dragons. Wild masters of the sky. They were bigger than the bonded dragons of the clan, more brightly colored, and as glossy as Ilst after a bath and polish.

The shaman was already chanting the prayers, leading the two sacrifices to the wide stone. Dane tried to hold Eryn's hand again, but as the women disrobed, Eryn stepped away from him. An ancient metal ring had been pounded into the stone generations ago, and the young men who would gain eggs in this exchange bound the women's hands to the ring. The sacrifices knew their duty and didn't pull on the ties, embracing the honor.

They knelt on the stone, jaws moving. Were they praying? Dane sighed at their piety. *Thank you, Lord Baltenn, for choosing them. They are worthy sacrifices, and willing.*

As the shaman's voice lifted in his chant, the words that entreated Lord Baltenn to accept the sacrifice to his children, the mighty dragons of the wild, the women bowed their heads, eyes squinted shut.

Two dragons stepped forward out of the mingling flock. Both males, one silver and one a midnight blue. Their scales shone in the morning sun as they approached the women. The shaman, along with the two warriors, stepped back, and the rest of the clan backed to the edge of the plateau.

"They always do it quickly," Dane whispered to Eryn.

And they did. In three bites, it was over, and all that remained of the sacrifices was a small puddle of blood, bright red against the brown stone.

Dane, carrying Calla on his back, led the group back across the path as the dragons dispersed. He glanced back at Eryn as they passed the nest, but her eyes were dark, face downcast. She didn't even glance up at the female who glared down at their passage.

When they reached the wide, flat entrance to the path that would lead them through the mountain pass, the dead warriors were gone, and two eggs waited on the ground. The warriors who would be bound to the dragons inside each took one, and together, the men and eindon of Dragon Clan passed out of the Valley of Dragons.

CHAPTER 22

No other dragonsworn would help Dane carry Calla. Eryn was not surprised. As she walked behind them, she could see that the pad Calla wore to protect her stump was crusty with dried blood. When they stopped for a break halfway back to the Stone of Baltenn, Eryn pulled her aside and sat next to her, both of them chewing on dried meat.

"Let me see that bandage," Eryn said, but Calla pulled away.

"It's fine."

Eryn frowned. "It's not fine. You've bled through it and it's no wonder you can't walk. When's the last time you changed it?"

A shrug from the woman. "A week? A month? It doesn't matter."

What treatment must she be used to that she doesn't even care.

"Please let me look at it. I have ointments and fresh bandages." Eryn patted her bulging healer's bag, full of as many species of plants as she could stuff in from the Valley of Dragons. She could hardly wait to get back to a real camp where she could sort them out.

"Maybe later," Calla said. "This won't be a long rest." Her eyes turned soft for a moment. "But you're so lucky. Your man has carried me all this way. Without him, I'm not sure I'd make it." She dropped her gaze to her lap. "Not that I care either way. Better to die alone on a mountain, I think. I wish Lord Balten had chosen me."

Eryn dug into her bag and pulled out a few more white poppy seeds, pressing them into the woman's hand. "When the pain gets bad, chew one or two of these. No more. This is a week's worth. They'll help."

With another shrug, Calla tucked them into her own small pouch. "Thank you for helping me. I'll probably get a beating tonight for letting Dane carry me, but not having to walk this mountain again…" once more she met Eryn's eyes. "Do whatever you have to do to keep him happy. There's no one else like him. None I've meet since I was taken from my own people. Do whatever you must to keep his love. And whatever you do," she said, gesturing to her missing foot, "don't try to run. If it gets that bad, kill yourself instead. You'll never make it, and your life will be even more miserable when they catch you."

Eryn thought about Calla's words all afternoon as Dane carried the unfortunate woman up the mountain, across the crest, then back down toward the wide flat area where Baltenn's stone waited.

Keep his love. *Is that what she thinks this is? Love?* Yes, Dane was kind. No one else had offered to carry Calla. But he didn't carry her up the mountain. Only on the way back, when it was clear she wouldn't make it. Yes, he was growing more comfortable at night, arms wrapping her in warmth and safety. And yes, the look in his eyes was something she never expected to see from a man. Not possessive. Not angry. Not controlling.

He doesn't have to look controlling. I wear his chain around my neck. She fingered the links and his rune.

But still. If any other dragonsworn had claimed her, she might be just like Calla, wishing Baltenn had chosen her to die this morning.

Poor Trinda. Poor Silva. As they disrobed, Eryn had noticed they were already clumsy, heads drooping. They were chewing the poppy she had given them, and she prayed that they felt no pain or fear when the open mouths of the dragons closed over their heads. At least they didn't tear them apart alive. She glanced at Calla's foot again. *Dragons are kinder than men.*

And so much more beautiful.

She smiled a little at the thought. The Valley of Dragons was the most beautiful place she had ever seen, and the dragons themselves, truly magnificent. The females with their rainbow spikes…why were they so different than the drab females of the Clan, just shades of brown and beige? Ilst was pretty in her way, but the wild dragons were transcendent. It must be in the bloodbonding. *Whatever they do makes them sterile, and it shows in their colors.*

Her stomach turned for a moment, and she grinned, thinking of the ointment she'd rubbed into the hair of the sacrificed girls. It might not do anything to a dragon. But she hoped it would work like it did on humans. Those two males would be miserable today.

Did they deserve that? It was the clan that made the deal. The clan that wanted the eggs.

But the dragons participated, giving up their own young for the chance to eat a human.

She pondered as they walked, climbing across the descending path. Dane had to put Calla down and help her scoot down some of the steeper passages. He waited at the bottom and didn't pick Calla back up until Eryn was safely down.

"Why do they give us eggs?" she asked him when the path widened enough for her to walk next to him.

"Because we give them sacrifices," he answered.

"Right, but we were fifteen people just walking into that valley. Why not just eat us all?"

He cocked his head, unable to shrug with the weight of Calla on his back, light as she was. "Because then we wouldn't come back next year. This way they get at least one girl a year."

"Hardly seems worth it for an egg that will become a magnificent dragon."

His grin was worth it. "They are magnificent, aren't they? But I didn't think you liked dragons."

She looked away, up toward the narrow opening to the sky above them. "I don't like what dragons do to our people."

"Your former people," he corrected. "You're Dragon Clan now."

"Sort of." She clanked the chain around her neck. "And why do they stay in that valley? Can't they just fly through the pass to our lands? Or over the mountains?"

"They could, but it's not easy. The mountains are too high in most places, and the pass barely wide enough, even up high, for more than one at a time to come through. Besides, you saw their valley, and that was only part of it. Their lands beyond these mountains are ten times what we have down on the flat. No one knows how many wild dragons there are, but they have plenty of room to roam and hunt up there."

They trudged on until they reached Baltenn's stone. Dane said that the bloodbonding would occur at midnight, and by midday tomorrow they'd be back to the horses and the dragons, and be on their way home.

No one had much appetite for dinner, so the men played the dice-rolling game. The two young men who would be bonding the eggs threw dice to determine who got which egg. One shell was swirled in green and orange, and the other, blue and purple. The shells were hard like birds' eggs, and neither was much bigger than a man's head. The egg Eryn had seen in the wild dragon's nest had looked bigger. The men had kept the eggs tucked inside their shirts on the entire walk, but now the eggs sat on fire-heated stones, covered by furs to trap the warmth.

At midnight, the first warrior brought his egg to the stone. While the shaman chanted, the warrior took a small awl and carefully drilled a tiny hole in the top of the eggshell. With a knife blessed by the shaman, he then cut a slice in his wrist, letting blood well up. Eryn remembered seeing a scar in a similar place on Dane's wrist.

The man held his wrist out over the egg, dripping his blood into the hole as the shaman entreated Baltenn to bond man and dragon into one blood, one being. In a few moments, the shaman pulled out a mixing mortar from his pouch, smaller than Eryn's but similar. He poured in a few drops of some liquid, added powder from a pouch, and mixed until he had a thick paste, which he applied to the hole in the egg, sealing it. The new dragonsworn wrapped his wrist in a clean bandage and took his prize back to the warmed stones. Then the second young man repeated the procedure with his egg.

The dragonsworn clapped them both on the back, sharing drinks through half the night. When Dane finally crawled into the bedroll with Eryn, she worried the alcohol might make him unpredictable. But he fell asleep within seconds, snoring louder than usual. She kicked him until he rolled over to face away from her, and she snuggled into his chilly back until they were both warm.

In the morning, they awoke to a groggy shout from Brinir.

Calla lay stretched across Baltenn's stone, cold and dead.

CHAPTER 23

Dane stared at Calla's lifeless body.

"She wanted to be the sacrifice," Eryn murmured from beside him. "I should have known."

He looked at Eryn's pale face. "You couldn't have done anything. She was very weak. I thought carrying her would help, but she's had a rough time since Brinir took her. He's not easy on his eindon."

Eryn's face hardened. "No, most of you aren't. The two women who died yesterday were happy to do so. Their lives as eindon were not worth living."

Her words echoed in his head as the camp was packed. For the first time, he looked at the other dragonsworn with their eindon. Really looked at them. There were only three left, including Eryn. Both of the other women had dark circles under their eyes, and lank, dirty hair. As he watched, one was backhanded across the face by her dragonsworn for moving too slow in the packing. The other stayed as far from hers as she could, always staring at the ground. She flinched away when he approached, barking orders at her. Both of them carried the larger of the packs.

That's not right. We're their dragonsworn, tasked with protecting them. Dane never let Eryn carry the heavier pack, though she insisted on carrying her herbs by herself.

We've lost our way. We weren't supposed to be like this.

Brinir interrupted his thoughts.

"You carried her yesterday. Carry her yourself now, or, she stays here to rot."

Dane scowled. "Give me her bedding. I'll take her the rest of the way."

He wrapped the dead woman in a thin blanket and gently pulled her up over his shoulder. It would be harder going this way, but he couldn't leave her here. Even an eindon deserved to be eaten and not rot. She must have felt she was dying and laid herself on the Stone to feel closer to Lord Baltenn. Her soul would never find its way to him if her body weren't either burned like a warrior or eaten by a dragon. Chern, Brinir's ugly beast, should have the honor, as Calla belonged to Brinir. And if Brinir forgot his dragonsworn honor, Dane did not. Eryn shouldered both of their packs and they slogged the final descent.

He could feel Ilst's joy increase with every step they took. As they left the closed walls of the cliffs and made the final descent down the open switchbacks that led down to the prairie, all the clan's dragons soared in close, flashing their bellies as they swooped and banked.

"I missed you, my darling."

Dane saw Eryn's head snap around before she realized he was talking to Ilst, not her.

Missed you. Back safe.

Her words were a balm for his heart.

What do you carry?

"It's Calla, Brinir's eindon. She died on the way home. Chern will eat her when we get to the bottom."

Chern was eyeing him from the sky. Brinir must be talking to him, telling him what happened.

Two eggs?

"Yes, two new dragonsworn. Three young men won't come home."

Eryn intruded on his conversation. "Why do you talk out loud to Ilst? Everyone else's lips move, but they don't make a sound when they talk to theirs."

Dane flushed. "I probably don't have to. She talks in my head, and her words are getting clearer all the time. But I've always talked to her, and I've only had her a couple of years. Just a habit, I guess."

"And what does it sound like in your head? Is her voice like a human's voice?"

"Sort of. It's as much pictures and feelings as actual words. I always know what she means, but I think she understands me better when I use words to talk to her."

Because your mind is messy. No focus.

Dane laughed. "She says my mind is a mess, and she can't focus on my words unless I concentrate on saying them out loud."

He'd been so scared until the choosing, wishing he had another eindon so Eryn could have stayed safely at home and not be at risk. But he'd never even thought of taking a spare. By next year, he'd take another eindon female so he didn't risk Eryn again. He pictured her watching him leave, heavy with his child. That's what he wanted for her. For them. Safety and a family. Not the whim of a god to take her from him.

They reached the bottom of the switchback to find the horses waiting where they had been left, kept corralled by the dragons overhead.

Dane laid Calla on the ground and unwrapped her.

"Brinir," he called. "She's here for Chern."

Brinir sniffed. "She was trash. Leave her to rot." He loaded his pack onto one of the horses and walked away.

Eryn was at his side. "We can't just leave her here. Can we bury her? Burn her body?"

"We don't have time to burn her properly, and if we bury her too shallow, something will just dig her up and eat her."

He sighed, watching the rest of the men load their horses. "And if we don't treat her properly, her soul will wander here forever, and never get to meet Lord Baltenn."

Eryn shivered. "She wanted to die. But she wouldn't want that."

"How do you know she wanted to die?"

She looked away from him, back to the body on the ground. "She told me."

He glanced back to the pack she carried. "Eryn, did you help her die?"

But she refused to answer directly. "She's happier now. But we need to treat her properly. Does it have to be Chern?"

"No, it just has to be a—" His words were cut off by a scream from above.

One by one, wild dragons poured through the crack in the mountains. The Clan's dragons roared as they met in the air, fangs and claws flying.

Chapter 24

On land and in the sky, there was chaos. Eryn stood frozen as wild dragon after dragon emerged from the pass, nearly a dozen of them, gleaming in the sunlight. She recognized the silver and blue beasts that had eaten the clan's eindon sacrifice. The clan's dragons met them in the air, smaller and lighter, maneuvering up and down to claw and bite at wings and tails and necks.

Dane shoved her back toward the wall. "Find a rock and get under it!" he shouted, pulling his sword and dashing toward a few dragons who had landed.

Horses bolted in terror. The screams of eindon and dragonsworn were drowned out by the roars of dragons in the sky and on the ground.

There were too many for the clan's dragons to fight. Outnumbered two to one. Eryn rushed back to the cliffside, searching for a place to hide. She found a small divot under a boulder and wedged herself in, scouring the field until she saw Dane's form. He stood before a huge green dragon, sword drawn.

Eryn's heart pounded. She was no warrior. She couldn't possibly fight a dragon, and she had no weapons. But she couldn't watch him die alone out there.

She pulled herself out of the crevasse and stepped forward.

One of the new dragonsworn rushed across in front of her, clutching his egg. Eryn watched in horror as a dragon swooped down from above and grabbed the man's shoulders, pulling him off balance. The egg rolled from his grasp as the dragon dragged him a few feet away before crunching down on his neck. Blood sprayed everywhere, dousing the golden scales in red.

The dragon looked at the egg, and without thinking Eryn rushed over to where it lay. "No! Not the egg."

Red, unblinking eyes stared down at her. The dragon stepped forward and Eryn backed away. *What are you doing? It's bound to a dead man. Let them have it back.*

The dragon picked up the egg in its foreclaw, glaring at Eryn before turning away and taking to the sky. She stood in the open, battle raging around her, and watched as the dragon carried the egg into the sky. Her mouth opened in a scream as the egg dropped from its grasp, plunging down to splatter in a sticky mess of white and yellow and swirled shell on the rocks behind Eryn.

She ran blindly into the fray, thoughts whirling.

They don't want the eggs back. They're useless now, bonded to humans.

More of the dragons had landed, Clan and wild. Three of them surrounded the other new dragonsworn, who had dropped his egg. It lay cracked on the ground behind him.

"Oh, sweet Lord Baltenn, no."

One dragon grabbed each arm, and one grabbed a leg, and together they pulled, tearing the man apart. He didn't scream, but lay bleeding on the ground where they left him, his one remaining leg flopping uselessly.

Eryn rushed over and knelt next to what was left of him. She met his eyes for a moment, watching as they stopped rolling in wide terror and shock, stilling in his head, staring straight at the sky.

I did this. I made the dragons sick and broke the contract. Now the eggs are wasted, and everyone is going to die.

She wasn't sad for the men. They were brutes, murderers.

Even Dane?

She batted the thought away.

Not the women. They don't deserve to die.

But as she looked around the battlefield, she didn't see the other two eindon. Were they already dead? Or hiding, like she should be doing.

She pulled the dead man's sword from its sheath and stood to race back to her hiding place.

A dragon snarled behind her, and she whipped around to face it.

A rainbow female hissed at her, claws scoring the ground, wings outstretched.

Hold on.

The voice felt like it came from outside of her body, pounding into her skull amid the battle cries and screams of dragon challenge. Was it Dane? Was he coming for her?

She raised the sword, pathetically aware of how small she was, how ridiculous with a sword she could barely lift.

The dragon moved around behind her again, and she stood stock-still as it sniffed her hair, hot breath blowing into her ears. It smelled lower, nosing at her pack.

It knows.

She whirled around, raising the sword, catching the dragon right in the muzzle. It reared back, green eyes widened in shock. Lowering its head to the ground, its neck slithered like a snake.

Dane. Where was Dane?

Eryn's blood was on fire, and she advanced on the dragon, raising the sword.

"You've had your revenge. The dragonsworn are dead, and the eggs are ruined. Why would you destroy your own eggs?"

Because they were tainted.

Again, the voice felt like it came from inside her.

Keep talking. Keep her distracted.

"Go back to your valley. We won't bother you again."

But could Eryn keep that promise? In a year, it might matter. But for today, the dragon just blinked at her. It surely couldn't understand her words. The rainbows on its spikes flashed and glowed in the sun.

"Eryn? Eryn, where are you?"

Definitely Dane.

"I'm here!" She dared not break the gaze of the dragon, acid dropping from its teeth. And she didn't move the sword.

All around her the sounds of battle reached her ears.

"Go. Just go. Leave us in peace."

The dragon pivoted around her again, sniffing at her backpack. Eryn whirled to follow it.

In an instant, the dragon was shoved away from her, bowled over by something huge and black.

A roar of challenge deafened her, and the rainbow dragon took to the air. Eryn was enveloped by a thick black tail, curling around her body, wrapping her into its heaving, obsidian side.

The head from her nightmares peered around from the long, snaky neck, midnight blue eyes blinking, nostrils smelling all around her.

Ardos. The dead chief's dragon curled around her body, giant wings shielding her shoulders.

The rainbow dragon circled above them, and Ardos roared his challenge. With her ears, she heard only a dragon's deep rage.

But in her mind, she felt his words.

This one is mine.

Chapter 25

The shaman was dead. Dane waded through the aftermath of the attack, stepping around pools of blood as the Clan converged.

It was over as fast as it began. The wild dragons were perched along the switchback leading up to the cliff face, just watching the warriors below.

"Eryn!"

Dane called across the field where clan dragons blocked his view, each with their dragonsworn. Ilst landed beside him.

"Are you alright? Where's Eryn?"

Fine. Will heal.

He wasn't sure if she meant herself or Eryn and paused a moment to look her over. Bloody scratches marred her scales, and a puncture to her face would have cost her an eye if it had been a handbreadth lower. But she walked without a limp, chest puffed with pride.

"Where's Eryn? Did you see her? Is she hiding?"

Ilst gave a mental chuckle. *Not hiding.*

"Dane! I'm here!"

He rushed to the sound of her voice, stopping only when two clan dragons moved to reveal Eryn, wrapped up by a huge obsidian dragon.

"No! Let her go!" He raised his bloody sword, but Ilst knocked into him from the side, rolling him onto the ground.

The sword clattered from his hand, and he jumped to his feet.

"I'm fine," Eryn said. "It's…It's Ardos."

Dane focused on the black dragon. Indeed, it was Ardos, returned from wherever he had gone since his dragonsworn died. And he wasn't attacking Eryn. He was protecting her.

Brinir strode up to the pair. "Ardos! Why have you returned? Why do you protect this eindon?"

From within the protection of tail and wings, Eryn straightened up. "He returned for me. He says…" her eyes unfocused for a moment. "He says I'm his dragonsworn now."

The men fell silent.

"Impossible," Brinir said. "You are eindon. A woman."

She shrugged. "I know. But here we are. Do you want to tell him he's wrong?"

Ardos lowered his neck, growling low in his throat. Dane could feel the sound vibrating in his own chest.

From behind him, Ilst approached Ardos, neck lowered. He touched noses with her, and she smelled him all over, reporting to Dane as she did.

Healthy. Fit. Not leaving.

Dane was flabbergasted. How was this possible? No woman had ever bonded a dragon before. She wasn't in the clan when Ardos was bonded by Chief Krunnan. She probably wasn't even born; Dane was only a child when the last chief took power. But here they were, and there was no denying that Ardos was behaving like a bound dragon did with its dragonsworn. And no one was getting near Eryn except through him.

"Ardos, may I come to Eryn? I need to make sure she's all right."

Ardos's eyes narrowed.

"It's all right, Ardos." Eryn murmured the way a mother might to a baby, or lover to lover. "Dane is all right." She looked at the dragonsworn around her, all staring daggers at her. "No one else. Never anyone else."

Dane approached, wary of the great obsidian head. He had to step over Ardos' tail to get to Eryn. When he reached her, he threw his arms around her, knocking her pack to the ground. He held her as long as she would let him, until she squirmed away, accompanied by a warning rumble from Ardos.

"Why didn't you hide? When did Ardos come? What's going on?"

She smiled, wearing a dreamy look that Dane remembered on his own face the moment Ilst hatched. *It's real. They're bonded, just like us.* He wasn't sure if the thought came from him or from Ilst, but it didn't matter. Dane's family of three was now four.

"I did hide. But then one of the wild dragons was attacking one of the new dragonsworn and dropped the egg. I tried to save it, but I couldn't. And then a dragon was on me, and then…" she glanced up at Ardos, pure love in her eyes. "Then Ardos knocked her away from me. He came to defend me." She looked back at Dane, and for a moment, that look of love warmed his heart. "He's my dragon, and I'm his dragonsworn. We will never be apart."

She tried to save the eggs.

You know she is special. Ardos knew. Ilst's voice was soft, caught up in the new love of Ardos and Eryn before her.

Brinir cut into their dreamy bliss.

"Well, it can't happen. Ardos, you belonged to our chief. You cannot belong to an eindon. You're no longer part of this clan."

A deep growl from Ardos said otherwise.

Eryn laid a hand on the huge black neck. "Ardos says neither you, nor any human makes decisions for him. He's chosen me to be his human. He's part of the clan as long as I am." Her eyes unfocused for a moment. "And he says you have a lot to learn about chiefs and eindon." She pressed her cheek to his shoulder, and again Dane's heart gave a squeeze.

Jealous of a dragon?

He smiled at Ilst's comment.

"A little," he admitted.

A crash from the cliff's edge made all heads snap around to look. The wild dragons had flown up the side of the pass, to the single, narrow crack that led into the path between cliffs. Dane watched in horror as they gripped rocks from above, sending boulders and debris crashing down the ravine.

From the top and side of the mountain, they dug claws into trees, stone, and dirt, which crashed into the path. In a few minutes, the entire entrance was blocked four men high. With a final roar and glare at the Clan and their dragons, they flew up over the pass, disappearing toward their valley.

For long moments, the Clan stared up at the blocked pass, unable to process what it meant.

With a shaking voice, Tornnen said, "We can pull it down. It will take all summer, but we can clear the path."

Dane snorted. "And then what? We march back into their valley? They've sent us a pretty clear signal. They don't want us anymore. The pact is broken." He shook his head. "But why?"

Next to him, Eryn took in a breath.

"Maybe they didn't like the sacrifices."

Every eye focused on her, and Brinir took two steps in her direction.

"What do you mean, eindon?" He spat the word.

"I…I just mean that one of them was blinded. Maybe they don't want brutalized castoffs." A growl from Ardos punctuated her words.

Brinir looked at the giant head high above his own. From behind him, his Chern rumbled, but did not challenge Ardos. Brinir spat on the ground at Eryn's feet.

"The chief will decide what to do with you when we get home. You're not my problem." He glanced at Dane. "But you," he chuckled. "You might have a very big problem here."

Without a backward look, Brinir stomped away, leaving Dane, Eryn, Ardos, and Ilst alone together.

CHAPTER 26

Eryn rode proud in the saddle, Ardos circling protectively above her with Ilst in his wake.

He's magnificent. I had no idea.

"You're seeing it now, aren't you?" Dane asked from his horse next to Eryn's. "I tried to tell you. There's no clan that can compare to a clan that's been chosen by dragons."

She thought about that for a long moment. "But you're not chosen. The ceremony with the blood…you bind them. They don't have a choice." *Not like me. Not like Ardos.*

Dane's face showed no regret. "It's bloodbinding, so the dragon knows its worthy warrior. But you didn't bloodbind Ardos. And you didn't do the Dance of Dragons." He shook his head. "I wish the shaman was here. He would know."

Images popped into Eryn's mind as they rode across the flat prairie. "What happens in the Dance? The dragon bites, and the warrior has a spasm of some kind, and then…" She trailed off.

The afternoon sun lit Dane's hair, gold like autumn grass. "I don't remember," he admitted. "When it happened to me, when it was my turn, I felt the bite, and then it just went black. I think I dreamed of Baltenn, but it's vague. I just remember waking up, and everyone was so happy." His face clouded. "I was the only one who woke up."

A dream of Baltenn. A dragon bite, and then darkness. Eryn looked down at the scars on her arms. "It's the venom." She glanced up at Ardos, high above her. "Their venom in our bodies…it's fatal. Unless it's not."

The memory of pain, of falling down a ravine, her arms cut and bleeding. A dragon standing above her, hot saliva dripping into her wounds. The descent into blackness, and waking up to Dane's face, and a chain around her neck.

"It was you," she murmured.

It was me, Ardos agreed. *But that's not why you are mine. It doesn't matter what dragon bites you. Only that your mind is open to hear me. I chose you. Your people call it heartbinding.*

The same warmth she felt in Dane's arms at night flowed through her, from the mind of the dragon in the air. "Why? Why did you choose me?"

She was aware of Dane watching her from the horse that paced alongside hers. A small smile curled his lips, and Eryn found herself annoyed. He looked so smug. But she did understand him a little better. The arrogance. The confidence.

I was alone.

Those three words from the sky broke Eryn's heart.

"You are not alone now."

A sweeping image flowed into her mind; a funeral pyre, and the sudden hole in the center of her soul where the clan chief had been, then there was nothing. A crushing loneliness filled her, and sent her howling into the sky, into the dark, starry night where the smoke curled up to nowhere. She was Ardos, and Ardos was her, and together they mourned the clan chief who had been the other half of Ardos since he was hatched.

"I tried to save him," she murmured.

I know, he replied. And the loneliness vanished, replaced in his heart with…her. Me. Us. The line between dragon and woman blurred.

"Is that why you chose me? Why you came back?"

She knew from the murmurs and black looks around the group that heartbonding was almost a myth. Warriors had died, leaving dragons bereft before. They disappeared and were never seen again. And dragons had died, leaving their warriors half-empty, descending into a muttering madness that usually ended when the former dragonsworn took his own life, desperate to reunite with their dragon in Baltenn's immortal Clan.

Partly.

"Did you go back to the wild dragons?"

He chuckled, a deep rumble in his chest. *Those arrogant monsters? No, they are not my family. They look down on bonded dragons, even if we are no longer bonded. They think they are better than us.* He rumbled again. *They were not pleased with your little trick.*

A chill gripped Eryn's chest. What had she done? She had seen the dragons that ate the groundrose on the eindon's hair. She intended it to make them sick. To make them regret eating those poor women. To make sure the women were remembered.

Now they would never be forgotten.

The pact was broken. Whatever ancient agreement had formed between men and dragons, however it evolved that women were given and eggs were received, that agreement was ended now, because of her.

If she had known it would mean the end of dragon eggs for the clan, she would have been even more eager to do it. Now, feeling the heartbeat of her soulmate in the sky, reveling in the beat of his wings against the air, his long neck looking down, watching over her, his elegant tail streaming out behind his massive form, now she wasn't so sure. No more dragons. No more Dragon Clan.

She looked around at the men and women on horses, spread out over the land. An empty wagon pulled by a pony should have been carrying two eggs, the future of the clan, the joy of those two young men. But the dragons had been very specific. The shaman was dead, the two warriors killed, others injured, including dragons, but no one else killed. They took out their anger on those who were on the stone when the poisoned-hair eindon were given.

And they would have killed her as well, had Ardos not arrived to protect her. They knew. They smelled it in her pack. But Ardos, the only Clan dragon as large as the wild ones, sheltered her under his wing.

"I'm not like him. Like the chief."

You're nothing like him.

The man had led the raid that decimated her clan. He took eindon slaves, and fathered Brinir, the most brutal of the dragonsworn she'd known. While he hadn't been cruel to her during the long wagon trip when she'd kept him alive, he was the leader of these barbarians. And Ardos was bonded to him.

I knew he was a bad man, Ardos said. *I saw his brutality. The things he did that hurt others. I was with him for decades. But I was bonded to him through no choice of my own. When he was happy, I was happy, even when he was a beast. That is not a bonding I would have again. I would not have chosen another warrior.* A wave of affection flowed down from the sky. *You are stronger than he was. You are better. Together, we are better still.*

From beside her, Dane spoke up. "You're talking with Ardos? Does he use words, or just pictures?"

Eryn shifted in the saddle. "He is more eloquent than you are."

I spent years learning to speak in Krunnan's head. I know your language. I am not a fledgling.

She smiled. "He says he's not a fledgling."

They rode through the day, heading west and south. The rest of the clan was on the move, herding the cattle from pasture to pasture. They would meet up with Chief Calnan,

Dane's father, along with the rest of the clan in another part of Den Woth as they circled the lands they controlled.

What would happen when they reached the clan? What would the chief do? A moment of panic flared as the sun set the sky aflame ahead of her.

No one can separate us. I am yours and you are mine. The clan has no say in our bond.

But they had a strong say in what happened to Eryn.

She turned to Dane, who had pulled up to a halt and dismounted from his horse. "Take off this chain. I will not be a slave. I am as much dragonsworn as you are."

Dane pulled the saddle from his horse and set it aside. "That's not for me to say. But my father will know what to do." He looked uncertain. Sadness lowered his eyelids.

He doesn't want to lose his property.

Adrdos chimed in. *He doesn't want to lose* you.

But when the meal was finished and the bedrolls laid, Eryn did not sleep in Dane's protective embrace. She slept with her head pillowed on a scaled tail, Ardos' body wrapped around her. She had never felt so safe in her life.

CHAPTER 27

Dane stood before his father, with the rest of the dragonsworn around him and Eryn at his side. Chief Calnan's tent was full, hot and close as the late morning sun beat down on the fabric from above. Most of the dragons were enjoying a meal of beef, but Ardos sat just outside the closed tent flap, his loud breaths reminding everyone inside that he had thrown the entire clan into turmoil.

The festival outside had already begun, but ripples of discomfort were spreading out as Dane and the rest of the party returned. There was no hiding the fact that they had returned with no eggs, with none of the warriors that left with them days earlier, with no shaman, and with Ardos in tow. The annual festival to celebrate the new dragonsworn should have been especially grand this year, as the new chief took up his mantle. Now the entire clan was at risk, and only those in the tent knew it.

"Tell me again," Chief Calnan said with a heavy sigh, seated on a heavy, fur-covered chair with a high back. "Tell me again how we are no longer welcome in the Valley of Dragons."

Brinir grunted. "We don't know what happened," he said, looking around the group. "The sacrifice was fine. Two eindon, both healthy."

Eryn cleared her throat, and Brinir turned a look of death on her.

"They were healthy," he continued, "and the dragons ate them just like normal. But then the dragons must have…changed their minds. They attacked us, killed the new dragonsworn, destroyed the eggs. They pulled down the stones of the pass. We could probably clear it, but the message seems pretty clear. They are angry with us."

The chief nodded. "And then Ardos returned and has heartbonded to my son's eindon."

Every eye turned to Dane and Eryn. She leaned toward him, and he raised an arm to lay it around her shoulder, but she suddenly seemed to realize what she was doing, and sidled away. Dane dropped his arm. *She doesn't need me. She has Ardos.*

In the distance, her belly full of beef, Ilst sent a wave of humor. *Have to win her on your own merits.*

He became aware that everyone was still looking at him. "Ardos has chosen Eryn. He won't say why, but over the past three days, it has been very clear that he will not be swayed. It's a true heartbond, the first in generations."

"Ardos is mine, and I am his…" Eryn was cut off by Brinir.

"Silence, eindon. You do not speak in the presence of your betters."

A warning growl from outside the tent made Brinir glance over his shoulder. Ardos' muzzle pushed into the tent for a moment, his huge eyes taking in every man in the tent.

The ice in Eryn's eyes could have frozen hot coals. "I am sworn to Ardos. I have no 'betters.'"

In spite of his trepidation, Dane beamed with pride. She was something.

Every man in the tent began to shout, and Eryn stood proud. Chief Calnan's voice rose above the din.

"Silence! This is my tent, and I am your chief. You will speak when you are addressed." His gaze swept the room. "That means all of you, not just the eindon."

The shouting dropped to muttering and angry glances.

"So," the chief continued, "we are left with the question of what to do."

Eryn raised her hand.

"Yes? You have permission to speak."

She cleared her throat. "I request the removal of the chain of slavery. I am dragonsworn, bonded to Ardos, strongest among dragons. He chose me, and I am as worthy as any man here."

The furor started up again, swiftly silenced by Dane's father. His mouth quirked as he looked at his son.

"I have heard nothing from you, Dane. What is your thinking on this matter?"

I want her. She's mine. The thought was all Dane's. But as he looked at her, standing tall among the hostile drag-onsworn, wearing the eindon chain and his runelock, he realized she was not his. She never was. He claimed her, but it took Ardos to make him see. She was no one's slave. But if she wasn't his, she would leave him. The nights she had spent sleeping in his arms were a sweet memory, but he feared it was only for warmth on a cold night and safety from the other dragonsworn who would happily force her submission. She was no fool. And the minute she had another source of safety, she left him to sleep in the curl of her dragon's wings. Everyone was looking at him, awaiting his answer.

"I think Eryn is special," he said. "I have known it since I first saw her, and Ardos has seen it as well. I would love to claim her as my own, but she belongs to Ardos now."

Eryn's ice visibly thawed, and he got a wave of approval from Ilst.

Chief Calnan sighed. "Those are wise words." He focused on Eryn, pulling at his beard. "And if you were released from the chains, what would you do?" He gave her no time to answer. "Would you stay with the clan, using your dragon for the betterment and protection of all? Would you choose a warrior husband and provide the strongest of sons, warriors and dragonsworn of the future?" At her scowl, he gave a snort. "Sons and daughters," he amended.

"Or would you, when the chain was removed, disappear in the night?"

Dane's heart pounded. His father just gave words to his worst fear.

"Would you take the sacred, secret knowledge of our rituals," Chief Calnan continued, "and return to your own clan, taking our most protected lore and your powerful dragon with you? Next year would we find that we are not the only clan with dragons, if the wild dragons of the valley chose to allow your people in?"

"We would never sacrifice our women…"

Chief Calnan cut her off. "Perhaps you would not. A lesser clan might not have the strength to make the necessary sacrifice, a life for a life. A woman for a dragon. And the dragons might not allow you to enter, or might slaughter your clan as soon as you descended into the valley." His hands stroked the fur stole he wore, the emblem of his chiefdom. "But we cannot take that chance."

Beside Dane, Eryn stiffened.

"You entered our clan as eindon, and eindon you shall stay." He nodded at Dane. "You are dragonsworn, and none can contest that. But you remain the responsibility and property of Dane Rowe, who claimed you. You shall wear the chain and the lock and shall not attempt to leave our clan; the punishment of eindon applies."

Ardos growled, and every head snapped to look at his muzzle poking through the tent flap.

"But," the chief continued, "you shall be treated with the respect owed to one heartbonded to a dragon. I'm sure Ardos would accept no less."

The look Brinir turned on Dane and Eryn would have melted steel. Dane sighed, never more relieved that the former chief had the wisdom to choose Dane's father as his successor.

Imagine if Brinir were chief. He turned from the thought.

There was grumbling around the tent, and Eryn's face did not reflect the swell of joy Dane felt.

She doesn't belong to me. But she's still mine.

CHAPTER 28

The chief demanded that the secret of the clan's true failure, their eviction from the Valley of Dragons, be shared with no one. Eryn and the other dragonsworn filed out of the tent, having sworn to speak nothing of their fear for the future of the clan.

Other dragonsworn. Who could possibly have guessed that Eryn would count herself among their hated number? But she would not give up Ardos, not even to have the chain and lock removed from her neck. She didn't really think the chief would let her go. But for the first time, she felt safe in the crowd of men. Dane had kept her from the whims of the warriors who would have made her life a misery, and she had to admit that she was the most fortunate among eindon, to have a man who didn't force himself on her. Didn't beat or maim her. Who honestly seemed to have some respect for her. It didn't change the fact that she was his property, and remained so.

You belong to no one but me.

Ardos met her at the tent flap, and she stroked the scales of his face.

Brinir's voice cut in from behind her. "She pets him like a child with a puppy. It's a disgrace."

She whirled to face him. "My relationship with my dragon is none of your concern."

His expression was rage, but a warning growl from Ardos stayed his hand. Instead, he turned to Dane. "She's your responsibility. Best you teach her some manners."

Dane gave a lazy smile. "She seems to be doing just fine on her own. Ardos didn't choose a weakling."

The look on Brinir's face was almost worth the chain around her neck.

Dane's not so bad.

She wasn't sure if the thought was hers or Ardos'.

The group of dragonsworn were given a wide path through the assembled crowd as they processed out of the chief's sweltering tent and through the twisting path among the tents. A wide field had been cleared of cattle, and the festival games began.

There were no speeches, no announcements. Just a list of competitions overseen by Chief Calnan. This was where the warriors were chosen who would be next year's dragonsworn candidates. She almost felt sorry for the young men, currently shooting targets with a bow from horseback. They thought they would have the chance to bind a dragon next spring. They had no idea the pass was closed. There would be no more dragons for Dragon Clan.

After the archery came the sword battles. Thirty young men had scored well enough at archery to compete, and Eryn's heart leaped in her chest when she realized they were using real, sharp swords, not dulled practice swords. A young man lost his arm at the elbow, and another went down in a spray of blood as his competitor sliced a lucky blow across the neck.

Eryn stood with Dane, dragons resting off to one side.

"You did this? You won last year?"

"Not last year," he said. "Ilst is two years old. But yes, I was one of the winners." He looked away from the young men waiting to fight. "It's part of why the other dragonsworn are so angry," he said. "It's not just that you're eindon, or a woman. They risked their lives to bond a dragon, and you didn't. They don't feel you earned the right."

Eryn's words echoed Ardos' thoughts in her head. "A dragon is not earned. It's not a prize. Dragons should all have their choice, and not be bonded against their will."

Dane's face was almost funny. *He's never even considered that Ilst might not have wanted him. That she had no choice in the matter.* She almost felt sorry for him.

When the warrior trials were over, only four warriors were selected. The rest failed to impress the chief or were too injured to continue. The four young men cheered, clapping each other on the back. *If they only knew.*

"Now it's time for the best part," Dane said. "Now it's our turn."

Ardos' excitement vibrated through their bond. He and the other dragons moved into the field, each one standing tall, shining in the sunlight. *Ardos is as handsome as the wild dragons.* But the females were so bland.

"You are an herbwoman, yes?"

Eryn looked down to see a young boy peering up at her through dark lashes.

"Yes, I have herbs," she answered.

"Can you help my mother? The real herbwoman won't help her."

Real herbwoman? Eryn bristled, then forced herself to relax. She was not of this clan. They didn't know her training.

"I'll help if I can."

She left the festival field and followed the boy, stopping at Dane's tent to pick up her bag of medications. The boy led her all the way to the outermost ring of the tent city, to a small, battered tent. Inside, Eryn found a haggard woman lying on a thin blanket. A younger woman, barely more than a girl, knelt next to her. She looked up at Eryn's approach.

"Eryn? Thank Baltenn you're here."

Eryn remembered the girl from Godseye Clan, the daughter of a herding family. She wore a runelock Eryn didn't recognize, and did not appear to have been beaten, though she was much thinner than she had been when she was captured along with Eryn. She smiled at the woman lying on the blanket. "It's OK now. My clan's caldera is here to help you. But I have to go before I'm missed." With a quick, tight smile, she scuttled out, leaving Eryn alone with the woman on the blanket, and the young boy who'd come to fetch her. The tent smelled of blood, and even in the dim light of the tent, the woman's face was pale.

Eryn set down her pack and approached the woman. "I'm Eryn, and I'm here to help you. What's your name?"

Her name was Cori, and when Eryn pulled back the blanket, the issue was apparent. A huge, purple bruise spread over the woman's abdomen, and dried blood coated the insides of her thighs.

"You were pregnant?" Eryn asked gently, opening her bag.

The woman nodded.

"And you took a blow to the stomach, and…"

"And the baby is gone," the woman murmured.

Eryn sent the boy out for a bucket of fresh water.

"I'm so sorry," she began, but the woman shook her head.

"It doesn't matter. And it's not the first time."

When Eryn looked closer, she saw the chain and runelock around the woman's neck. She was Brinir's eindon. As she rummaged through her bag, she spoke more quietly.

"Who did this to you?"

The name came on a sigh. "Rina."

Brinir's woman, the warrior who looked at Eryn with such hatred. Was the young boy Brinir's son? Did Rina treat all of his eindon this way? The bruising covered the woman's entire abdomen. It had taken quite a beating to make her lose the baby.

The boy brought the water back, and Eryn cleaned the blood from Cori's thighs. She made a salve using taruna leaves that would make the bleeding stop. "I don't know if you'll be able to have another baby. I'm very sorry."

A shrug from the pale woman. "Brinir has plenty of eindon who are younger and more interesting than me. If I prove barren, maybe he'll forget about me."

The little boy moved in to snuggle under his mother's arm. "Father won't forget you. He's the strongest dragonsworn, and Chern is the strongest dragon. I won't let him forget you."

"He will never forget you," the woman murmured. "You'll be dragonsworn one day, and you won't forget your old mother."

And you won't be dragonsworn, Eryn thought as she packed up her kit. *No one will ever be dragonsworn again.*

CHAPTER 29

Dane watched Eryn return to the festival field and met her at the edge.

"Where have you been? You missed all of the dragonsworn games. It's down to just the dragons now. The race is halfway through."

He was just as glad she'd missed the dragonsworn's portion of the festival. He'd come in second in archery, second in knife-throwing, and in the last wrestling event, he'd been paired with Brinir for the final battle. He was every bit as strong as the bearded brute, but of course Brinir had cheated with a knee to the groin that took Dane to the ground. The man had no honor. He couldn't shoot an arrow to save his life, but when it came to fighting dirty, no one could match him. No, Dane was just fine that Eryn hadn't seen him almost win every tournament, but come away empty-handed.

She didn't look anywhere near as excited as she should be. It was her first festival, and she had a dragon to compete.

"Ardos isn't racing—the race is just for females," he said, gesturing to where several of the large males awaited their own turn to compete. "But Ilst is, and she's doing great." He paused, tuning into Ilst's thoughts. "She's in third place, and she's feeling strong."

There were two events for the dragon competition, with runelocks as the prize. Seven dragons were flying the race now. The final competition, a strength challenge, was for the big males.

"Brinir is livid," he confided, leaning close to whisper so none of the other dragonsworn could hear. "With Ardos gone, Chern was almost certain to win the strength challenge. Now he's got competition." Brinir had complained at the start, but no one was going to tell Ardos he couldn't compete.

Ilst popped back into his mind. *Tired. Flying.* She barely had the energy to talk to him, all her energy focused on the race.

A small group of warriors had ridden out early in the morning to mark the turnaround point, hours away on horseback. Each dragon had to pick up a small fabric flag from the warriors, and the first to return would win a runelock and pride.

Dane chuckled, taking Eryn's hand amid the press of people. *She would say we already have plenty of pride.*

They crowded in with the other dragonsworn at the finish line to await the racing dragons. The heavier males moved in behind them, and Eryn faded back to stand with Ardos. Dane tried to control the jealousy that flared up. He remembered the early days, bringing the egg that hatched into Ilst down from the mountain. Heating stones by the fire, tucking them in under blankets to keep her egg at just the right temperature. Then, a month later when Ilst was newly hatched, nothing could take him from her side. He fed her by hand, barely taking his own meals. Kept the fire stoked, warming her small body in his arms at night. Just like with Eryn.

Those days were gone now, for both of them. Ilst no longer needed his warmth, and Eryn no longer needed his protection. She had Ardos now, and though she would still sleep in his tent as his eindon, he had no illusion that she would return to his bedroll.

I'll win her somehow. Ilst loves me. One day Eryn would love him, too.

But did Ilst truly love him? He reached for her mind, and found her exhausted, flying like the wind itself. *I'll win for you.* A week ago, he would never have questioned her devotion to him. She'd been in his mind since before she hatched, floating in the egg, bonding with him even then. But did she have a choice? He turned to watch Eryn and Ardos now. The huge obsidian dragon bent his neck around her, and she polished his scales with a soft cloth, cleaning every trace of dust from around his huge blue eyes. The way she looked at him, and he at her… Dane could only wish someday she would look at him with that kind of love.

Ardos chose her. He didn't have to. He wasn't blood-bonded. He returned to the clan of his own accord, because Eryn's heart called to his own.

I chose her, too.

But he was coming to realize that it wasn't the same. Not even close.

A cheer arose from the crowd around the finish line as the first of the racing dragons came into view. They were too far away to tell one from another, just dots in the sky speeding across the prairie grass, cattle scattering before them.

He reached out to Ilst's mind again, looking through her eyes.

Only one dragon was ahead of her, and only by the length of a dragon's tail.

"Come on, Ilst!" He shouted with the crowd, eyes on the sky.

They came speeding over the grass, wings pounding the air. The crowd around him yelled, a wordless cheer as the winners streaked through the sky. Nose to nose, the first two approached the finish line.

"You can do it!"

The other dragon, a lithe seven-year old female, faltered as they came in over the crowd. With a final push of speed,

Ilst edged her out, nose crossing the finish line barely a head's length in the lead.

He felt a pair of arms wrap around him from the side, and spun to see Eryn, face alight.

"She won! Ilst won! Ardos says that's amazing for how young she is! Congratulations!"

Dane hugged Eryn, caught up in the joy not only of the win, but of her excitement. "I knew she could do it. She's light and strong, and she never gives up."

She joined him in running over to where Ilst landed, sides heaving, head held high.

"You're the most amazing dragon."

Ilst preened. *Of course I am.*

The fullness in his heart shone out of Dane. *This moment is perfection.* Ilst was resplendent, adored by the crowd. And Eryn was happy, rubbing Ilst's neck next to him, like a true partner. He let the happiness flow over into words.

"There's no one I'd rather share this moment with than you."

Eryn's head snapped around, looking from Dane to Ilst.

Dane clarified, "With you, Eryn. I'm glad to share it with you."

For just a moment, her face relaxed, a glimpse into the woman she must have been with her own people. Then her hand fluttered to the lock around her neck.

"I'm happy that Ilst is such a wonderful dragon."

The words cut Dane. In all his jealousy over Eryn's love of Ardos, he'd hoped it might bond her fully to the clan; help her realize that she was better off here, and if she'd only let herself, she could be happy with him as his woman.

That's all she can *be.* Ilst's rebuke was another slap in the face.

His woman. Never his wife. She was still eindon.

Dane's father had decreed that despite Ardos' heart-bond, she was still his property. Dragonbound, but lower than the lowest clan-born. Though she was safe from the beatings and abuse common to so many eindon women, she was still property. No different than a horse, a dog, or a sword.

But his father was chief. In time, he might change his mind.

In the lull of excitement before the final event of the festival, Dane took Eryn's hand, refusing to let her pull away.

"Eryn, I know you hate being eindon. Even with Ardos' love, you hate us all for taking you from your home." The force of her gaze stopped his words for a moment. "But my father only said that so you wouldn't leave. If we can prove to him that you're truly committed to the clan, he might change his mind. He might let us remove the chain."

Her soft blue eyes took his breath, lit by the afternoon sun on her face. Wind blew wisps of her hair from its braid, and her lips parted gently as she looked into his heart.

"Maybe…" she began, but a shove from behind him sent him barreling into her, nearly knocking them both over. Brinir's laugh boomed over the murmurs of the crowd.

"Your eindon seems to think she's one of us," he said, looming over Eryn's small form. "Better teach her some manners, or I will."

Ardos's head appeared over Eryn's, a deep growl vibrating right into Dane's chest as the dragon stared death into Brinir. Chern answered Ardos' growl, lumbering up beside him. The two dragon's eyes locked, spines on their back raised in aggression.

A shrill whistle split the air.

"Settle it on the field," the chief said from behind Dane. "We'll have no dragons fighting in my clan."

CHAPTER 30

Eryn's blood boiled, partly her own anger, and partly Ardos' rage. She had no idea how dragons in the wild behaved, how big their territories were, or if they had structure with dominant males, but the smell of Chern nearby always got Ardos' hackles up. Too many males with no chance to breed. It wasn't natural.

Our females are not arousing.

Eryn looked at Ilst, still preening about her victory. She was a lovely dragon, cream and chocolate-colored, with an elegant neck. But to Ardos, she smelled like nothing. Not female. Not alluring.

I do not look at her the way Dane looks at you.

Even though no one but her could hear his words, Eryn flushed. Dane's words were rattling around in her head. *He might let us remove the chain.* Us.

He's trying.

And again, she wasn't sure if the thought belonged to her or Ardos. Then again, all their thoughts belonged to both of them now. And Dane was trying. Even before she had the protection of a dragon, he'd been respectful, kind. His arms around her in the chill of the mountains hadn't been unpleasant. He couldn't help where he was born. And he was right about dragons. They truly were astounding.

Chern was still bristling, but Ardos had relaxed. The chief led a procession of dragonsworn and dragons, followed by the rest of the clan, over to a cleared patch of land. A large woven basket with rope handles sat ready next to a large pile of stones, each one larger than a man's head. Eryn was surprised to learn that dragons couldn't carry much more than their own body weight in the air. Argos chuckled. *We're strong, but we're not shaped like birds or even bats. Perhaps your god made us this way so we couldn't carry you straight to his realm in the sky.*

The chief addressed the crowd. "The final competition is for dragon strength. The dragon that can carry the heaviest load from here," he pointed to a line of stones on the ground, "to there," and he pointed to another ten dragon-lengths away, "will be the winner."

Only the males would compete, with their massive structure and muscle. The females moved over to one side to watch, and the crowd made a semicircle around the clearing, vying for the best viewing spots.

Ardos took his place next to the other males. Only Chern and Kalg matched him in stature. Five other males looked determined, but Eryn had no question who was really in competition.

One by one, each dragon gripped a basket with a stone in his front claws, pushing off the ground with heavy hindquarters and beating the air with muscular wings. Each one managed to take to the sky with a single stone loaded into the basket and make it across the line. Seven of the eight were able to succeed in the next round with two stones, and five were able to fly the distance to the line with three stones.

Dane stood behind Eryn, cheering along with her and the crowd as another stone was loaded into the basket. "Come on, Ardos! You can do it!"

She had to laugh along with his enthusiasm. Across the field, Ilst pawed the ground, obviously sharing her dragonsworn's excitement.

Four stones proved too much for all but Ardos, Chern, and Kalg.

Chief Calnan gave the order. "Load the fifth stone!"

Kalg made the first attempt. The basket stretched under the weight of the stones as the big blue dragon strained against the weight. He managed to lift it a foot off the ground, but halfway across the distance, it dropped from his talons, and he popped skyward, suddenly relieved of the weight.

"It's all right, Kalg, good job!" Eryn was shocked to hear the words pop out of her mouth.

The location of the drop was marked, in case none of the dragons could make the whole distance. Whichever made it the farthest would win in that case. Five warriors rushed onto the field to carry the stones back to the starting line and re-load the basket.

Ardos was next. Eryn's shoulders tightened, her face drawn as her dragon gripped the handles. Through their bond she grimaced as wing muscles she didn't have ached. Her hands clenched into fists, mirroring his grip on the taut rope.

"Come on, Ardos; come on, Ardos." She could barely hear Dane's voice behind her, blood pounding into her head.

Barely a man's height off the ground, the basket lifted and swung across the field, held in Ardos' talons. Eryn screamed along with the crowd as Ardos beat the air, fanning the crowd with dust. With a crack of rocks, he crossed the finish line and dropped the basket, heaving in the spring sunshine.

"Yes!" Eryn's heart leapt and she jumped into the air, arms above her head. Ardos' pride filled her and she yelled his name, voice mingling with Dane's and the rest of the clan.

Let's see Chern do that.

Eryn forgave Ardos the arrogance in his thought. He earned it. He truly was the greatest dragon that ever lived.

The warriors carried the stones back to the starting line and loaded the basket. Chern gripped the handles, and Brinir moved in next to Eryn, his shoulder bumping into hers.

"Now watch how a real dragon flies."

She felt the heat of Dane moving in even closer behind her, but brushed off his arms as he tried to hold her. She didn't need his protection.

"He'll never get off the ground," she replied.

But he did. With a bellow of effort, Chern lifted the load. Barely a foot off the ground, it skimmed forward, Chern's wingtips almost touching the ground with every beat.

The crowd went wild and Eryn's vision went red, watching the other male heading for the finish where Ardos waited.

Five dragon-lengths to go.

Four.

Three.

The basket dipped, scraping the ground. It tipped over, stones spilling out. Chern popped into the sky, still clutching the empty basket. He roared with rage, flinging the heavy basket right at Ardos, who leaped into the air, catching the basket with his front talons and settling gently to the ground.

Eryn led the crowd rushing over to surround him. "He did it! Ardos is the champion!"

Her joy bubbled over at Dane's shout, and she turned to him, jumping into his arms. Ardos wrapped them both with his neck, holding them as they held each other, the two humans laughing until tears streamed down their faces, adding his rumble of pleasure. Another rumble joined the throng as Ilst moved in, nudging Dane and Eryn with her soft-skinned nose.

Eryn pulled back from Dane's shoulder, and for a moment, they grinned at each other, happy as children. Her legs were wrapped around his waist, and he held her without effort, lost in the moment of joy.

For a few breaths, nothing else existed within the embrace of the two dragons entwined around their humans.

Chapter 31

That night, torches burned in a wide circle in the center of the tent village under a black sky, the smoke curling up toward the stars. On any other year, Dane would be heartened by the clear night, a sign that Baltenn could look down upon them with no clouds in his way, and smile upon their victory. Tonight, however, his heart was heavy. No one had yet spilled the secret, that there would be no more dragon eggs for Dragon Clan. No more bloodbonds. No more dragons.

The full impact was starting to take root in the hearts of the few who knew. Tempers were short, anger covering the fear that their way of life, their dominance in battle, might be in its last generation. Even without the dragons, they were the strongest warriors in Den Woth. Of course, they were. But they had never needed to find out. Other clans scattered, running for their lives when the dragons roared from the sky. The warriors only had to sweep in and clean up.

When the truth was finally revealed, the clan would panic. He didn't envy his father, who would be remembered as the chief who let it all fall apart. Of course, he had nothing to do with it; he wasn't even there when the wild dragons voided the ancient pact. But this was his clan, and these were his people. Dane was glad his mother was no longer around to see his fall.

"Dragon Clan, rejoice with our warriors, these brave men who have been found worthy to travel to Baltenn's Stone and seek the egg of a dragon!" Chief Brunan's voice boomed out over the assembled clan that ringed the circle of torches.

The old man stood in front of his fur-covered throne, which had been carried out to the edge of the torch ring and placed on a waist-high wooden dais, torches glowing at all four corners. Next to the platform stood a young man dressed in the shaman's regalia, bones clicking when he moved. The shaman's apprentice was now the clan's only holy man. What knowledge had been lost when the shaman fell to the claws of the wild dragons?

Dane's shoulder brushed Eryn's from their position on the edge of the circle. Knowledge and lore, that was her training. He hadn't considered it important, more a woman's fancy, a chance for a beauty like her to avoid the attention of the inferior men of her former clan. None of them were good enough for her, so she chose the solitary life of—what had she called herself? Caldera. He smiled in the torchlight. *Saving herself for me, though she didn't know it.* Ilst intruded into his thoughts. *She still doesn't know it.* But her words were pushed with gentle humor, and Dane's smile remained. *No, she doesn't know it. Not yet.*

This was the ceremony where the awards for the festival were given. Where the four young warriors who had survived their trials were officially named as Baltenn's chosen, the honored future dragonsworn who thought they'd travel to the mountains next year and hopefully return with an egg. *Poor fools. They have no idea.*

Each of the young men approached the chief, bowed before him, and received the high honor from the shaman, a necklace of bone with their rune etched into it. Each rune was unique to the warrior, a combination of his name, and an honorary title. It was a gift from the chief and worn with pride forever. Dane touched the bone that hung around his neck. Dane Row: Kind and Honorable. He hadn't appreciated it when it was given to him three years ago. Kindness was not a valued trait among warriors or dragonsworn. He'd thought it was a slight from Chief Krunnan, Brinir's father. But he'd come to appreciate it, and to realize it defined him more than he'd realized. It honored his own mother and father; the kindness from her, and the honor from him.

The four young men received their runes, their titles variations on victory, strength, fierceness. Each wore his bone amulet as if it carried the wisdom of Baltenn himself, and the crowd cheered for their future.

Next came the awards for the dragonsworn tournament. The rankings were read, with runelocks as the prizes. Brinir turned a wicked grin on Dane as the wrestling results were announced and he accepted the runelock with his title on it. Brinir: Aggressive and Proud. It suited him.

Eryn murmured beside Dane.

"You came in second in every competition? That's amazing. Nobody else is good at everything."

He thought his heart might actually explode with joy. *She's right,* came Ilst's voice. *Everyone else is good at one thing, or none. But there's nothing you can't do well.*

The derision of Brinir fell away. Dane didn't need the approval of a brute like him. He had the praise of the only ones who mattered.

Finally, it was time for the dragon awards. Chief Calnan beamed across the crowd.

"The fastest of our dragons, and the youngest ever to win the dragon race, I'm proud to honor Ilst, bloodbound to Dane Rowe!"

With wingbeats that made the torch smoke billow into the sky, Ilst landed in the center of the circle. Dane strode up next to her, glowing in the cheers of his clan. He laid a hand on her shoulder and received an affectionate bump from her nose. His father handed him a runelock, a matching bronze disk to the one that held Eryn's chain. Dane held it up for the crowd to appreciate, and they roared approval. Ilst launched herself into the sky, and Dane returned to his place in the circle. Eryn took his hand and gave it a silent squeeze. She would have dropped her hand, but Dane held on, and she blinked at him for a moment before relaxing her hand in his.

"And finally," Chief Calnan said, "We award the prize for the strongest dragon, our greatest honor. Dragon Clan lives by the strength of our bloodbonded dragons, and when one is lost to us, it is a most terrible day. But when a dragon returns to us by his own decision, when he chooses to rejoin the clan and selects another to share his life with, this is the rarest gift Lord Baltenn can give to our clan."

He looked out over the crowd.

"There are those among you who might question that choice. Who might think that an eindon is unworthy of a dragon's bond. That only a strong warrior should know the power of a dragon at his side." He zeroed in on Dane and Eryn. "And yet, this was not the choice this dragon made. Instead, he chose the lowliest among us, an eindon who wears the chain of the foreign-born, who was brought to our clan to serve us, as befits the station of one born to a lesser clan. What does it mean?"

The silence around the circle stretched all the way to the back of the crowd, where the eindon stood ringing the clan-born.

"It means that even the lowest of Dragon Clan is worthy of the name. It means that when a dragonsworn takes one of another clan, his choice is led by Baltenn himself. It means that the eindon taken by Dane Rowe, who has given up her former clan and embraced her role as servant to a drag-onsworn, is herself worthy of a dragon's bond. If the lowest among us can be chosen by a dragon, truly we are the people of Lord Baltenn, and no clan shall ever be as honored in his sight! The strongest dragon of Dragon Clan is Ardos, heart-bound to eindon Eryn Rowe!"

Dane's pulse shot into his head.

Eryn Rowe.

His father had named Eryn as a Rowe, as if she were not his property, but his wife. No eindon he had ever heard of had earned the right to bear her dragonsworn's name. She was not his wife. He had not claimed her as such and couldn't wifebond her. That honor was only for clan-born women.

The crowd was hushed for a moment, until Ardos dropped into the center of the circle, wings making the torches flicker. He roared into the sky, and the clan responded, roaring back, either in approval or disbelief, Dane couldn't tell.

"Go up and bow to the chief," Dane whispered.

Eryn stepped forward, and the cheers died down. But as she approached her dragon, and Ardos bent his neck to encircle her, touching his huge wide forehead to hers, every voice was hushed. They stood together in the middle of the circle for a moment, face to face in the silence. Dane blinked back tears, reveling in the obvious show of their bond, and feeling the joy of his own bond with Ilst.

Chief Calnan stepped down from his dais and reached into his cloak. He approached Eryn and Ardos, and the dragon moved his tail to allow the chief into their little circle.

"Such a thing has never been recorded in the history of our clan. But the prize for our strongest dragon is a runelock for his dragonsworn. So has it always been, and so it shall be today." He pulled a bronze disk from his pocket.

"Today I present this award to Ardos, heartbonded to eindon Eryn. Her rune is recorded in our lore." He held up the runelock, which glittered in the torchlight. Dane couldn't see the unique symbol on it, but his father read it for the crowd.

"Eryn: Wise and Adored!"

The cheer started from the back of the circle, as every eindon screamed into the sky. It rippled up as the joy of the chained spread like fire from the lowest clan-born up through the most honored. Dane took up the howl, and in the center of the circle, Eryn accepted the runelock prize while Ardos roared his glory up to the stars.

CHAPTER 32

Eryn ground dry sunroot into a powder, mixing a bit of fermented potato alcohol to make a paste. The young man in front of her peeked out from under his hood of tattered cloth, the chain and runelock around his neck declaring him the property of one of the older dragonsworn Eryn hadn't met.

At least, this one looks well fed.

Since the day of the festival two weeks earlier when she had treated the young woman whose unborn child bled out of her, Eryn had become the eindons' unofficial healer. Ragna, who remained the clan's herbwoman even after taking on the markings of mourning for her husband, the former chief, did not treat eindon wounds or sickness. But the past week had seen the trickle of sick or injured eindon turn into a daily flow of patients.

"You'll have to make this last," she told the man as she smeared the paste onto the flaking red patches that partly covered his face and arms. "I'm running low on almost everything."

He thanked her profusely, tears shining in his eyes. "Thank you, dokkas," he said. "May Baltenn's eyes always smile upon you."

This eindon wasn't the first to call her that. An eindon taken from another clan in the far north had given her the name, which fell from their lips like rain in the desert. Dokkas. In the old dialect, it meant hope.

It was a heavy name to wear. The eindon who had a dragon. The eindon who brought hope to all those in chains, that one day their lives might not be the misery of slavery.

But I'm still a slave.

Ardos was enjoying a late afternoon rest in the sun, but he gave Eryn a mental hug that felt as real as a pair of arms around her shoulders. *You wear a chain. But you serve only those you choose to help.*

Of course, she would help the other eindon. Anything she could do to alleviate their suffering was worth her effort. It was the only way she could share her amazing good fortune with them.

The chuckle from Ardos was a light breeze dancing through her mind. *Such good fortune,* he agreed.

His words in her head startled her. It was her own thought reflected back at her, put into the dragon's deep mental rumble. Good fortune. Would she ever have believed she could consider herself fortunate? Her hands stroked the smooth chain around her neck, as they did a thousand times a day. She still despised it with every bone in her body. She was still a slave. But with her captivity had come Ardos, who was part of her soul. Without the chain she would never have felt the comfort of his mental strength, and the protection of his midnight wings. She no longer needed Dane to keep the other dragonsworn at bay. No one would cross Ardos.

Her pocket clinked as she sorted the dwindling herbs in her pack. The runelock with its chain in her pocket was the most confusing thing she had ever owned.

Eryn, Wise and Adored. That's what her unique rune said, what the chief had named her. And by the eindon of Dragon Clan and the children, she was certainly adored. Whenever she left the tent, she attracted a following of young girls, full of questions about Ardos. Dane's little sister was her constant shadow. They all wanted to see the runelock she kept in her pocket. It sickened her that they were so impressed with something so cruel—the lock for an eindon chain. But they didn't see the inhumanity, only the honor. No woman had heartbonded a dragon in hundreds of years. And no eindon ever had, in the history of the clan. She didn't want to acknowledge the pride that filled her when she saw Ardos in the sky, or when she groomed and polished his scales and claws. The runelock was the clan's symbol of that bond. She would never, ever use it to bind another human to her service. It was just a plaything for the children to admire, the hope of the eindon. One of her names.

Rowe. Eryn Rowe. That was her other name now.

The chief, Dane's father, had called her by their last name. As if she were his wife, and not his property.

She wasn't anywhere near ready to think about that.

The packets of herbs and remedies she had brought from her own clan were running low. The sunroot for skin rashes. Mountain maiden, which she brewed into a tea to stop the hot flashes in the women who were past childbearing. Rock laurel, to heal bruises. Poppies for pain. Red dandy leaves for nausea. She had used a lot of rock laurel on Dane after the festival games. Her face warmed at the memory.

Still flushed with victory, they had retired to his tent. He winced as he pulled off his sweaty clothing.

"You're injured," she said. "Let me see."

There was a long cut down his left bicep, and his chest was covered in bruises.

"I'm sorry I missed your fights. It must have been exciting to watch."

He shrugged, giving another wince. "You were busy, and I didn't win anyway."

She found that hard to believe. Here, so close to him, he was massive. His chest was wide, with just a bit of blond hair up near his throat. Shoulders so broad... She remembered how it felt to snuggle with her back against him in the early days before Ardos became her protector. *Focus on the task at hand.* She threaded a needle with a long thread of gut suture and set it on top of her pack. From her herbs, she pulled the antiseptic garlic and mixed a quick paste. "Hold out your arm. I need to clean the wound before I stitch it."

He opened his mouth, but the expected protest didn't come.

Her hand held the underside of his arm while she gently rubbed the antiseptic paste into the wound and wiped it around the dirty edges. His muscles were firm under her fingers, and she lingered for a moment. "Does it hurt a lot?"

"It's bad, but I'll survive."

She glanced up at his face, and he had a tiny smile.

He likes this attention.

If she admitted the truth, so did she.

Deft fingers sewed the skin edges together, and she wrapped a clean bandage around his upper arm. "Now let me rub this into the bruises. They'll heal faster."

She made another paste of the rock laurel, using fermented beet alcohol instead of water. With a small amount on her fingertips, she gently rubbed it into the worst of the bruises. Dane said nothing, just quietly breathed, eyes closed at her ministration. Long moments after she got them all suitably anointed, she continued the soft massage. *It's good for circulation.*

Sure it is. Ardos chuckled in her mind.

Oh, so you're a human healer now? she sent back to him.

No answer. Just a smug, knowing emotion.

"All right," Eryn said to Dane. "Anywhere else?"

He caught her looking at his leather pants, and she flushed.

"No more wounds. But bruises you could rub that ointment into."

Oh, sweet gods. Not sure I'm ready for that.

She took a clean shirt from his pile of clothing. "Take the pants off and cover yourself with this."

He took the shirt, and she turned away.

"I'm ready."

He lay on his bedroll, with only the shirt covering his groin.

He is a beautiful man.

But Eryn didn't want a man. She had never truly wanted a man. But this one, lying here, trusting her, and her…trusting him? *He keeps me in chains. There can be nothing between us when one of us is in chains.*

She sat next to him on the bedroll and rubbed the rock laurel ointment into the bruises on his thighs. After a few moments he stopped her and rolled over abruptly.

"OK, that's good enough. Thank you."

His words puzzled her for a moment, but Ardos laughed in her mind. *A shirt doesn't hide what the thigh massage was doing to him.*

Heat rose up Eryn's chest and neck. She was glad Dane couldn't feel what it had done to her in the same region.

Dane had played up the wounds for a week, and she obliged, rubbing in the ointment after the bruises had faded. She had never been so sorry to see a patient recover so quickly.

Now, Dane burst into the tent, almost tripping over the packets she had lying all over the rug.

"My father has been talking with the senior dragonsworn," he said, plopping down beside her. "He's preparing a list of our strongest laborers to go start pulling down the rocks in the pass to the Valley of Dragons."

Eryn sat back on her heels, pushing sweaty hair out of her face. Her fingers were stained with sunroot paste, and she wiped them on the front of her tunic. "Why? The dragons won't let us in."

Dane picked up a packet and raised it to his nose. Eryn swiped it out of his hands before he could sniff it and tucked it into its place in the pack.

"He thinks if we make a peace offering before winter sets in, they'll forgive us and everything will be fine."

Peace offering. The words chilled Eryn's heart.

"What do you mean?"

Dane's gaze dropped to the chain around Eryn's neck. He flushed, looking away, turning another small packet over and over in his fingers. "It won't be you. Ardos would never allow it to be you."

No, he wouldn't. But it would be someone.

"How many?"

Dane mumbled an answer.

"I didn't hear that. How many eindon?"

He sighed. "A hundred."

Bile burned the back of Eryn's throat. A hundred eindon. A hundred people, sacrificed to the wild dragons. Because of her. Because she just had to play the trick that got them banned from the valley.

I have to fix this.

"They won't all come from here," Dane continued, tapping the packet against his knee. "There will be raiding parties through the summer to take as many as we can from other clans…" he trailed off when he could plainly see his words weren't helping.

She plucked the packet from his fingers and stared into his eyes.

"What do you think of that plan?"

He held her stare for a moment before looking away. "I wish there was another choice."

Eryn's hands trembled, her sick dread crystallizing into resolve.

"I don't know what to do," she said, "how to fix this." She stopped and blinked back tears. "But I have an idea of someone who might."

CHAPTER 33

Dane brought Eryn's idea to his father. To his surprise, the chief agreed.

"We've never had need of anyone else's wisdom before," he confided to Dane alone, "but these are new and disturbing times. If Eryn thinks this person has any secrets that might help us, we must know them."

The thought of traveling to wherever this wise person was, just Dane and Eryn along with their dragons, filled Dane with joy. It was just what they needed…some time alone, away from the things about the clan that bothered her. Away from the other dragonsworn, with their sneers and slurs at Eryn. Away from the herd of children that followed her everywhere; that Ardos graciously allowed to climb all over him, behaving like a kindly old uncle instead of the most powerful dragon in the clan. The four of them would travel, just like Eryn had wanted, to get the wisdom she most valued. And along the way, he would figure out what she wanted of him. What she liked, what she desired—and find a way to become that.

With his next sentence, Chief Calnan dashed Dane's hopes.

"It's too dangerous for you to go alone. You'll take Tornnen and Rina along with you."

Dane protested, but there was no swaying the chief. Tornnen, with his female dragon Urrgar, and Rina with her snide remarks and derision of Eryn—those would all accompany Dane and Eryn on the journey east.

Eryn knew where they were going, up to a point.

On the eastern border of Den Woth, far south of the Greyfang Mountains—and the rolling foothills where Dane had first found her in the early spring grazing lands of the Godseye flocks—those foothills grew into a proper mountain range. No sheer cliffs like Greyfang, but endless forested green slopes that would still have snow on top, even as the days grew longer and warmer. A wide pass wound between those mountains that led all the way to the border of Concadia, a land that Dane had always thought was myth, but Eryn assured him was real and full of wonders. But they weren't going all the way to Concadia. Partway through, the river that flowed down from those mountains split into a fork. The lower path led to Concadia, where Dragon Clan was banned, and dragons were not permitted to follow. Dane had bristled at that, insisting that there was nowhere a dragon's might would not prevail. Eryn's descriptions of catapults and great siege weapons that fired arrows as thick as a tree trunk and could drop a dragon from the sky gave him pause. She hadn't actually seen them, as she'd never been to Concadia. But she'd seen drawings, heard descriptions from those who had been there. No, they would not follow the flow of the river. But the upstream fork that led higher into the southern hills—somewhere along that river was Tiezahal, the City of Stone. Eryn had never been there either but expressed confidence that they would find it easily. As long as they left their dragons out of sight, they could claim to be from any other tribe to gain admittance.

So they packed their possessions, loaded packhorses with food, tents, bedding, and weapons, and left the clan, trailed by a dwindling tail of children and eindon, weeping as their hero rode away.

Dane felt no jealousy that the hero wasn't him. Eryn was beloved in a way no other clan member had ever been. The dragonsworn detested her, but the common people whispered prayers when she walked by, and she always had a kind word, some food for the hungry, or a remedy for the sick or injured.

Torrnen grumbled every step of the way.

"I should be with the raiding parties," he said from his horse plodding along ahead of Dane's. "Getting eindon for the big sacrifice. Not babysitting on some errand to some weakling in the mountains. Dragon Clan has no need for the 'wisdom' of any other clan." He twisted the word until "wisdom" sounded like a curse word.

Rina rode next to Torrnen, agreeing with everything he said. Dane and Eryn kept away from them as much as they could, setting up their tent on the far side of the cookfire at night.

They both insisted that Eryn do all the cooking, and Dane was shocked when she didn't object. A few meals in, he noticed that she was very careful about which bowl of beef stew she handed to each person, and further noticed how often Tornnen and Rina had to stop and run for the bushes. They were looking paler by the day. Dane was able to gauge Eryn's mood by how much gastric distress her two enemies were in—not enough to slow the journey much, but certainly enough to make riding horseback a nightmare. He also noticed that he himself had no such issues.

She doesn't hate me. Not like she hates them.

It wasn't much, but it was enough for now.

On the fifth night of travel, Eryn retired to their tent right after dinner and her nightly grooming of Ardos, who was so clean he practically glowed in the dark. Dane groomed Ilst at the same time, admiring the sheen of her beige scales.

The base of her neck spines reflected the red of the firelight and the orange of the setting sun as he rubbed her down. Her claws were bloody, and her breath smelled of whatever mountain creature had been her dinner.

It was a goat of some kind. Delicious.

She burped in his face, and he was torn between his own revulsion at the raw meat smell and Ilst's delight in it.

"Well, whatever it is, it suits you. Wild game and mountain air are doing you good."

He left Ilst and joined Eryn in their tent. She knelt on the ground, illuminated by a lantern from below, golden braids hanging over her shoulders as she sorted the day's harvest; all the flowers and roots and things she picked during their frequent halts.

Watching her so absorbed in her work gave him a pang. *This is what I took her from. This is what she wants.* She was practicing her craft as best she could, taking care of the lowliest of her new clan. But her joy was in these herbs, in caring for the sick.

And in her dragon, came Ilst's voice.

Yes, her dragon. And without Dane, if she had never come to Dragon Clan, she would never have known him.

"Eryn, are you happy?" Even Dane wasn't sure where the words came from. He expected her usual dark look, the way she shut down any attempts he made to help her see how fortunate she was.

Instead, she sat back on her heels, holding a small bunch of blue flowers in her hands. She picked at the petals, setting them aside as she spoke. "It depends when you ask me. When I'm with Ardos, with my cheek against his chest, hearing him breathe—yes, I'm happy. It's the joy you must feel with Ilst, and I see now why you are all so arrogant. With a dragon at your side, it feels like you can do anything, and nothing can touch you."

She scraped the pollen from the center of the flower onto a sheet of waxed parchment. "It's not true, of course. If it were, I wouldn't have Ardos because Chief Krunnan wouldn't have died." Her eyes unfocused for a moment, the way they did when Ardos spoke in her head. After a moment she smiled.

"Ardos is happy. He says this heartbond feels different than his bloodbond with the chief. It's free will, not slavery." She touched the runelock around her neck. "And when Ardos is happy, it's hard for me to be sad. He's not a slave anymore. And I'm not sure what I am." She folded the packet of pollen into an envelope, carefully tucking in the corners to make a sealed packet. Only then did she look at him.

"It's all mixed up in my mind. If you hadn't taken me, I wouldn't be a slave now. But I wouldn't have Ardos, and there's nothing I wouldn't give to keep that bond. Of all the dragonsworn I've met, you're the only one that...." She picked another bunch of flowers off the floor and started peeling the roots away from the stems. "If anyone else had taken me, I would be dead by my own hand already. Long before Ardos, I would have ended it. If it was Brinir, or Tornen..." She shivered. "You were well named. Kind and Honorable."

After another few moments, she set down the flowers, still staring into her lap. "Back at my old clan, there was a man who wanted me for his wife. And I say "wife," but being wife to him would have been so much worse than being an eindon. When a man wants a woman, the easiest way is to take her by force. Take her purity, render her unfit for any other man. Then he can graciously marry her, saving her from a life of shame as a plaything to any other man who wants to take her. So that man tried to take me, and he would have succeeded. But my brother heard my screams and found us before—. That's why I became Caldera to my clan. I never wanted any man's hands on me again, and only the Caldera is protected. I would live alone and die a crone, and that was the best I could hope for."

She turned to look at him then. "So…am I happy? Honestly, compared to the life I might have had in my old clan, there are joys here I couldn't have imagined. I'm still able to practice my craft, and I'm going to see the Tieza just like I always hoped I would"

Dane's breath filled his chest. "You can have a good life here. With Ardos. And with me, if you choose. I will never force you to do anything you don't want to do. But you have no idea how much I want to touch you, not like that other man did, but…like Ardos touches your heart."

Oh, very good. You're learning, Ilst purred into his mind.

Eryn's smile was worth all the frustration, all the waiting.

"You're giving me time." And again, she touched the runelock around her neck. "I don't know what my future is with this clan. I know I will never leave Ardos. And I know," she said, glancing down at her herbs, "that I'm running low on runwort, so I'm going to have to switch to cararoot and see if constipation suits Rina and Torrnen better than diarrhea does." Her lips curled into a smile.

"Eryn, may I kiss you? Just on the forehead?"

Her eyes opened wide.

"Yes."

He stepped forward, gently taking her hands in his. She lowered her head, closing her eyes. His fingers gently pushed away a strand of her hair that had fallen out of her braids, then rested on her cheek.

Her forehead tasted of salt and smelled of lavender. When his lips rested against her skin, she sighed. He wanted to hold the chaste kiss forever, breathing in her hair, her softness, one hand in hers, the other gently stroking her cheek. But after a moment, she pulled back.

"You're nothing like the rest of them," she murmured.

"Neither are you."

The moment might have lasted forever if the sounds from outside the tent hadn't intruded. Brina and Torrnen had waited only a few days on the trail, but tonight she must have gotten tired of convincing him that she wouldn't tell Brinir. Or maybe he'd been unable to catch a wild animal to torture, staking it alive to the ground and cutting off bits, hearing it scream until it died, one of his favorite pastimes in the absence of an eindon to torment. The sound of Brina and Torrnen's gasping, screaming rutting broke the sweet tenderness inside the tent, and Eryn knelt by the herbs again, stripping off the roots of the flower and sealing them up.

Dane tucked into his bedroll, alone, but warm, flying high on the taste of Eryn's skin still on his lips.

Chapter 34

They followed the fork of the river up the foothills, stopping only when they had to. It was mostly pine forest, with plenty of rhododendron, their sagging green leaves of little use to Eryn. Nothing medicinal there, unless you wanted someone dead. Which she certainly did. Torrnen and Rina's animal sex noises had kept Eryn up half the night, and their constant complaining made her feel like a mother of toddlers.

"How long until we get there?" Torrnen asked for the hundredth time. "This is a waste of time. I should be getting eindon right now."

Eryn thought they'd make it today. She had never been to the Tiezahal before, the stone city in the hills, where people from Den Woth and Concadia came to have audience with the Tiezan and learn from their wisdom. She would have come with Nora, her sister-in-law, this summer, but the Dragon Clan raid had ended those hopes. Like every day, she offered a silent prayer that Nora and her daughter, Filina, had found safety that night. And that her brother, Falnar, had found them when he returned from hunting. *Please let them be safe, and far away from the raids that are gearing up right now.*

Everything hinged on this mission. The lives of a hundred innocent women, and possibly all those who would go to make the sacrifice, relied on her finding some way to prevent it. Dane would almost certainly be among those who entered the mountain pass. He'd said she was safe from sacrifice and that Ardos would never allow her to be taken, but Ardos wouldn't be on that side of the pass. He wouldn't be in the Valley of Dragons, and if she were made to go with Dane, she had no doubt that she would end up tied to a rock with the other women, regardless of the wrath of Ardos after it was done. She wasn't doing it for herself, though. Too many other lives were at stake.

I started this. My little trick caused all of this. So I have to fix it.

The flatter path around the river opened up as they climbed, packhorses picking their way. They led three extra horses, which would be left as payment for whatever knowledge they gained and for room and board while they were in the city. The dragons swooped on thermals, wind buffeting up the mountainsides. When the footing was easy, Eryn opened her mind to him, soaring above the pines, diving with the other dragons, scaring the local wildlife.

They crested a hill, and below them sprawled a village.

"Thank Baltenn, we're finally here," Tornnen grumbled. He turned to Eryn. "Get your books or whatever we're doing here, and let's get home."

Below them stretched the city of the Tiezan. The hills on each side had been cut to level terraces, and plow-lines showed that the land had already been planted. Like stairs for a giant, each flat level curved around the hill, clearly human-made, but also looking natural, as if the hill had just grown that way. The river they had followed continued up to the right of the pass. The party looked in awe at the city that sprawled over the bottom of the valley. Permanent dwellings of stone and wood, roads of flat, placed rock… Eryn had never seen anything like it. And so many people, bustling from building to building. It looked both small and huge from the top of the hill. They stood staring at a sign etched in stone proclaiming that dragons were not welcome. For those who couldn't read, there was a drawing of a dragon with a large X through it.

You have to stay up in the mountains where they can't see you, Eryn thought to Ardos.

Be careful. You don't know these people. His concern made her itchy.

A group of six armed fighters met them as they descended. They were dressed plainly, but each carried a stout sword.

"Welcome. How can the wisdom of the Tiezahal help you?"

Eryn started to answer, but Tornnen cut her off. "The wisdom of…"

Dane stepped in. "Thank you for the welcome. We are here to learn about the dragons of the valley."

Every eye shot skyward. "Are you Dragon Clan?"

Tornnen's chest puffed, and he answered before Eryn could. "Of course, we are."

The lead warrior nodded to one of the others, who rushed away down the hill. "No one from your clan has ever darkened our hall before, but we know of you. Dragons are not permitted here. If we see them, we will shoot them. Is that clear? Tell them to stay in the mountains, or return now to your lands."

"If you shoot them—" Torrnen began, but again Dane cut him off.

"We will happily abide by your rules. This is your home, and we have come here to learn. This is Eryn," he said, and she rode up next to him. "She was to be her clan's Caldera, but has joined our clan instead. She is our most learned, and we hope to find answers here that will help us."

The warrior eyed the chain around Eryn's neck.

"Joined you, did she?"

Eryn flushed. "I am Eryn Drys—" she stopped for a moment. "Eryn Rowe, formerly of Godseye clan. Heartbonded to Ardos, who will not shadow your city with his wings. We graciously accept your hospitality."

The warrior led them down the path toward the village. It was busily swarming with people, moving from building to building. Eryn had never seen buildings of wood or stone before, as both of her clans were nomadic, living in heavy tents that followed the flocks or herds to seasonal grazing. She marveled at the construction. Logs hewn to planks, fastened with iron nails. Or stones stacked and joined with some kind of hard amalgam to stick them together. Roofs of waxed bark shingles. Some of the buildings were several stories high, with windows overlooking the streets below.

They stopped at a long building that housed other horses and dismounted, all stretching their legs after days of riding.

"We will take your belongings to our guesthouse and get you settled in. When the Tieza wishes to see you, you will be summoned."

Rina grumbled about that. "I thought we were here so she could read some books or something. No one 'summons' Dragon Clan."

But they followed a young boy who carried their packs like they weighed nothing, leading them to a stone building that stretched up the side of a hill, partially dug into the earth. He led them up the staircase, a wide, stone climb, its smoothness cool under Eryn's boots. People bustled around, and the smell of something spicy and foreign made her stomach growl.

"We have two rooms available to you," the boy said. Eryn and Dane took the room that faced the front of the building, nearest the stairs, while Torrnen and Rina took the one across the hall. They would have no windows, but she thought they might be more comfortable that way. Neither of them looked the least bit pleased to be hemmed in with so much stone. But it was amazing, and after the boy left, she rushed to the window. Dane came up behind her and wrapped his arms around her waist.

"Did you ever believe there could be a city like this? Where everyone lives in the same place all the time, and you can build a structure like this one? We're three floors up! It's like flying with a dragon over the grasslands, but we're standing still."

He chuckled into her hair. "I think I'd go crazy living in the same place my whole life. How do you know the seasons if you're not going to the summer fields, or the winter grazing? How do they sleep with a solid roof like this over their heads? And…" he looked around. "What do you do when you have to—go?"

Eryn did know that. Nora had described it all after her own trip here. "There should be a clay pot or something, probably under that thing with the short legs, which I think is where we are supposed to unroll our bedding."

Indeed, there was such a pot, but Dane shook his head. "No pot for me. I'll go where the horses are. No one will notice."

The room also held a small chair and table, with quills and ink and more fresh parchment than Eryn had ever seen. There were no books here to read and she had no idea how long it would be before they were called for, so she watched out the window, looking over the street below.

It was easy to tell who was whom. The locals dressed in simple pants and tunics, similar to what Eryn and Dane wore, but with fewer beads and adornments. The women's hair was in single braids down their backs, not the multiple thin ones that the clans wore. There were people from other clans, some with clan emblems on their tunics. But others were exotic, like nothing Eryn had ever seen.

Men in high boots and tight pants with close-fitting shirts and leather vests, fine silver on their sword hilts, and colorful designs on the sheaths. Women draped in fabric from head to toe, with their legs hidden in the folds. How could they possibly walk in that clothing? How could they ride a horse? *They must be Concadian.*

A knock on the door pulled her from the window. Dane accepted two bowls of something that smelled of unfamiliar herbs and two mugs of weak beer. They perched on the edge of the bed and sniffed the food warily.

"I don't like eating food I didn't prepare," Eryn said.

"Can't imagine why not."

They shared a grin.

"Well, I'll go first," Dane said. "If I'm still all right in an hour, you should be safe to eat yours."

She smiled. "They're not going to poison us. It just smells—weird. Let's eat it together."

They each dipped in with their spoons, pulling out broth and small chunks of what looked like root vegetables.

"Here we go." Dane took a bite at the same time Eryn did.

The spice traveled up the back of Eryn's throat and right into her sinuses, causing a pleasing burn behind her eyes. She closed them, inhaling, the bowl held right under her chin. The soft vegetables rolled around her tongue, and she sighed.

"Oh, this is something special," she murmured and opened her eyes.

Dane was looking at her face, a soft smile on his lips. "I love to see you happy. It's good here, and not just the food."

Eryn scooted back on the bed and tucked into the meal. While they ate, they shared stories, him growing up with the dream of a dragon, the fears he hid when he was chosen to be judged by Baltenn. Would he be worthy? Would the Dance of Dragons kill him, or make his dream come true? And the joy of carrying Ilst's egg down proudly from the mountain, sharing his blood with her, watching her hatch and helping her grow.

They set down their bowls, each lost in thoughts of their dragons, the great winged beasts that made them whole inside.

Dane reached a hand to Eryn's cheek, setting his empty bowl on the bed. "May I kiss you on the forehead again?"

She set down her bowl, nesting it into his. Her heart pounded with the words that burst into her mind. *This road leads in one direction only. You cannot go back.* She let the words tumble out before she could reconsider. "My lips are on fire from the spice. I would rather you kissed me there."

His eyes widened for a moment, then warmed as he held her gaze. He scooted nearer to her on the bed and leaned in as Eryn held her breath. He tasted of peppers and heat, lips gently touching hers. His hands feather-touched the back of her head, not holding her, but tracing the intricate knots of her braids, trailing down her back. In a moment, she parted her lips, allowing his tongue to taste hers, sharing the heat that did not come from the meal.

Heat spread through her, and she laid her hand on his chest, feeling his muscles through his shirt. His breath sped up, matching hers.

A knock on the door broke the kiss. Dane pulled back and blinked at her for a second, then leaned in for one more small kiss, lingering on her lower lip. The knock sounded again, and he sighed, standing, hand still gently sliding over one of her braids.

The boy waited just outside the door.

"The Tieza will see you now."

Chapter 35

Of course, Tornnen and Rina protested, but the boy held firm. Dane sighed, embarrassed at their behavior. *Is that what I look like? Rude and filthy?* He was acutely aware of the smell of horses and dragons on his clothing. The contrast with the boy, who had almost no odor at all, reminded Dane that this was not his world.

He took Eryn's hand, and she did not resist. "The boy says we all go together, or we don't go at all," he said. "We haven't come all this way to turn back now." He chuckled. "I know you're frightened, but Eryn knows what to do."

The remark got exactly the reaction he hoped for, a spluttering protest from Tornnen and Rina.

"Frightened?" Torrnen puffed up his chest, glaring daggers at Dane. "Nothing frightens a dragonsworn." But as the boy led them down the stairs and through the streets, Dane grinned at Tornnen's obvious discomfort.

For the first time, he saw Tornnen and Rina as Eryn must have originally seen him. Barbarians. He knew he was no better. Without Eryn on his arm, he would be just as uncomfortable, following the boy over the smooth, even streets. But her delight in everything she saw traveled right from her hand into his, filling him with the same wonder she must be feeling. These people knew so many things he didn't know and had never even thought to ask.

They turned a corner around a building that smelled of wax and tallow, and Dane stopped in his tracks. The road led straight into the side of the mountain. A huge cave mouth opened into torch-lit darkness. Around the mouth of the cave, giant stones had been smoothed and carved, making a dramatic, open archway. Columns of stone were etched with vertical lines, topped with scrolled carvings with flowers, vines, and snakes. The arch rose from those carvings, curling up to the head of a dragon that looked down at them as they passed underneath it. The skill of the carver was unmatched; every scale, every tooth, every ridge of the stone dragon's face was a work of precision.

"Looks like Urrgar," Tornnen said from beneath it.

But this carving was far more beautiful than his plain female. It was almost as beautiful as Ilst herself.

The road led straight into the cave, rows of torches illuminating the path. It narrowed as they wound in and down, and the air chilled the sweat on the back of Dane's neck. He pulled Eryn a little closer and wasn't sure if the comfort was for her or for him.

It's unnatural to be underground like this.

With a start, he realized he could barely feel Ilst in his mind. It was as if his connection with her, usually a vast ocean of communication, had been reduced to a slow drip off a melting icicle. She was there, but so distant she might as well have been on the moon.

"I can't…" he began, but Eryn squeezed his hand.

"I can't either. We're blocked from our dragons. It must be all the stone around us. Ardos feels a million miles away."

Behind them, Tornnen's steps slowed.

"I'm not going any further. I can't hear Urrgar."

Dane dropped Eryn's hand and turned around. "We're all going as far as we need to. Our chief sent us here to find whatever answer this place holds, and that's what we're going to do." His hand rested on his sword hilt. "You were a warrior before you were dragonsworn. You can breathe without her for a little while."

His words were as much for himself as for Tornnen. *You can do this. She's fine. You're fine.*

Rina snorted. "Can't wait to tell everyone you were too scared to walk down a dark tunnel."

Tornnen bristled, and backhanded Rina across the face.

She held a hand to her cheek but did not back down. "Brave man, aren't you? Brinir will laugh until he throws up if you run away."

Through the exchange, the boy had stood silently, awaiting their decision. When Tornnen set his jaw and pushed past Dane, shoulder-checking him to be first down the tunnel, the boy sighed and led on.

After a few more minutes of walking, the tunnel opened into a large chamber, clearly carved by humans from the rock. There were long wooden benches in the middle, and passages led off in four different directions.

"We will wait until we are called for," the boy said. "By entering the Tiezahal, you agree to submit to the Tieza's judgment. You may each ask one question, and it will be answered with the wisdom of the ages. One question only. The Tieza knows everything that has ever been known, and you will be considered individually. A scribe will be provided if necessary. You will not speak except to ask your question. Are the rules clear?"

Dane's head was starting to ache without Ilst. It felt hollow, like a bleached skull with empty eyes. But Eryn was nearly bursting with excitement.

"We understand," she said. "Thank you for your guidance."

The boy left them, footsteps echoing back up the tunnel through which they had entered. They sat on the benches, looking around at the hall. The walls were smooth stone, and the passages that led off it were curtained with fabric, except for the tunnel they had come down. The passage to the right let voices murmur through, like owls in the night. It sounded like a number of people, but he couldn't make out any words. The passages to the left and straight ahead were quiet.

This is no place for a dragonsworn. Dane sweated though the underground space was cool. *It's wrong to look up and see no sky, only stone.*

After a long, uncomfortable wait, a young woman appeared through the curtain straight ahead.

"Please follow me."

They jumped to their feet and followed her, with Tornnen in the lead. Rina was next, then Dane, and finally, Eryn. The tunnel was short, and opened onto a small, dim room. The floors were carpeted with thick rugs, muffling their footsteps. To their left were four stools in a line against an ornate wooden wall. Carved with more flowers and serpents, the thick wood panel stretched from floor to the low ceiling. To the right was a single chair, unadorned, with fabric covering the wall behind it. Straight ahead was a small table with parchment and ink, and a chair. They filed in and were directed to sit on the stools. Dane eyed the carvings on the wall as he turned to sit. There was space behind it, with darkness visible through holes in the ornate woodwork. He couldn't see through the holes. The chill in the air spread down his spine. His back would be against those carvings when he sat on the stool. *Is someone back there, peeking at us?* But he couldn't show the speeding of his pulse. Not after what he'd said to Tornnen, who was already sitting on the far stool, slouched against the wall behind him.

They sat in a line, Eryn to Dane's right and Rina to his left. The chamber smelled of exotic spices, which he traced to a brazier along the back wall that glowed with whatever was burning inside. It was not unpleasant, and he found himself relaxing despite the strangeness of the surroundings and the enormous hole in his mind where Ilst felt so far away.

"Remember, you may each ask one question," the girl said, before disappearing out through the curtain.

They sat in uncomfortable silence for ten breaths, then the fabric wall they faced rustled, drapes parting. An old man stepped through and shuffled over to the writing table, pulling out a quill, which he held at the ready. A woman emerged, wrapped from head to toe in black, with long, draping sleeves and a hood that shadowed her face in the dim light. She was followed by two large men in black leather, both armed. The woman sat on the chair, flanked by the men, and a long moment of silence passed before she spoke.

"I am the Tieza, gifted by OrAdor with the power of memory."

Dane knew that in other lands they worshiped other gods besides Baltenn. The way she said "OrAdor" left no doubt that this was the name of a god.

The woman in black looked at each of them in turn, taking deep breaths. "The power of OrAdor takes many forms. I have read your memories, as I have read the memories of so many others, including the Tieza who served before me. His mind held the memories of the Tieza before him, and so on since the power of OrAdor was first given to humans. I have the knowledge of the ages, of every Tieza since the first, and of every supplicant who has ever sat in this chamber. I know what you have never told a soul. I know the memories you have long since forgotten. I know you all better than any of you know yourselves."

Her eyes swept the room, moving from face to face as she spoke.

"I know everything that has ever been known."

CHAPTER 36

Eryn's heart pounded and she longed to reach for Dane's hand, but forced herself to sit still, back against the carved wooden wall. The Tieza herself sat before them, peering into their memories from under her hood. Eryn had known that the Tiezahal was a repository of knowledge, full of scribes and scholars. But the power of OrAdor, to allow this woman to read memories? She shivered. What had she seen when she looked into the depths of Eryn's soul? Beads clacked as Eryn worried the hem of her tunic with nervous fingers.

The woman turned her shadowed eyes to Eryn. "I will hear your question first."

Why do I have to go first? Eryn cleared her throat and forced her hands to be still. She took a deep breath and spoke.

"How can our clan get more dragons since we are no longer welcome in the valley?"

If the woman was telling the truth, Eryn didn't need to say more. *She knows what you did. She knows why the dragons rescinded the pact. She knows everything.*

The woman peered at her for a long moment before speaking. "The knowledge of dragons is sparse. Your clan has not entered our city for long ages. What I know of dragons comes from Tieza memories of the distant past, words in a language no longer spoken." Her eyes rolled back in her head as she began to murmur, with the scribe scribbling furiously, taking down her words.

Eryn strained to hear them. She knew a little of the old tongue, those words that survived into modern language, however twisted and changed. The Tieza spoke of eggs and twins, and her words chilled Eryn's blood when they appeared to mention the sacrifice she had witnessed.

The woman finished speaking, and the scribe sprinkled sand on the paper to set the ink.

"I have no clear answer for you," the Tieza said. "But take the words I have spoken and consider them. If you are wise, you will find the answer you seek."

Eryn's heart sank. Why was it up to her? The scribe shuffled over and handed the writings to Eryn. She wanted to pore over them immediately, but the Tieza spoke again.

"And now, for your judgment."

The younger woman had mentioned submitting to the Tieza's judgment. Would she tell everyone what Eryn had done, and how the closing of the dragon pass was her fault? If Tornnen and Rina found out, they would certainly tell the chief, who would doubtless order her death. They might just kill her here, where Ardos couldn't protect her. Dane wouldn't be able to fight both of them off if they knew what she had done. *Please don't tell them.* She closed her eyes as the Tieza gave her judgment.

"You are a blade of grass in the wind, bending as you are blown. But the heart of a dragon beats alongside yours. Trust your heart, overcome the hurts that shackle you, and take the life that has been given to you. You are judged worthy."

The Tieza turned her gaze to Dane, and Eryn sighed, clutching the parchment in her lap. *Thank you, Tieza. I will heed your words.* She had no idea if the woman could read her active thoughts or only her memories, but a tiny nod her way indicated that her thanks had been heard.

Dane took a sharp breath. "Oh, wise Tieza," he began, clearly unsure how to proceed, "how can I be truly worthy of my clan and my dragon?"

The Tieza smiled. "Listen to Ilst."

There was no need for the scribe to write that down.

"Your judgement," she continued, "is just as simple. You have often failed to do what you knew was right. You have stood by and witnessed great evil. But you have grown. You are learning." She gave a tiny smile. "You are judged not for your worthiness now, but for the worthiness you strive for."

She turned her attention to Rina, who sat up straight and spoke directly.

"How can I get a dragon?"

"Be worthy of one," the Tieza replied. She shook her head. "I judge you now on your actions and your intentions. You are the product of the evils done to you, but unlike some, you have made those evils your own. You delight in cruelty and torment. Ambition rules you." She paused. "For yourself, you are not worthy to leave this chamber. The world is no better for your presence."

Eryn heard the anger in the woman's voice. *Good. Keep her here. We don't need her.*

"But," continued the Tieza, "I do not judge you alone. The child you carry is blameless, and it is not my place to judge that life along with yours. The child is judged worthy."

Eryn looked past Dane at Rina, whose eyes flickered over to Dane.

"It is not his child," the Tieza said. "If your child has any hope of being better than you, allow it to be raised by someone else."

Eryn's heart stopped for a moment. *Not Dane's child? Of course, it wasn't.* But Rina looked to Dane, not Tornnen, upon hearing the news. And Dane didn't meet Eryn's eyes now, though he must surely feel her stare.

Dane and Rina? When? Why? She could still feel the taste of his lips on hers, but the spice turned sour and bitter. Of course, they were together. How could she not have seen it? Rina had hated her from the beginning. She always looked smug when Dane was around. She was beautiful, in a hard, angry way. A warrior. And Eryn was…a blade of grass in the wind.

Dane finally looked over at her, but she turned away, staring at the paper in her hands without seeing it.

"You may ask your question." The Tieza's words were meant for Tornnen.

"How do I become clan chief?"

The woman adjusted her hood. "A clan chief must be wise. He must lead his people to security and plenty. He must put the needs of others over his own wants and desires." She stared right at Tornnen, her face pale in the weak light of the brazier. "You will never be clan chief."

She stood and pulled her hood back, revealing a head of white hair piled in intricate braids on top of her head. She was younger than Eryn expected, and there was no kindness or mercy in her expression.

"You are judged a danger. You are a follower, not a leader, and have chosen to follow the worst instincts of all of your clan. There is no gentleness in your heart, no nobility. You are unworthy of the dragon who is bound to your cruelty. You take pleasure in the suffering of others. The world is a darker place as long as you draw breath. I have judged you as unworthy."

It happened in the space of one breath. Two black spears erupted through Tornnen's chest. Blood spouted from around them, splattering onto the dark rugs. Tornnen grunted, hands flailing at the spears, twitching on the stool. Red foam bubbled out of his mouth, and his head went slack. His body remained pinned from behind by the spears.

They came through the wall behind us.

All three of the Dragon Clan jumped up.

The holes. In the intricate carvings of the wood were holes at chest height to a person sitting on a stool. Someone was behind the wall, waiting for the judgment. Unworthy. The Tieza meant "unworthy to live." Her sentence was death, carried out immediately. Whoever thrust the spears through the holes, through Tornnen's chest, would not have seen his face. Only the word of the Tieza, delivered without mercy.

When Eryn spun around, the Tieza and her guards, and the old scribe were gone. Eryn, Dane, and Rina were alone with Tornnen's body, anchored to the wall behind him.

Chapter 37

Dane tried to grab Eryn's hand as they backed out of the room of judgment, but she snatched it away. His head was whirling, filled with the image of Tornnen's bloody face hanging limp over his chest, and with the shame that Eryn knew he had been with Rina.

It was before Eryn. She'll understand when I can explain.

He wasn't sure he'd get the chance. Eryn strode forward, papers clutched in her arms, not looking at Dane or at Rina. She looked pale in the torchlight, and her lips were trembling. He wanted to grab her and shake her and tell her that he hadn't touched another woman since he found her. That other women were only candles against the raging bonfire of her beauty and intelligence. But now was not the time. She was clearly shaken by the shocking execution of Tornnen.

It could have been any of us.

He looked behind him to where Rina was splattered with Tornnen's blood on her left side.

It could have been her.

He didn't know or care whose child she carried. It wasn't his; somehow the Tieza knew that. Nothing else mattered.

The boy who had guided them down waited in the room with the benches, holding a sheaf of papers bound with twine. He pressed it into Eryn's hands. "You'll need this. It is a gift from the Tieza." He did not comment on the fact that four had entered, and only three emerged. Surely the boy knew what happened to those who were judged unworthy. Unworthy of what? Of life? Of mercy? Dragon Clan was not known for mercy, so why would he expect it here? The boy beckoned them to follow and led them back through the torch lit hallways of stone.

Ilst, I need you.

As they wound through the stone passages, Dane's connection to his dragon swelled from the tiny trickle into a faint stream. It reminded him of their tenuous bond when she was still in the egg; merely feelings without words or images.

Ilst was afraid.

Eryn finally looked back at Dane. "Ardos—something's wrong."

Dane pushed ahead, heart pounding as Ilst's fear pulsed in his veins.

When they finally saw the light of the tunnel entrance, they broke into a run, leaving the boy behind. The sound of screaming, of shouts and weapons echoed around the buildings.

Ilst was fully in his mind, frantic with worry.

What happened? You were gone. Urrgar went mad.

He could see that Eryn must be having a similar exchange with Ardos.

"Tornnen is dead, Ilst."

They rounded a corner to see Urrgar in the middle of chaos. The roofs of buildings lay smashed around her, and she roared her rage at a circle of soldiers that surrounded her, weapons drawn. She had clearly gone on a rampage when the tiny connection she had to Tornnen snapped, leaving her alone with no idea what happened. The cobblestones beneath her bore deep grooves from her claws.

"Urrgar, stop!" Dane yelled, rushing past Eryn.

The dragon swiveled her neck to hiss at him, venom dripping from bloody fangs. She was injured, with arrows sticking out of her belly and deep sword cuts on her legs and wings.

Dane pushed past the soldiers to stand before her. He was aware of Ilst in his mind. She was flying in from the hills beyond the city to defend him. *No, Ilst. Stay away. They will kill you if they can.*

He held his hands out, showing no weapons to the enraged dragon. "Urrgar, Tornnen is dead. He's gone. You are no longer bound to him."

She hissed again, eyes wild.

"His death was a punishment for his past crimes. It was just, and he submitted to that judgment willingly." *The fool had no idea what he was submitting to. None of us did.* But Urrgar didn't need to hear that.

The dragon panted, mouth open, eyes unfocused.

Eryn moved in next to him. Dane tried to push his way in front of her, but she stepped to the side, eyes locked on the dragon before them. "You're free, Urrgar. Fly from this place and choose another or live free. Tornnen no longer holds your life in his hands. You are no longer tied to his cruelty and evil. You're free."

Urrgar blinked, mouth closing. She looked around at the circle of armed guards, at Dane, and finally at Eryn. Her back arched, wings low against the ground as she roared into the scarred street, a sound of anger and heartbreak.

Her eyes cleared. With one more glance around the circle, she launched into the sky, arrows still protruding from her flesh. Dane swayed in the wind of her passing as she beat the air, circling the city. Behind him, the guards all nocked arrows, aiming at her form.

"Don't shoot," Eryn said. "She's leaving."

With one final roar, Urrgar sped across the sky, disappearing over the hills.

The guards stood down, and Dane breathed. A wave of relief poured from Ilst.

She could have killed you. Her words had never been so clear.

But she didn't.

Beside him, Eryn sank to her knees, still clutching the parchment and book from the Tiezahal. Dane knelt next to her.

"Are you all right? Why did you do that?" He echoed Ilst's thought. "She could have killed you."

Looking at the ground, taking deep breaths, Eryn shook her head. "I know what it's like. Because Ardos knows what it's like. When your dragonsworn dies."

He wanted to hold her, to gather her in his arms, but her shoulders were turned and tight, her body language closed to him.

"I never thought about that. Of course, Ardos would know."

The soldiers cleared away, and the street babble picked up as the square filled with people staring at Dane and Eryn.

"I think we need to leave."

Eryn raised her head at his words and looked around at the wreck Urrgar had made of the buildings around the square. Roof tiles littered the ground, wood planks and stone. A statue that had stood in the middle of the pavement was crushed beyond recognition.

Dane stood and turned, scanning the crowd. Rina emerged from behind a half-destroyed building. With a rustle of paper and clicking of beads, Eryn stood. She didn't look at Dane or at Rina, eyes unfocused, clearly communing with Ardos. Without a word, the three of them retraced their steps, picking their way back to the long building where they had expected to spend the night.

"Gather your things," Dane said in the stairwell to Rina. "We'll get the horses and go."

The room smelled of the spiced stew that now sat in Dane's belly as a heavy wet mush. *She kissed me here on this bed. She chose to kiss me, and it was bliss.*

Now she wouldn't even look at him. Their bags were still packed, and she stuffed the papers and book she held into hers, hoisted it onto her shoulder, and pushed past him to exit the room without a backward glance.

Damn you, Tieza. Damn you, Rina.

He picked up his own bags.

Damn you, Dane.

CHAPTER 38

He was with Rina. He thought he might be the father of her baby.

Eryn thought she had made her heart into a glacier years ago in her own clan when a man had tried to claim her by force. In her terror, she had closed herself away from the thought of men as anything other than predators. All except for her brother Falnar, who had saved her that wretched night. Love was not meant for Eryn, the Caldera of Godseye Clan, alone with her studies and her healing herbs.

Her heart was ice and stone, frozen in the depth of winter. It was not meant to thaw for any man—certainly not for a barbarian. A killer. A man who attacked her people and took her as his property. But thaw it had, growing shiny and wet in the warmth of his arms, protecting her against his own clan brothers on chill nights in the mountains. He was nothing like those brutes. He had been nothing but kind, nothing but gentle, nothing but patient. He didn't treat her like property, even before Ardos made her more than any eindon before her. And so she finally let the heat of his eyes begin to melt the ice inside her, meeting his lips with her own, tasting their sweetness, feeling the beat of his heart against her own thawing pulse.

Then she learned the truth.

And why does that matter?

She fretted and mulled through the afternoon, descending the path from the Tiezahal, following the branch of the river and the figure of Dane on his horse ahead of her.

You know it was before he met you. Ardos glided above her, enjoying the warm sun on his wings.

His shadow passed over her and she glanced up at him, the joy of his presence in her mind making it hard to stay angry. But every time she looked ahead to where Dane rode, with Rina riding ahead of him, she couldn't erase the image her mind had created. Rina's lips on Dane's. Rina's hands on his chest. Rina's legs entwined with his. Since she had come into the clan, Dane had hardly been away from her long enough to meet up with his former lover. He'd been nothing but attentive to her, and she'd never suspected a thing. But now she couldn't see anything else. *No wonder she hates me.*

Clouds rolled in at sunset, blocking the moon's light and forcing them to halt their travel. They were a quiet trio setting up camp by the river's edge. Dane made a fire, and they each ate dried meat from their own packs. No spiced stew. Eryn pushed the thought from her mind.

She itched to start translating the parchment that the scribe had given her, the dictation of the Tieza's memories of those with ancient dragon lore. The book she carried was a dictionary with all that was known of the old tongue— words, and how to decipher a grammar long lost to modern clans. She'd glanced through it when they dismounted in the fading light and seen enough to know she had a difficult job ahead of her. But Ardos came first.

She chewed her strips of meat as she rubbed him down, cleaning his claws and scratching the places he couldn't reach.

You should talk to him. Ardos pressed his head against her back as she wiped dust from the scales under his wings.

"I have nothing to say."

Really? Nothing at all?

"Nothing."

All right, then. That's settled.

Eryn wouldn't have believed a dragon's voice in her head could somehow be patronizing, sarcastic, yet totally understanding and full of love at the same time. She knew he was right. And she knew that he knew she knew he was right.

She wondered if Dane and Ilst were having a similar silent conversation.

"Hello, Ardos."

She whirled around at Dane's voice behind her. Ardos lowered his head to allow Dane to rub his forehead, a privileged greeting she had never seen any other dragon accord to someone not his own dragonsworn. Except for Ilst, who had let Eryn touch her that way almost from the start.

I wonder why?

"Shut up, dragon," she muttered.

The light of the fire was behind Dane, silhouetting him with light but leaving his face in shadow. She couldn't see if he was smiling at her comment or not. He hadn't spoken to her, so she was under no compulsion to answer, and turned back to grooming Ardos.

"I just wondered if you needed anything," Dane said.

Without turning around, Eryn answered, "I'm fine, thank you. We're both fine." *We're both fine without you.*

"Okay, well, I'm going to set up my bedroll by the fire. If you need any help with the translating or anything, I'll be over there, where the light is better."

A snappy comeback stopped on her lips, something snarky about his ability to read one language, let alone two. But she held it back. A few weeks ago, she would have said it to insult him. A day ago, she would have said it to tease him. Today she didn't say it at all.

"Thank you. I'll stay here with Ardos tonight."

She moved around to the dragon's far side, putting his enormous obsidian bulk between her and Dane. No need to look at him. No need to see if he was hurt or sad, or relieved.

When she groomed her way back around to the fire lit side, admiring the iridescent reflections in Ardos' scales, Dane was gone. She peered over at the fire and saw him nearby, tending to Ilst. The female dragon also gleamed in the firelight, pale under the dark sky.

He deserves a chance to explain.

Eryn bristled. "He doesn't need to explain anything," she whispered. "I don't need anything but you." She sighed. "And some light to read by."

The papers were stuffed on top of her bedding. She pulled them out gently, along with the translation book. *Why didn't I bring quills and ink?* The Tieza's words were in a clear, neat hand, she had seen that at first glance. There had been no chance to examine the book, but with the number of scribes at work in the city, it was sure to be equally pristine.

The firelight was already dimming. Not bright enough to read by. From over by Ilst, Eryn heard quiet voices.

Dane and Rina.

Her hands balled into fists at her side.

Stop it. They're the only two people for miles, and you won't speak to him.

Ardos sent a wave of understanding. Dane must be rattled by Tornnen's death, even if he hated the man.

Did he hate him?

Ardos sighed. *Tornnen was troubled. He never should have been chosen to bond a dragon. Urrgar was half-mad from his cruelty. Her bond to him made her love him despite his many flaws. It is only when we are freed from the bond that we see them as they were.*

Eryn set the book aside and pulled out her bedroll, spreading it on the ground and snuggling into it. Ardos lay next to her, tucking her under his wing.

"I never even thought about how hard that must have been. I assumed she was as evil as he was."

It is why she snapped when he died. She saw the horrors he had committed for what they were, and that she was a party to them.

"Did you feel the same? When Chief Krunnan died?" She knew he had felt deep grief, and empty loneliness during the time he was unbonded, before he chose her to heartbond. She knew he had truly mourned his former dragonsworn. But Krunnan was not a good man. He was no Tornnen, but he ordered his clan to attack others, to take slaves, to kill and plunder.

My former bond was forced upon me. Ardos tucked his neck under his wing, warm breath blowing on Eryn. *I loved him in a very different way than I love you. He was in my blood, in my body. When he died, a part of me died with him. But yes, I saw his faults. He was not a good man, but he was mine.*

Eryn pressed her face into Ardos' chest, feeling the beat of his heart against her cheek.

He was in my blood, but you are in my heart.

From over by the fire there was quiet. Eryn couldn't see where Dane had chosen to spread his bedroll. Did he share this night with Ilst, tucked up against his dragon as she was? Or did he share his warmth with Rina?

Dane lies with Ilst tonight. Rina sleeps alone.

Eryn was never so glad for a dragon's night vision, though she would never have admitted it.

She is crying.

That gave Eryn pause. *Crying for Tornnen? Who would weep for such a monster?*

But tears welled in Eryn's eyes as the vision of the man with spears bursting through his chest filled her mind again. The horror of it, the shock of seeing such a swift, efficient, brutal execution crashed down on her. She trembled, and Ardos folded his wing in tighter around her, reminding her of how Dane had once held her in the cold darkness of night.

Sleep, my heart, he crooned in her head. *You are loved.*

She let the tears fall, tasting their salt on her lips. Her heart had never been so full, nor so empty.

CHAPTER 39

Dane led the way once they reached the fork in the river. The clan would be moving east, driving the herds toward the summer grazing lands in the middle of Den Woth. Spring was well over the foothills they followed, flowers in bloom and the air alive with insects and the calls of birds from the trees. Last night's clouds followed them, both overhead and in Dane's heart.

She hates me. She wouldn't even speak to me. How can I explain if she won't talk to me?

Ilst, high overhead, said nothing, but sent a wave of compassion. He had communed with her late into the night, wishing he held Eryn by the fire. Ilst was sure Eryn would come around. That she was overwhelmed by the shock of seeing someone killed, as well as learning that Dane and Rina had been lovers. Ilst was certain that time would heal her. But Dane wanted to heal her. He wanted to throw his arms around her and cover her with kisses, and swear to her that no woman had been worth a single thought since the moment he'd first seen her. Only the fear that she would turn away held him back. If she turned from him, refused him, he would be broken. Better to wait. She kissed him once. It had taken time that he willingly spent. Ilst was right. He would give Eryn time again.

They wouldn't reach the clan tonight, but if they pushed hard, they would join them tomorrow. One more night in the field.

Rina rode up next to him. Her eyes were red but held their usual hardness. He'd heard her crying but would never in a million years have gone to comfort her. Eryn would never forgive him if he had.

"Tornnen would be livid," she said, looking straight ahead.

"At what?"

"That he died like that. Stabbed from behind. Not a warrior's death."

Dane shrugged. He looked behind them to where Eryn rode. She wasn't looking at them, keeping her eyes on the trail between them. "He didn't live an honorable life. He didn't deserve an honorable death."

That got a snort from Rina. "Honor was never a word he understood." She was silent for a long time. "They would have killed me, too," she finally said.

The Tieza had called Rina unworthy as well, and had spared her because of the child she carried. Was it Brinir's? Tornnen's? Dane didn't really care. At the time the Tieza had said it, he'd only been full of panic that it might have been his. He hadn't even realized what the Tieza was threatening.

"Do you think Urrgar might come back and choose me?" Rina asked.

It was the most vulnerable thing he'd ever heard her say. It almost made him soften to her, just for a moment. "I don't know," he said. "You haven't done…" He fell silent. No one outside the dragonsworn and the shaman knew about the dance of dragons, the bite that proved them worthy. "Maybe you should ask Eryn. Maybe Ardos would tell you what a dragon looks for when they get to choose." *Not a calculating schemer like you.* But maybe Tornnen's judgment would change her. Maybe the baby would. It was up to her.

He turned his horse, letting Rina lead. Eryn was looking right at him but dropped her eyes when he faced her. He waited on the trail until she was almost to his position, then turned his horse again to ride next to her.

"Are you all right?" he asked.

"I'm fine."

The set of her jaw and the hardness of her eyes said all the words her voice didn't.

"Eryn, I need you to know that there is nothing at all between me and Rina," he began, but she cut him off.

"You have no need to explain anything to me. I'm eindon. You owe me nothing."

He tried again. "You're far more than eindon. Ardos knows it, and I know it, too." He moved his horse a step nearer to hers. "There were other women before you, Eryn. I told you that from the start. None of them, including Rina, were anything more than a night's enjoyment. And I have touched no other, wanted no other, since the day I found you. I swear on Ilst's life that this is true."

She looked at him then, face still set. "Thank you for telling me." Her fingers stroked the links of the chain around her neck, never a good sign. She kicked her horse, pulling ahead of him, and he let her go. *Don't push. Let her think about what you said. At least she let you say it.*

They forded the river at its widest, shallowest point, icy water splashing up and soaking into their boots. The forest around it was thinning, the hills flattening. Their path left the river, turning north toward the wide prairie that made up the center of Den Woth. The vast grazing land was bordered all around by hills, mountains, and at the far western border, the sea, or so Dane had been told.

Up ahead, Rina stopped. She cocked her head, looking up toward a small outcropping of rock overhung with trees.

"Do you hear that?" she asked. "Wait here." She hopped off her horse and disappeared into the trees.

"What's going on?" Eryn said, pulling her horse up next to Dane's.

"I'm not sure," he answered. "Rina heard something and went to check it out." He pulled the short bow from his saddle and nocked an arrow in case there was trouble. He should go after her. But there was no chance he was leaving Eryn to run off after Rina.

A high-pitched cry carried through the trees, and in a moment, Rina emerged, dragging a small, skinny girl by the arm. The child's hair hung over her filthy face, her clothing ragged. Rina pulled her down the hill, a huge smile on her face.

"Look what I found all alone in the bushes!" She flung the child down in front of Dane. "Tornnen would have loved a little thing like this. He liked them young. But there are plenty of others that will fight over her once she's cleaned up." Rina preened over her prize.

From behind him, Dane heard Eryn gasp. She flung herself off her horse and rushed over to the child.

"Filina? Is that you?"

The weeping child raised her tear-streaked face. "Aunt Eryn?" She threw herself into Eryn's arms, and they both collapsed to the ground, rocking back and forth, the girl's face buried in Eryn's neck.

Aunt Eryn? She knows this child? Someone from her old clan?

Rina pulled the girl right out of Eryn's grasp. "I found her. She's mine. And whoever claims her as eindon will pay me well for finding such a nice little prize."

The girl, Filina, Eryn had called her, strained against Rina's grip. Eryn leaped to her feet and stood nose to nose with Rina.

"She is my niece. She is Godseye Clan, and you will unhand her this very moment."

Wind buffeted Dane's back, and his horse danced under him as Ardos landed on the path with a low warning growl.

Dane dismounted as Rina released her hold on the girl, still staring death at Eryn.

"You don't order me to do anything, eindon. Dragon or no dragon, this girl is going back to the clan. And soon she'll be someone's eindon, just like you."

Eryn turned to Dane, the horror of that truth on her face.

He stepped up to the three of them and crouched next to the child. "Filina? Is that your name?"

She nodded, wiping her nose, arm still clutched in Rina's nails.

"Filina, where is your family? Your mother and father?"

She sniffled. "Gone."

"They left you here alone?"

The tears started again, great wracking sobs.

Eryn crouched next to them. "My brother and Nora would never have left her alone," she murmured. "If they lived, they would be with her."

Another low growl finally made Rina drop her hold on the girl and step away as Ardos approached. "Either she comes back to the clan with us," she said icily, "or we leave her here alone to die."

Beside him, Eryn trembled. Filina fell into her arms again, sobbing. But Rina was right on all counts. They couldn't leave a child alone out here. And when they took her back to the clan, she would become the eindon of whoever was willing to fight the hardest to claim her. And there were a few men, like Tornnen, who would be thrilled to have a little thing like this, for as long as she lasted.

We truly are barbarians. No wonder Eryn hates me.

Eryn seemed to work through the same thoughts, awful as they were, and acted before Dane could move to protect the child himself. With one arm around the girl, she rustled in her cloak. She wrapped her arms around her niece's neck, and Dane heard a soft clink.

When Filina sat back, her little hands flew to a chain around her neck. A chain closed with Eryn's runelock, earned for the strength of Ardos in the competition that seemed like ages past.

"Filina Drysel," Eryn said. "I claim you as eindon. You belong to me, and me alone. No one shall touch a hair on your head without my permission. And no one shall ever, ever have my permission." Her face was wet with tears as she pulled the child back into her embrace.

Chapter 40

Eryn flipped through the book the Tieza had given her for the thousandth time, holding her quill in her mouth.

"You have ink on you."

Filina's voice still warmed Eryn's heart after nearly a week back among the clan. She turned to see her niece sitting on the thick rugs of Dane's tent. The girl had a pile of flowers next to her and had begun to braid them into a chain.

"I'm sure I do," Eryn replied. "And I'll keep having ink on me until I can figure out what all these words mean."

The flowers dropped from Filina's hands, landing in a pile with the rest. She knee-walked over to where Eryn sat with the book in her lap and the pages from the Tieza off to her side. With a thoughtful frown, she picked up one of the pages, sounding out the letters of the words Eryn had already translated.

"D-R-A-G—" Her face split into a huge smile. "Dragon! Like Ardos!"

"Yes, dragon like Ardos."

From the moment she slipped the chain around Filina's neck, stomach in knots as she carried the girl to her horse, Eryn had never imagined how easily the child would adapt. She loved the chain with Eryn's runelock, delighted that she and her aunt had "matching necklaces." When Eryn told her that her own lock looked different because it had Dane's name on it, Filina smiled at him. "You gave her this?"

Dane's eyes widened. "Yes, I did. It says my name, and Eryn wears it because we're bonded together."

Not exactly. Eryn had not corrected him, and Filina was satisfied that Dane was alright.

But nothing compared to Ardos. Godseye clan lived in fear of dragons, of the attack from above that took their people and their belongings. Filina had been raised to watch the sky for the silhouette against the clouds that meant run and hide. Flying dragons were a terror.

Ardos on the ground, gently offering his neck to be hugged, was apparently a completely different creature to Filina . She was instantly smitten with the way his scales shone, the sheen of his wings, and the soft skin around his eyes that felt like velvet. Eryn was almost jealous of the way Ardos let the child climb all over him, but the dragon just laughed in her mind.

She is yours and you are mine, and I am yours. I love her as you love her, and of course she loves me. I am glorious.

It was a welcome distraction for a child who had just lost both of her parents.

Eryn's brother had not come home from the ambush that failed to retrieve them. It felt like forever ago that she rode in the cart, a new eindon trying desperately to keep the hated clan leader alive for fear of her own death, all under the watchful eye of a great black dragon. Many of Godseye's hunters were killed that day, and Falnar was apparently among them. It might have been Dane that killed him in the battle. She couldn't think about that.

The clan was scattered, their flocks decimated. Nora, Filina's mother, had set out with her child toward the Tieza-hal where she knew they would be safe. Days into the journey on foot, Nora stepped into a nest of vipers. It took her nearly a day to die of the venom, despite all the healing herbs she carried. Filina was alone in the wilderness for almost a week before Rina found her weeping in the woods.

All this came out during the journey back to the clan, as food and the comfort of her aunt's arms soothed the sobbing, starving child. Now, nearly a week later, Filina had recovered in the way of children. She still cried at night for her mother and father. Eryn cried with her. They slept together in Dane's tent with Ardos and Ilst always alert outside.

"Aunt Eryn? What's this word?"

Filina's voice startled Eryn back to the present. The child held up the parchment, pointing to letters in the old language.

"I have no idea," Eryn said. "It's in a language that nobody really speaks anymore. The words are different, and they didn't write the sentences the same. And only some of the words are in this book, and half of those don't make sense when you put them in order." She sighed. "But I'll figure it out. A lot of lives depend on it."

The clan had already sent men and dragons to start working on the path to the valley that the wild dragons had filled with rock and rubble. And other bands of warriors and dragonsworn were returning with eindon taken in raids, ready for the enormous sacrifice that was planned to try and appease the only source of dragon eggs the clan had ever known.

"Uncle Dane!"

Filina jumped up and rushed over to the tent flap, throwing her arms around Dane's legs. He laughed and crouched down next to her. "Hello, little flower. How has your day been?"

"It's good. I'm making a flower chain, wanna see?" She took him by the hand and led him past Eryn to her pile of petals on the floor. "Here hold this." She pulled Dane down and plopped a handful of flowers into his lap. "Which one do you want me to braid in next?"

Despite her anger, Eryn couldn't help but smile at the two of them. The huge barbarian warrior, dragonsworn killer, sat covered in flowers while a little girl wove them right from his hands.

Pushing hair out of her face, Eryn set down the book. "Filina, are you making that flower wreath for Dane?" She gave him a wicked smile, knowing that if Filina asked him to, he'd have no choice but to walk around the camp in a daisy necklace until it rotted off his shoulders.

"No, it's for my friend."

The tent flap opened, and Dane's little sister stood in the gap. "Filina, are you done?" She held out an armload of flowers, different colors than the ones Filina used. "I found more. Come to my tent and let's finish them."

Filina grabbed her flowers off Dane's lap. "Can I go, Aunt Eryn?"

The refusal was on Eryn's lips when Ardos spoke in her head. *I will watch over them. She is safe with me.*

"Stay where Ardos can watch you."

The girls scampered away. Dane stood and brushed off loose petals that clung to his pants. Eryn caught herself watching, picturing the strong thighs under the leather. *Stop it.* She picked up the book again.

"Making any progress?" Dane flopped down next to her and looked at her parchment without touching it.

Eryn shrugged. "I've sorted out a lot." She picked up the parchment and showed him a mostly translated paragraph. "This talks about dragons breeding. The females almost always lay just one egg. If they lay two, the second one is always smaller than the first, and they push it out of the nest and let it die." The memory of the eggs left by the wild dragons at the valley's opening popped into her mind. "They just gave us their castoff eggs. Ones they would have abandoned anyway."

"Why? Why not raise two baby dragons?"

"Not sure," Eryn said, and pointed at a line of text. "I think this bit here is saying that the smaller egg makes a smaller dragon, but it might mean weaker." She thought for a moment. "Or an infertile one? Could that be why our females don't go into season?"

It certainly does not mean weaker. Eryn smiled at Ardos' indignation at the thought. He sent her an image of the two girls sitting in the sun, braiding flowers around the spines on his tail.

Dane shook his head. "No one knows why our females don't want to breed." He said it strangely, and Eryn blinked at the tiny smile on his lips. Was he making a joke? A suggestive tease? Heat warmed her belly, and the memory of a spiced kiss warmed her cheeks.

"Maybe they just need a lot of time. Maybe they have a hard time being bloodbonded and knowing they didn't get to choose their dragonsworn."

Dane scooted an inch closer to her. "Maybe. But maybe they also know that just because it's a bloodbond, doesn't make the feelings any less real. Bloodbonding is the way of the clan, and even if it's wrong, sometimes maybe it can turn out right."

Heat and ice warred in Eryn's mind. The image of Dane with Rina. *Before he met me.* The look in his eyes right now. The taste of his kiss, and the gentleness of his arms. The way he welcomed Filina into their tent without question, knowing how heart-wrenching it must have been for Eryn to lock the hated chain around her neck.

"No one else?" she whispered. "Not since we met?"

He shook his head. "Not since. Not now. Not ever."

The book made a soft thump as Eryn set it on the carpet. She pushed the papers aside, setting the little pot of ink safely out of the way, and rolled up onto her knees.

Dane mirrored her posture.

She reached for him, touching his cheek. The blond stubble of his jaw was rough against her palm. He stroked the fingers of that hand, gently moving up her wrist and arm, under her shoulder and down to her waist. They leaned in as one, lips meeting. This time he tasted of honey instead of spice. Both of his arms wrapped around her waist, pulling her close. She let him explore her lips with his, then her tongue with his own. His hands tugged gently at her long braids hanging down the back of her neck. She wound her fingers into his hair, pulling it free from the strip of leather that held it away from his face.

From behind her came the sound of someone clearing their throat.

They broke the kiss but stayed entwined, eyes locked together.

"Yes?" Dane called, still looking only at Eryn.

"Chief Calnan, um, requires you, dragonsworn."

Finally, Dane looked away, over Eryn's shoulder at whoever stood in the entry. "Just me, or both of us?" he asked.

"Just you. The dokkas is not called."

Without looking, Eryn knew the messenger was eindon. Only they called her that. Dokkas—hope. She sat back on her heels. What hope had she given to Filina ? Life as a slave?

Life with her aunt, Ardos chided gently. *Life with you and Dane and me.*

"Tell him I'll attend directly," Dane said.

The tent dimmed as the flap was lowered, and Dane started to speak, but Eryn waved him away.

"Go and see what your father needs. I have plenty to keep me busy here."

He leaned in and kissed her again, soft and sweet. "I'll be back as soon as I can."

And then he was gone, leaving Eryn with the taste of honey on her tongue.

CHAPTER 41

Dane sat on the ground in his father's tent. *The chief's tent,* he reminded himself. His father only used it for official business, preferring to actually live with his children and the elderly eindon who cared for them since Dane's mother had died. His father had never taken a wife, and Dane's mother had given his father all of his children. One day he might choose a wife or take another eindon to bear him more sons and daughters, but for now he seemed content to raise Dane's two younger brothers and his little sister, the pride of their father's heart.

Chief Calnan eased down in front of Dane. He looked tired. More gray seemed to fill out the chief's beard, and more lines around his eyes. Small wonder. His clan's future depended on the dragon eggs they couldn't have.

"Has Eryn come up with anything yet?"

Dane shook his head. "She's learned that the eggs the wild dragons give us are castoffs, ones they have rejected and would leave to die anyway. So if we can find a way to appease them, they'll surely let us have them again. Those eggs are useless to them, and everything to us." He would never speak openly of such things to anyone but his father, but only the young shaman was in the tent with them, kneeling silently behind the chief, and the warriors posted outside would not hear through the thick tent fabric.

"Is there anything about how the bargain was originally struck? What offering was made to gain the dragons' trust in the first place?"

Dane glanced at the shaman, who looked at the ground. *Poor fool.* He should have had years more training under the old shaman. He should have had time to learn all the secrets before he had to fill the role. The wild dragons had cut that training short when they killed the shaman along with the future dragonsworn on the bloody plain outside their valley.

"I don't think so," he said. "The Tieza, the woman who reads memories, she said she knew the memories of everyone that had ever held the position. But she said our clan never came to them for guidance. So everything she remembered was ancient, just bits and pieces of the old memories of someone that's been dead for ages. And it's all in the old language of the shamen."

The first day they had returned, Eryn had called for the young man who wore the bones of his office. She hoped he might know more of the old tongue, but he knew even fewer words than she did. He had learned the chants by rote and had no idea what they actually meant. The old shaman probably wouldn't have known, either.

Chief Calnan took a long drink from the mug on the floor next to him. "Then we have no choice but to proceed the only way we know how. The dragons have always traded on our sacrifice. One eindon for one egg. We will have to hope that a hundred eindon in exchange for whatever slight the last shaman made that angered them so much will be enough."

Dane's heart sank. On the floor near the fire was a giant pile of runelocks and chains. The locks were not marked with the name of a dragonsworn, but only the symbol for "dragon." The eindon they would claim would not belong to any man, but to the entire clan, until the autumn blood moon, when they would be taken to the valley in the hope that their blood would appease the wild dragons into honoring the old agreement once again. Whoever took the eindon would be in as much danger as the offering. If the dragons didn't accept it, they might show their answer by killing them all.

Dane's father sighed, shoulders low. "The clan is restless. Despite swearing everyone to secrecy, rumors are flying that we can't get any more dragon eggs. The people have always looked to the skies, seen the power of our dragons, and known that we are safe. Our cattle are the finest in Den Woth, our people the most fortunate. Now they're unsettled, and it won't take long before that turns to fear, and then to panic." He gestured back toward the shaman huddled in the corner. "On the advice of our young shaman, I've decided to announce that Lord Baltenn has demanded this sacrifice, these hundred eindon women, to prove our worth and secure our prosperity for the next hundred years. It should satisfy the people and avoid the inevitable questions when we leave in the autumn for the journey."

They sat quietly for a moment, the fire crackling in two huge braziers at the sides of the chief's empty chair. Finally, Dane's father shook himself and took a long drink before speaking again.

"We believe that Lightning Clan may be driving their herds north of us, heading west," Chief Calnan said. "I need you to take a couple of warriors and Ilst and scout them out. Don't engage, just get close enough for Ilst to send you images of their camp. We need to know how many there are and if they've brought their women and children along. You'll leave as soon as you're packed."

A protest died on Dane's lips. The chief had spoken. As much as Dane hated to leave Eryn just when she was warming to him, there was no point in questioning his father.

"How far north?"

"A day's ride. If you leave shortly, you should reach them by midday tomorrow."

Dane nodded. He stood and held a hand down to help his father, but the old man waved him away. "I don't need your help to stand up. I'm not ancient yet." His knees cracked as he stood.

"Father," Dane said. "Will you keep watch on Eryn and Filina while I'm gone? I know Ardos won't let anything happen to them, but—"

"But more eyes are always better," the chief agreed. He smiled. "Your mother would be very proud of you, son."

A lump tightened Dane's throat, and he took a moment before speaking. "You loved her, didn't you? Not just as eindon, but as a woman?"

Chief Calnan smiled, eyes misty. "Eindon is nothing but a word. I never treated her as property. And yes, I loved her. She was the most exciting woman I ever met, and she loved you kids more than her own life," he said. "I always hoped you'd find a woman as special as your mother." He chuckled. "And then you brought home Eryn."

Dane smiled. "She is special. I knew it even before Ardos heartbonded her."

"But she despises the chain," Chief Calnan said with a knowing look. "I know what the other eindon call her. She's their hope—the hope that they could be worthy of a dragon themselves."

"It's more than that, but yes, she hates the chain." Dane leaned down to pick up his father's mug. "She hates that she had to chain her own niece to keep her safe, I think worse than she even hates her own."

The chief slung an arm around Dane's shoulders. "She did what she had to do. She's smart." He gave a squeeze, still strong enough to hurt. "She's worthy of Ardos, and she's worthy of you."

Dane smiled remembering the feel of her lips on his. "I just hope I'm worthy of her."

Chapter 42

Eryn sat in the sun on the far edge of the outermost tents. Ardos lay behind her in the tall grass, letting the two little girls play Mountain Chief, climbing all over him. The book sat to her side, parchments on the ground before her.

Dane will be back tomorrow, by nightfall at the latest. The tent was cold and empty without him. She slept with Filina now, but Dane's presence made it more like a home than she would ever have imagined. *Maybe one of these nights the girls can have a sleep-party at Dane's family's tent.*

The thought heated her more than the sun on her shoulders.

It's about time. Ardos chuckled in her mind.

Maybe it was time. This was her life now. When she'd arrived, she'd wanted nothing more than to escape. Now she would never leave Ardos. She was Dragon Clan until she died. And she didn't want to leave Dane. The clan was far from ideal, and the chain around her neck would always weigh far heavier than its links. But she had Dane, and Filina . They were her family now, and they were here. Despite her misgivings about being part of such a warlike clan, and the knowledge that Dane was part of those attacks, she couldn't ignore her attraction to him. He was a product of this clan, as she was of Godseye. His nature was kind, but his training was aggression. Strong, but gentle—that was Dane. He was the best he could possibly be, given his upbringing. And he was trying so hard to please her. It was time she pleased him as well. *Tomorrow. He'll be back tomorrow.* She fanned her face, glad no one was around to question the blush in her cheeks.

She turned back to the parchment in front of her. The work was fascinating. When she'd first seen the wild dragon females, she was instantly struck by their colors. They were rainbow-hued, scales almost glowing with prisms of color. All the clan's females were shades of brown or cream. She knew it was part of the key to why the clan dragons never went into season and wouldn't breed. The parchment section she was working on seemed to be talking about dragon breeding. She wondered whose memories were written here. Had some ancient caldera studied dragons in the wild? Had the ancestors of the clan once bred their own dragons with a secret that was here in her hands, half-translated and waiting to be discovered?

The laughter of the girls was drowned out by a low growl from Ardos. Eryn looked up to see Rina approaching. The girls slid off Ardos and hopped over his tail to stand behind him. He stood up and moved in closer to Eryn.

Rina smiled and held out her hands. "Hello, Eryn."

It was the first time Eryn remembered the woman calling her by her name.

"Hello."

Rina sat down next to Eryn, ignoring the grumbling of Ardos from behind her. "How is the work going? Have you learned anything?"

What is she playing at?

"I've got some things translated, but they don't make much sense yet."

Rina nodded. "It must be hard work if you need that huge book to figure it all out."

The conversation felt surreal. It was as if Rina had forgotten all the dirty looks, the cutting remarks. And Eryn had not forgotten for one second that she once had Dane, if only for a night here or there.

She has fresh bruises.

Ardos had noticed them before Eryn did. Rina's left cheek was faintly purple, and there was a clear bruise around her left wrist. She had displeased Brinir somehow. For a tiny moment Eryn felt pity for the woman. Brinir was a monster, as cruel as Tornnen had been, but smarter, more controlled. It must be a nightmare to be his woman.

"Are you all right, Rina?" Eryn asked. "I have ointment that can help heal bruises if you want some."

Rina's face darkened, and she pulled her sleeve down over the bruise. "I'm fine."

Eryn sighed. "What do you want, then?"

But Rina was looking at the parchment. She snatched it up, peering at the words Eryn had translated. "What does it say?"

Eryn read it to her. "To bring the color to the scale, the female must consume the maid of the mountain."

"What does that mean?"

Eryn shrugged. "Wild dragons are brightly colored, at least when they are fertile. I think this is talking about how to make wild dragons go into breeding season. Some kind of ancient ritual."

"Maid of the mountain," Rina murmured. Her eyes flashed over to where the girls stood behind Ardos. "Interesting." She smiled at Eryn, her usual cruel grin. "See you later, eindon."

Ardos growled again as Rina hopped up and trotted away.

Well, that was just…strange. She had seemed honestly friendly at first. And then…Eryn shook her head. There was no telling with someone like Rina.

She returned to her parchment. The female must consume the maid of the mountain. Surely this was the ancient pact. She had thought the deal was a trade, a woman for an egg. But this seemed to indicate it was more than that. Did the gift of the women actually cause the wild females to conceive the eggs for the following year? Had the ritual warped into a trade of some kind over the ages? Her stomach turned to think that the horrible plan, to sacrifice a hundred women to appease the dragons, might have some basis in fact.

Ardos stood, stretching his wings. *I'm hungry. I'll be back soon.* He launched himself into the air, and Eryn watched through his eyes as he took to the sky, flying over the grazing herd, choosing his prey.

"Here, it's right here."

Eryn snapped back into her own eyes at Rina's voice. She led Brinir and Chief Calnan straight up to where Eryn scrambled to her feet.

Rina pounced on the parchment, handing it to the chief.

"It's right here. She knew and wasn't telling anyone, because she knows what it means."

The chief read the paper silently. "Please explain."

"It means," Rina said, "that we don't have to go back to the wild dragons. We can make our own dragons breed. We just have to feed them a maiden from the mountains, and they'll become colorful and fertile. It says so right here."

She dashed over to where the girls were playing in the dirt and grabbed Filina by the arm. She pulled her over to the chief. "This child is from a mountain clan. She'll make a fine sacrifice."

Bile choked the back of Eryn's throat. "No, that's not at all what…"

Brinir grabbed the parchment. "It does seem to say that if a female dragon eats a maiden like this, she will change colors." He looked at the chief. "You've seen the wild females. They're like rainbows, and ours are drab and brown. If we could breed our own eggs, we would be untouchable." He grinned an evil smile at Eryn. "And all it costs is one little girl to find out."

The chief turned sad eyes to Eryn. "Is this true?" He took the paper from Brinir. "Is this translation correct?"

"Yes, I think so," Eryn said, "but you can't possibly…"

Brinir cut her off. "That's what eindon are for," he said with mock kindness. "That's what eindon have always been for."

Ardos, I need you. Eryn's head was spinning.

"She's just a child…"

"She's perfect," Rina said. "A maiden, just as the parchment says." She pretended sympathy. "I'm sure it's hard, but you were there. The Tieza wouldn't have lied. It's terribly sad, but it's necessary for the good of the clan."

Still clutched in Rina's grasp, Filina began to cry. She couldn't possibly understand what they meant, but she could tell it was upsetting Eryn.

"Take me instead." The whisper popped out of Eryn's mouth.

"What did you say?" the chief asked.

I cannot let them take Filina .

"Take me instead. I am also from the mountain clan. I qualify. Leave the child alone and take me. I will be the sacrifice."

"You qualify?" Brinir laughed, spraying spit at Eryn. "All this time and you're still a maiden?" He turned to the chief. "Didn't you teach your son what eindon were for?"

Ardos landed just behind her, looming over them with outstretched wings. Rina, Brinir, and the chief jumped back.

What is happening? What are you doing?

Trembling shakes coursed through Eryn. *I'm saving Filina's life. And maybe I'm righting what I wronged.*

The chief spoke to Eryn and Ardos together. "Eryn, you are a maiden of the mountains? You do this of your free will?"

She nodded, no longer able to speak.

His shoulders slumped. "It will be done. Alert the shaman. Tomorrow at noon."

Ardos roared his rage to the sky.

Chapter 43

Dane crouched behind a low rise of ground, looking down at the distant flatland through Ilst's eyes. She soared overhead, high in the sky, being careful to stay on the dark side of the twilight as the sun set. No shadow passed over the tiny dots below her; another clan moving their herds between grazing grounds. On any other year, Dragon Clan would have let them pass. They were no threat, and no one attacked Dragon Clan for any cause. But this year they needed eindon, and plenty of them.

Some would come from the clan's own, the women taken over the years. But they needed a hundred, and some of the dragonsworn were attached to some of their own women. Better to capture new ones and keep them separate from the rest of the clan until the autumn sacrifice.

This is for Eryn. For all of us.

He kept reassuring himself as he scouted through Ilst's vision. If they didn't take enough captives over the summer, Eryn could be in danger, Ardos or not. They needed plenty to choose from so that Eryn was never in the running. It would be different; no Stone of Baltenn to help them choose. A hundred would go, and none would come back. If Lord Baltenn were kind, he would make the dragons understand the offering, and next spring everything would be back to normal.

What's normal? Ilst's voice in his head was strong and clear.

Indeed, what was normal? Sacrificing innocent people to be eaten by dragons? Forcing hatchlings to bond with a warrior they didn't choose? But it was the clan's way. It had been the ritual for generations.

Would you have chosen me if we weren't bloodbonded? He sent the thought up to the sky.

You are my dragonsworn. There has never been any thought of another.

Ilst's words didn't soothe him. He'd had long talks with Eryn and Ardos since their heartbonding, and more since Tornnen's death and Urrgar's departure. Ilst was his beloved, as much a part of him as his arm or his head. Eryn felt the same about Ardos. But the bond Ardos felt for Eryn was different than his former bond with Chief Krunnan, or so he said. He'd known Krunnan's faults but was compelled to love him anyway. When he was free of that bond, he'd truly realized some of the awful things the clan had done at Krunnan's orders. Things he'd been a part of, never questioning if it was right or wrong. Now, he claimed, he could see clearly. Make his own choices. He was his own warrior, and not eindon to a dragonsworn.

Did Ilst feel the same?

I love you, and everything you are. If I could choose, I would choose you.

He warmed under Ilst's reassurance.

He hoped Eryn was coming to feel the same way.

When the chief had ordered this scouting party, they'd had no time for the goodbye Dane would have wanted. He'd packed his travel kit and weapons, and taken her into his arms, covering her lips with kisses, warm and sweet. She pressed her body into his, hands behind his neck, pulling him close. The sweetness turned to heat that coursed through him, but there was no time. He didn't want their first explorations to be rushed, knowing his team was waiting. When they finally came together, when she finally opened herself to his love, he wanted no time limit, no distractions. He imagined the softness of her flesh, the flush of passion in her skin. When he returned from this mission, they would send Filina to stay with Dane's little sister, and the night would belong only to Eryn and Dane. He was glad he waited, and so thankful to Ardos, who had opened Eryn's heart to Dragon Clan and the life she could have with them.

Ilst finished her patrol and circled back toward where Dane and the two young warriors with him waited. She'd shown him what he needed to see.

"Time to head for home."

They mounted their horses and headed south. As they traveled, Dane taught them what he knew of warfare. Places to stage an ambush. Places to avoid where an enemy might have staged their own. By the time they came back to raid the clan they'd just scouted, their herds would have moved further west, so Dane led his party on a westerly course for home, evaluating the terrain as they traveled. He'd report to his father when they arrived, and the raid would likely happen before the week's end. Based on the number of tents and horses Ilst had seen, they could easily take a dozen eindon without decimating that clan's numbers. If they took women past childbearing years, they might take up to twenty.

Is it worth it?

His bond to Ilst screamed that any price was worth paying. But, of course, that depended on who was paying. It was easy to trade the lives of strangers for the glory of seeing through a dragon's eyes, sharing a dragon's heart. Easy to pay for that supreme privilege at the expense of others.

He'd never looked at it that way before Eryn. Until she became his eindon and captured his heart, he'd blissfully ridden on the knowledge that Dragon Clan was superior, blessed by Baltenn. Whatever they did was done in Baltenn's name, because he had chosen them to bond with dragons, elevating them above all other clans. He never even thought about the eindon who died for Ilst's egg. Sacrifices were necessary to please the god and the wild dragons for the incredible gift of their eggs. And eindon should be thrilled to be taken as part of such an exalted clan, even if they were the lowest members, and subject to the often cruel whims of their owners.

You are better than them.

Ilst's words didn't alleviate the guilt. But what was the alternative? Would he deny future generations the joy of bonding with a dragon? One day he would have sons, young warriors of his own. Didn't they deserve the same chance he'd had, the same honor in raising a dragon of their own? They would be Eryn's sons as well. And daughters. Surely he wanted this same kind of love for them?

But it wasn't up to him anyway. His father had given the order. Maybe by the time his sons were grown, things would be different. Better for eindon. Better for the whole clan.

He smiled to think of his future sons. It was time to start working on that. He shifted in the saddle as darkness fell across the prairie, anxious to get home. The young warriors would complain, but they would ride all night and join the clan in the morning.

And tomorrow night, if he was reading her correctly, Eryn would willingly join him in making that new generation of Dragon Clan babies.

He squeezed his horse into a trot, imagining soft lips and warm, inviting limbs.

CHAPTER 44

Eryn sat alone in Dane's tent as darkness fell. Ardos circled overhead, roaring his anger to the stars. His feelings of betrayal and abandonment pulsed through their bond, making Eryn's legs weak from grief.

I don't want to leave you, Ardos. I never want to leave you. I'm so sorry.

But she had no choice. She would not see her niece fed to a dragon. If it meant her own death to show the clan that this was not the answer, she would pay that price to save Filina's life. At Eryn's request, the chief had already pre-claimed Filina as his eindon, effective upon Eryn's death. He had promised to raise her as his daughter, as a sister to Dane. She would be safe and kept far away from the horror of tomorrow's sacrifice.

And Dane would be devastated. But he would survive. *He was fine before me, and he'll be fine after me.* She couldn't think about that.

She sat on the floor of her tent, pulling her hands through her hair. As the only sacrifice, she would spend the night and the morning alone. The shaman had already said his prayers, and offered to sit with her overnight, but she shooed the young man away. Ardos in her mind was her only company, and he was enough.

"Aunt Eryn?"

A tiny voice came from the back of the tent. Eryn scurried over and lifted the bottom of the heavy fabric. Filina crawled through on her belly, wriggling up to throw her arms around Eryn's legs.

"Why? Why are you leaving?"

She'd only told her niece that she was leaving the clan, trusting in the chief's promise to keep the child away from the sacrifice tomorrow, which would take place in the middle of the open circle in the center of the camp.

"I have to leave, darling, but you won't be alone. You'll still have Uncle Dane, and Chief Calnan."

"And Ardos?"

Eryn's heart broke. Ardos would never stay with the clan when she was gone. She wished he could somehow choose Filina and heartbond with her, but the little she'd managed to glean from the parchment before it was taken confirmed that the ability to bond a dragon depended on the near-death experience of being envenomed by one and surviving—not at all guaranteed. She would not risk Filina's life. She was literally dying to save her.

She led her niece over to her herb corner, where all her healing flowers and roots were laid out. It was Nora's favorite place, smelling all the spices, helping Eryn organize and pack them.

"Come on and help me get all this put away, will you?"

They sat surrounded by botanicals, just as Eryn had once sat with Filina's mother and Godseye Clan's old caldera who taught them. She picked up a handful of bare roots. "This is sunroot, which is good for skin irritation and blisters." Filina took the roots and laid them on a piece of parchment, sniffling and wiping her nose on her sleeve. Eryn picked up a handful of dried yellow petals. "And this is mountain maid, which helps with hot flashes in women who are past childbearing…" Her words and mind ground to a halt.

Lord Baltenn, I'm a fool.

She remembered the rainbow-hued female dragons soaring over the vast fields of golden spring flowers. She remembered the herds of deer and goats fleeing before the bright-colored wings through those fields.

The deer eat the flowers—the flowers we call mountain maid. The dragons eat the deer.

Her hands shook as she held the dried petals.

It's the flowers. In an old woman losing her fertility, they make her feel like a younger woman again.

In an infertile dragon… Could it be that simple? Could a dragon's fertility come not from within her, but from whatever power the flower had over a human woman's breeding cycle? The dragons of the clan were spoiled, eating cattle that were grazed on flatland grass. No mountain maid for the cattle meant no mountain maid for the dragons.

She bolted up and rushed to the door of the tent. "Chief Calnan! I need Chief Calnan!"

The guards on each side of the doorway moved in to block her. One of them was Brinir, who gave a low chuckle. "I just bet you do. But he's given strict orders. Nobody is to go in or out of this tent and risk sullying the sacrifice." He looked her up and down. "Such a damned shame. Such a waste."

From above, a roar from Ardos sent him back a step. An answering roar from Chern, Brinir's dragon, was almost a challenge.

No, Ardos. Please don't risk yourself for me.

Eryn closed the tent flap before anyone could see Filina inside. She rushed back to her pack. How many mountain maid flowers would it take to bring the color to a dragon's scales? How fast would it happen?

She paused, thinking of their trip to the Tiezahal. Mountain maid grew along those slopes, and the dragons hunted their own prey on the journey. She'd noticed flashes of color in Ilst's scales, but thought it was just a reflection of the fire-light. Could it work?

There was no way her small packet of dried petals would be enough. And no way anyone was likely to listen to a con-demned eindon on her way to be sacrificed.

Filina picked up the flowers. "They're pretty. We used to pick them in the hills. You and me and mommy."

Yes, they did, back before the world turned upside down. *Can I really ask this of her? She's just a child. But small. And light.*

"Filina, are you the bravest girl that ever lived under the wide blue sky?"

The little girl smiled. "I'm the bravest girl ever."

"Do you trust me and Ardos?"

"Forever I do."

Could she ask this? Could she possibly take this risk?

She conferred with Ardos in her mind. *You're the strongest dragon in the clan. Ardos, can you carry Filina to the hills and keep her safe in the darkness?*

The answer was immediate. *Of course I can.*

Ardos, my beloved, do you trust me?

His answer was a wave of love, with a glimmer of hope overriding his despair.

She pressed a flower into Filina's hand. "Tonight, you're going to have a hero's adventure. Do you think you can find these flowers in just the moonlight? Can you pick a whole basket full of them if Ardos helps you?"

A nod.

"And to do that, will you let Ardos carry you as he flies? It's a long way, and it will be scary."

Her eyes shot open. "Fly with Ardos! He would carry me?" Filina bolted to her feet and grabbed a large basket. "Can I go right now?"

Eryn's eyes filled with tears. She hugged Filina too tightly, thanking Baltenn for bringing the child back into her life. "You have to sneak out the back, and you can't let anyone see you. Ardos will keep you safe, but you have to hurry."

Filina nodded. "If I get you a basket of flowers, will you stay and not go?"

Eryn sighed, letting her tears fall. "I hope so, darling. I hope so."

Filina hugged her again and scuttled out of the tent, crawling under the fabric in the back.

Keep her safe, Ardos. Bring her home to me.

She watched through his eyes as he gently held the child in his claws and launched them into the night sky.

Chapter 45

The outer tents at the camp were deserted when Dane and the young warriors arrived, weary from riding all night. They released their horses to graze, and wove their way through the small, battered tents of the eindon and lower classes, seeing no one. A murmur of noise told Dane that there was a large group of people ahead. His travel pack was hot on his back in the morning sun as he traversed the labyrinth of dwellings, pushing toward the huge open circle in the center of the camp.

It was bursting with people. He strained to see what was happening in the middle, but the crush of the clan kept him away. His own tent was one of the privileged that ringed the open circle, and he edged his way around the crowd to drop off his pack and see what was going on.

A small figure flashed past him, running from behind his tent around the edge of the circle. He recognized Filina's yellow curls, but the child didn't stop to greet him.

Two dragonsworn met him at the door to his tent.

"You can't go in there right now."

Dane scowled, feeling gritty dust in his eyes. "It's my tent. I'll go in if I want to."

The two men looked at each other. "Chief Calnan said no one goes in or out until it's time. He didn't make an exception for you."

The pack slid from Dane's shoulders and thumped on the ground. "I've been riding all night. I need a wash and a meal, and to know what in Baltenn's name is going on here. Step aside and let me in, or you'll regret it from the ground."

A tap on his shoulder made him whirl around. His father stood there, eyes downcast.

"Son, come with me." He nodded to the two drag-onsworn. "You can push his pack inside the tent, but do not enter."

This can't be anything good. A roar from Ardos made him crane his neck upwards.

"Why is Ardos raging? Is Eryn all right? What's going on here?"

Chief Calnan led him around to the side of the tent where it was a little quieter. "Dane, there's no good way to say this." He told Dane about the translation, and how Eryn had volunteered to take Filina's place as the mountain maiden sacrifice.

Dane's vision went red. "This is not happening. She translated it wrong. This is madness, and I won't allow it." His hand rested on the hilt of his sword.

"Easy, son," Chief Calnan murmured. "I hoped it would be over by the time you got back. It would have been easier for you."

"Easier? To come home from scouting and find that the love of my life has been eaten by a dragon?" His hand quivered on his sword, itching to lash out, strike, and kill. Didn't matter whom. Any target would do.

"Yes, easier. You need to go away, son. Ride out a ways so you don't see or hear anything. Take Ilst hunting far afield, and don't come back until after the noon sun. You can't help her, but you can make it a lot worse for her if she has to see you suffer as well." He glanced up at the sky. "Go now. I command it."

"I will not. I will stand at her side, and you will have to kill me to keep me away." He almost wished someone would try.

Eryn. Oh, Eryn, what were you thinking?

She would do anything for the child, came Ilst's voice clearly in his head. *Or for you.*

The chief nodded. "If you must. I'm sorry, Dane. I wish there was another way."

"When?"

"Noon." His father checked the sky. "I'm heading to the center now. Come with me if you insist on being part of this."

"I need to see her right now."

The chief shook his head. "You cannot. The shaman has said she must be alone until she comes to be sacrificed. We have no Stone of Baltenn here, but he had the woodcarvers make a stand and carve the runes." He placed both hands on Dane's shoulders. "It's for the good of the clan. If it works, we will have a way to breed our own dragons. Ilst could lay her own eggs. We will never have to risk the wild dragons again."

Hang the clan. Hang everything until it was rotted and dead. Nothing mattered without Eryn.

I'm still here.

"Yes, Ilst," he whispered. "You're all that's holding me together."

With a backward look at his tent, he followed his father up to the hastily built circle in the middle of the cleared field. The crowd parted to let them pass, and dragonsworn moved in to keep them parted, leaving an empty path from the tent to the wooden structure. It was wide and round, raised a foot off the ground, with runes around the edges. In the center was a heavy metal ring with a coil of rope next to it.

Dane joined his father on the platform, every muscle rock solid, his eyes on the tent.

The shaman arrived and opened it, and Eryn preceded him through the flap. Every voice in the crowd went quiet.

She looked like a goddess. She had dressed in a plain cream-colored tunic and pants, and her hair was in a hundred tiny braids, each festooned with fresh yellow flowers braided in. Her whole head was wreathed in golden blooms.

As she passed, eindon on each side reached out to touch her. She glided slowly up the path, taking the hands of every person that wanted to make contact. But her eyes were forward, locked on Dane's. She did not look frightened, but had the look of resolve she got when she was working with her herbs.

Dane offered her a hand to step onto the platform.

"Thank Baltenn you came back. You have to do this for me, Dane," she whispered. "Ilst. It has to be Ilst that eats, and you have to do exactly what I say. Cut off each braid one at a time and make her eat them first. Do it very slowly and make sure she gets every flower…"

Chief Calnan cut them off, pushing them gently apart.

"Dane," Eryn said to the chief. "I will only allow Dane to do the sacrifice. I am his eindon, and it is his responsibility."

The chief looked to his son. "Will you do this? Dane Rowe, Kind and Honorable, will you make this sacrifice of your eindon to your dragon?"

How can I possibly do this? But she asked him, and the look in her eyes was a plea.

"I will."

He turned to Eryn. "And Eryn Rowe, Wise and Adored, will you give yourself willingly for the good of the clan, that we may prosper, and let none forget your name and the gift you have brought us?"

She nodded, eyes on Dane. "I will."

"Then let it be done."

Ilst, come down here. We need you.

The crowd parted as Ilst left the formation of dragons flying overhead and landed right in front of the platform. The shaman tied Eryn's hands behind her, and she knelt over the ring. He secured her to it, chanted a few words, and stepped away to continue his chanting from a safe distance.

Dane approached her.

"The hair," she whispered. "The flowers. Slowly."

Why would she want to prolong the agony? But it was her final request. *Baltenn, give me your strength.* But his faith in the god was shattered. What kind of god would ask this of him? *We've been doing it for generations. This is the first time it's been someone you cared about.*

His throat closed as he pulled out his knife and made the first cut, a long braid from the back of her neck.

Ilst, you have to eat it all. We have to do it braid by braid.

He handed the braid to Ilst, who swallowed it whole.

Another braid, another swallow.

Dane's eyes filled with tears. Eryn raised her head between each braid, peering at Ilst. She was murmuring under her breath. "Come on, Ilst. Show us your colors."

Another braid, and another.

The crowd was growing restless, muttering. This must be unbearable for the eindon at the back, to see their hope destroyed like this.

"Hurry it up!" Brinir's voice shouted over the crowd. "Get to the blood!"

From the back of the circle, the muttering grew louder.

Another braid.

Dane looked at Ilst, swallowing each braid whole. Light refracted through the prism of his tears, making her pale cream color shine in pale rainbow colors around the ridges of her eyes.

Eryn's face lit up. "It's working. More. Give her more!"

He cut another braid, wiping his eyes on the back of his hand. "What's working?"

She was almost beaming. "The flowers! Dane, it's the flowers!" There were tears in her eyes as she tore her gaze away from Ilst's face. "Remember the wild dragons!"

She's gone mad. And who wouldn't?

But he did remember the wild dragons, shining like rainbows, sitting on their nests full of eggs. The same colors that were starting to appear on the unscaled skin around Ilst's eyes.

He cut another braid. The back of Eryn's head was all shorn now, nearly a third of her hair close-cropped from his knife.

"The flowers make the colors?" he whispered.

"Yes! And the colors show a dragon is fertile!"

He sheathed the knife and grabbed a handful of Eryn's braids, ripping out just the golden flowers. "Ilst, eat the flowers. Don't miss a petal."

Handful by handful, he pulled the flowers from Eryn's hair, stuffing them into Ilst's waiting jaws.

From above, Ardos roared. The crowd scattered as he winged in to land behind Eryn, still tied and kneeling on the platform.

Dane summoned his father. "Look at Ilst! Look at the colors!"

The chief smiled. "It's working. The sacrifice is working."

"It's not my hair," Eryn said, voice raised above the rising murmuring of the crowd. "It's the flowers. Mountain maid is the flower. The wild dragons eat it, and ours don't. It was never a human sacrifice at all. The flowers make them fertile, and our dragons will breed if we get enough for all of them."

The skin around Ilst's eyes was positively glowing with red, blue, and violet. Her lips showed green and yellow.

"Ilst, you're so beautiful," Eryn said. "I wish you could see how beautiful you are."

Chief Calnan held up his hands to silence the crowd.

"Dragon Clan, hear my words. There will be no eindon sacrifice today. The flowers are the magic that will make our dragons breed. Eryn's sacrifice is unnecessary, and our clan is forever in her debt!"

A cheer started in the back of the circle, eindon thanking Baltenn for the chief's words.

"Nonsense!" Brinir's voice boomed over the cheering. "She ate the hair from her head. It's the eindon, not the flowers." He stormed onto the platform, hand on his sword.

"You dare to challenge your chief?" Calnan said.

"I dare to save my clan."

He drew his sword and raised it, aiming at Eryn's neck.

Dane kicked him backwards, sending him to the edge of the platform.

Brinir's eyes narrowed. "You would tell any lie to save this woman. But I will not let you ruin this chance to save our clan. You're a liar and a traitor, and you will die here with her."

He raised his sword and charged.

CHAPTER 46

Eryn lunged away from Brinir as he charged Dane. The rope securing her hands to the ring behind her held steady and she flopped to her side, rolling onto her shoulder.

Hold still. Ardos' breath was warm against the shorn back of her head.

She lay where she was as steel rang against steel, Dane and Brinir trading vicious blows just a few feet ahead of her. All around the raised circle the crowd was going wild, screaming and pushing forward. The rest of the dragonsworn formed a ring around the platform, trying to keep the clan at bay.

Are they cheering for Brinir, wanting my death? Or are they screaming for my life?

Hold still, Ardos repeated.

She felt his teeth pulling at the ropes around her wrists, but they were too tightly bound for him to slide a tooth between rope and flesh.

From across the platform, Ilst roared a challenge. She reared up, flapping her wings and launching herself at Brinir, who whirled around, shoving Dane between himself and the enraged dragon. Her brand-new colors shone bright in the sun. A red blur flashed past Eryn's vision as Chern, Brinir's huge male, slammed into Ilst, sending her flying.

"Ardos! Help Ilst!"

Her beloved's huge black head popped up from behind her, casting his shadow over her body where she still struggled against the ropes.

"Go! I'm fine!"

Eryn shut her eyes as Ardos flung himself into the sky, lowering his head to crash into Chern from behind. The huge red male careened forward, tumbling into a row of tents. Ardos dove down after him, and his rage filled Eryn's head. She bellowed a wordless scream.

"Eryn, don't move!"

A figure stood over her, sun at his back, eclipsing his features. He held a long knife aimed at her. The rage of Ardos erupted, and she kicked at the figure, pulling against the rope that still held her fixed to the platform. It was wet and ragged where Ardos had bitten it, but still held.

The figure darted around behind her, and with a pop, the rope let go. It still bound her hands together behind her back, but she bounced forward as it released from the ring. Strong hands pulled her to her feet.

"Come with me!"

Chief Calnan held her by the arm, knife still clutched in his hand. He tried to pull her from the platform where Dane and Brinir fought, but she stood her ground.

"I won't leave him. Cut me loose!"

She held still as the knife sawed between her wrists.

"You can't help him. He would be disgraced if you did." The chief's words were spoken directly into her ear, penetrating past the wild noise of the crowd all around. Her hands popped free, the wet rope falling to the ground. For a moment she stood still, rooted to the spot.

Chief Calnan still held her now free arm. The platform was ringed with dragonsworn, holding the line against the screaming crowd pushing in from all sides. Dane's back was facing her, the huge muscles of his shoulders shining with sweat as he blocked an overhead swing by Brinir. The bearded dragonsworn's face was a mask of hatred, spattered with blood, mouth open in a snarl.

Whose blood? Was Dane injured, or was Brinir?

If you go to him, you'll distract him. Distraction means death against a warrior like Brinir. Whether her thought or Ardos', it was true. She could do nothing but watch as the two men traded blows, steel ringing over the din of the crowd.

And above, another battle raged. Ardos and Chern tumbled through the sky, claws scrambling for purchase on each other's slick scales, teeth snapping at darting necks. Ilst circled them, swiping at Chern, but unable to get a clean strike. The dragons broke apart, wings beating the air to gain altitude before crashing together again.

Be careful, my loves. The thought was inane, and a crazed laugh escaped Eryn's lips at the absurdity of the words. Be careful, Ardos, battling in the sky against a dragon who wanted him dead. Be careful, Dane, fighting for his life and hers, just steps away.

With a grunt, Chief Calnan's grip on her arm relaxed and he crumpled to the ground behind her. A face appeared in the place he vacated, eyes shining with hatred.

"This is all your fault. You are not worthy to be eindon."

Rina held a knife, its blade dark with blood.

Eryn dared not glance down at Chief Calnan, struggling to rise at Rina's feet.

"You," Eryn replied, eyes never leaving Rina's, "are not worthy to be Dragon Clan. And you will never, ever be worthy of a dragon."

Rina lunged, a wild strike with the knife. Eryn leaped back, feeling the wind of the strike passing just in front of her face.

"Ardos should have been mine!" Rina screamed, slashing with the knife again.

Eryn jumped to the left, barely avoiding the blow. "Ardos wouldn't bond with you if you were the last human in the world. You have no honor."

Chief Calnan struggled to his feet and shoved Rina from behind. She fell to her knees, the knife clattering from her grip and sliding across the platform. In an instant, she was back on her feet. She threw herself at Eryn, crushing them both down on the hard wood.

The air whooshed out of Eryn's lungs, and a sharp pain zapped from the rib that had yet to fully heal. She raised her hands, arms in front of her face to block the blows that Rina rained down from above her. The larger woman held herself up on one arm, pinning Eryn's shoulder to the ground, punching her with the other arm.

"Dokkas! Dokkas!"

The word echoed around Eryn's head. The punches stopped, and she felt the weight of Rina ripped off her body.

The line of dragonsworn around the platform had collapsed under a crush of eindon surging in from the back of the clan crowded around it. Chains clanking against their runelocks, they flowed up onto the platform, dragging Rina off of Eryn.

With a final cry of rage, Rina disappeared under a flood of eindon, all chanting Eryn's name.

Chapter 47

Dane faced Brinir, swords between them. Both men were bloodied, drenched in sweat, and feeling no pain from the wounds they had traded.

Spit flew from Brinir's lips as he panted, eyes locked on Dane's. "You betray your clan. You are not worthy of your dragon." He lunged at Dane, who parried the blow, stepping to the side.

You're slowing down. Dane's muscles strained, exhaustion taking its toll on his swing.

"I am saving my clan. It's you who betrays us."

Dane swung at Brinir, a blow that would have shattered any other man's arm. Brinir blocked it, swords sparking in the sun.

Sweat dripped into Dane's eyes. Both men panted, circling each other on the platform. The roars of dragons from overhead blended with the noise of the crowd all around them, but no one approached the fighting men.

A wall of people erupted over the platform's edge behind Brinir. They flooded past Dane's vision, carrying someone off the edge. In their wake, Eryn was helped to her feet by several other eindon. Her face was bloody and she winced as she stood, but she smiled in the brief moment their eyes met.

Brinir pounced on his moment of inattention, swinging at Dane's neck. Dane barely got his sword in the path of the oncoming blow, which knocked him hard to the side. He stumbled, and Brinir pressed in, sword raised for a killing strike. He paused, grinning through bloody teeth.

"Don't worry," he taunted. "I'll take good care of your eindon when you're dead." He spat red onto the platform. "By sundown, she won't be a maiden anymore. By fall, she'll beg to be one of the hundred we'll sacrifice to the wild ones."

Brinir struck down with his sword.

Every ounce of rage welled up in Dane, flowing through his back and down his shoulders, through his wrists and into the sword in his hands. He knocked the blow aside, springing upwards. In a flash, his sword bit downward, hacking straight into Brinir's side just below his ribcage.

Dane pulled his sword free. Brinir tried to raise his own, but his arm didn't cooperate. He looked down to see his own guts spilling from the deep wound in his side. The sword fell from his hands, and he dropped to his knees in a pool of his own blood.

Dane towered over the panting man who grew paler with each breath.

"You will never touch Eryn. You will never dirty our clan's name with your filth." He crouched in front of Brinir, smelling the hot metal stench of the blood bubbling out of Brinir's mouth. "And your body will be left for the scavengers. You will never join the immortal clan of Baltenn. Your name will be forgotten forever."

The light left Brinir's eyes, and he flopped forward at Dane's feet.

A great roar split the air, quieting the riot from the crowd all around them. Dane looked up to see Chern break away from Ardos in the sky. Everyone around the platform backed away as the giant red dragon landed, crouching over the body of his dead dragonsworn.

Narrowed black eyes turned toward Dane, who still held the bloody sword.

"You're free, Chern. You are bound to Brinir's hatred and anger no longer." Dane stood tall in front of the dragon.

Chern shook for a moment, tremors radiating down his body. He bled from wounds all over his neck, where scales were missing. His claws were bloody as well, along with his teeth. A brief mental tap from Ilst assured Dane that she was all right.

Ardos.

Before Dane could complete the thought, Chern raised his head, roaring straight up to the sky. He sprang upward, fanning the air with battered wings. In moments, he was gone, soaring over the distant fields without a backward glance.

Arms crushed around Dane's waist, and he winced at the pressure, suddenly aware of every wound he sustained in the fight. He looked down to see Eryn wrapped around him, face buried in his chest. Her hair stuck up from the remaining braids, golden flowers crushed and dangling. When she looked up at him, her lip was split, and her left eye already bruised, heading for purple and swelling shut.

She had never looked more beautiful.

He dropped his sword and took her in his arms, lips meeting hers gently. But her kiss was fierce, and though it must be painful, she crushed her lips into his, hands tangling in his hair. For a long moment, nothing else existed beyond the heat of their bodies, pressed together in the middle of chaos.

"Healer, we need you."

Eryn broke the kiss at the voice behind her. A dragonsworn stood there, eyes not meeting Dane's.

"What is it?" Dane asked. "Get Ragna. She's the clan's healer." *And leave Eryn to me, just this once.*

"He's asking for Eryn."

The crowd milled around the platform, still murmuring in their excitement, but no longer surging against the dragonsworn that circled it. Dane followed Eryn and the man, heart sinking as he recognized the tent they were heading for.

"My father? What happened?"

Eryn took his hand. "Rina stabbed him. They took him away before I could get to him."

The rage boiled back up through Dane. "Where is she? I'll kill her myself."

A squeeze of his hand. "She's dead. She attacked me as well, and the clan's eindon rose up. Nothing could have held them back. They saved my life."

The chief's tent was cool inside. Chief Calnan sat on his wooden throne, waving away the dragonsworn that surrounded him.

"Eryn, you're here. Patch this up and get me out there. We have to end all of this now." He turned with a grunt to reveal a large stab wound just under his ribs in the back.

Eryn rushed forward. Someone had already brought her healer's pack from their tent, and as she went to work on the wound, Dane opened his mind to Ilst.

"Are you all right? Completely all right?"

Through their bond, he felt her aches and pains. But she was flying overhead, keeping an eye on the restless crowd below. *I'm fine. Better than you.*

His own pains were starting to scream at him, but there would be time later for his own wounds.

"Ardos? Is he injured?"

But even as he asked, he knew the black dragon must be all right. Eryn would not be functional if Ardos wasn't okay.

He fought. He bleeds. He will recover.

Eryn wrapped clean bandages around Calnan's torso. At the back of the tent, guarded by a dragonsworn and two eindon, Dane's little sister and Filina strained to see what was going on. Dane hurried over to give each girl a quick hug.

"Everything's okay. You girls just stay here and do what you're told." He turned back to his father, who pushed up on the arms of his chair, coming to an unsteady stand.

"You have to rest," Eryn began, but he cut her off.

"I will," he promised. "And you will care for me until I'm well. But our people need us right now." He raised his eyes to Dane. "All of us. Help me, son."

Despite their protests, the chief insisted, and they flanked him on each side. He straightened up as they reached the tent flap and walked unaided into the sun. The crowd parted as the three of them approached the platform. Ilst, Ardos, and Dalna, the chief's big female dragon, all landed in the clearing, making a ring around the platform. Eryn's eyes unfocused for a moment, and she smiled. *Yes, Ardos must be all right.*

From the middle of the platform, Chief Calnan addressed his people.

"Dragon Clan, hear my words. We have been given a gift this day. Eryn Rowe, Wise and Adored, has offered her life for our future. That gift is not needed. The flowers known as Mountain Maiden are what will make our dragons fertile, providing eggs for our dragonsworn forever."

A voice called out from the crowd. "What if it's not the flowers? What if it was her hair?"

The rest of the crowd murmured, and voices of anger came from the group of eindon who stood defiantly at the front.

Eryn scowled. "You can take every hair from my head and feed it to any dragon you want," she muttered. "Without the flowers, it won't do anything." She glanced over at Dane. "And I don't intend to qualify as maiden for long." A crimson blush bloomed in her cheeks.

"How long?" Dane whispered, feeling the same heat in his own face.

She smiled. "As soon as this fiasco is over?"

Chief Calnan gave them a stern look but punctuated it with a wink. He addressed the people again. "We must prove it."

Eryn sighed, and pulled the cords holding her braids, dropping them to the ground. She untangled the flowers from her hair, handing each one to the chief, careful to make sure not a single golden strand clung to the petals. The underside where Dane had cut the braids away revealed her pale scalp, long hair from the top hanging over it.

"I like the new hairstyle," Dane murmured. "By tomorrow morning, every woman in the clan will have shaved the back of her head."

The chief fed the flowers to his dragon, one by one. Dalna dropped her head, taking them gently from his hands.

Across the platform, Ilst rumbled. Her colors were even brighter, spreading onto the scales of her neck and pulsing through her wings. Her body was still cream colored, but the spines of her back were veined with blue and purple.

Never before had a dragon's meal been watched by so many. Flower by flower, Dalna chewed and swallowed.

The color started in the ridges above her eyes, a glow of pink that blossomed to orange as it crept around her cheeks.

Ilst rumbled again.

"Don't be jealous, my love," Dane murmured to his dragon. "You were first. And you're still the most beautiful by far."

Dalna raised her head, chewing the last flower. Her lips were rippled in green and blue, and her brown wings were already shining red-gold in the sun. A cheer rose from the crowd.

Chief Calnan raised his arms for silence.

"Dragon Clan, you have witnessed a miracle. A great change has come to our clan, and our dragons will rule the skies forever!"

The cheer erupted, but the chief wasn't finished.

"In the days of our fathers from ages past, our eindon have long been the sacrifice, given to the wild dragons in exchange for the eggs that we cherished. That need is no more." He nodded to his shaman, who approached them with a heavy metal tool in his hands.

"From this day forward," the chief proclaimed, "Dragon Clan eindon are free. You may return to your former clans or remain with us as full members. You belong to no one. Your lives are your own."

The shaman lifted the tool, and Eryn raised her chin. With a snap of the jaws, her eindon chain fell to the platform, Dane's runelock broken into pieces at her feet.

She stepped forward. "I am Eryn Rowe, Wise and Adored, heartbound to Ardos, and free woman of Dragon Clan!"

The screaming of the crowd faded to a distant thunder as she turned to Dane, tears shining in her eyes. Dragons roared and his father beamed, but there was nothing in Dane's site but Eryn as she stepped into his arms and met his lips with the kiss that changed a clan forever.

CHAPTER 48

Eryn left the Chief's tent as the sun sank over the prairie. The sky glowed gold and red, fading to blue and purple. Torches burned all around, and the smell of cooking meat heralded a feast.

His wound was deep, but the man was strong. He would listen to her. She had packed it with honey and started him on a regime of herbs steeped in boiling water. The next few days would not be easy for him, but unlike his predecessor, this chief would survive.

Filina was staying with Dane's siblings tonight. She begged all afternoon for another flight with Ardos, but he was injured from the battle with Chern, and it would have to wait. The girl would be devastated when she got too heavy for him to carry, but her role in the miracle would never be forgotten, and she was the most popular girl in the camp right now, as the girl who flew with dragons.

The free eindon are calling you a new name. Ardos was having his own feast out in the field, but his voice was clear in her head as she breathed in the clean night air.

"What do they call me?"

"Danska."

She'd been steeped in the old language for days. She knew what the word meant.

"I am no queen. The clan has no queen."

Ardos chuckled. *In time, it will not mean queen of the clan. I suspect in a hundred years, the shaman of Lord Baltenn will mention a daughter, a queen to rule with him in the afterlife.*

She chilled at the heresy. "I am no god."

You are to the eindon.

The walk back to Dane's tent—their tent now— took ages. Former eindon, now freed of their chains, wanted to touch her clothing, to weep at her feet.

Told you.

She had feared the reaction of the rest of the clan, but the dragonsworn with female dragons were all possessed by the happiness of their dragons, who had all flown off toward the nearest foothills to gorge on mountain maid flowers, forgoing the prey that ate it and going straight for the blooms themselves. Ilst, who had told Dane if she never had to eat hair again it would still be too soon, was among them, and Ardos was feeding in her absence.

There will be fights among the males when they return.

Eryn took in a breath. "You are injured. You cannot fight again until you are healed."

He chuckled again. "I will not fight. I need only one female, and she has already chosen me as her mate. Given our bonds, we could both have no others."

Chilly night air prickled Eryn's skin, warm at the thought. By this time next year, Ilst and Ardos would be the proud parents of a newly hatched dragon. And it would be free to bond with whomever it chose. The Dance of Dragons would persist, to open the minds of the hopefuls with the gift of Baltenn. But the dragons would choose on their own. Perhaps some would not bond to clan warriors but fly away to join the wild dragons. Ardos was certain most would stay and heartbond, as long as the right candidates were available.

She reached their tent and ducked inside. A fire crackled in the center, and Dane looked up from where he knelt on the far side.

"I didn't have mountain maid. The dragons ate it all." He grinned. "But I thought these would do."

Where had he gotten so many flowers? The floor of the tent was covered in blooms. He'd carefully picked the thorns off the ones that grew on the prickly vines. And as she looked closer, she realized that a few of them were toxic. She kicked those away from the fire with a smile. "They're perfect."

There was a meal waiting on the small table, but she stepped past it, hungry for the taste of his lips.

He stepped back as she approached, and her hand fluttered to her face. *I must look hideous.* Her eye was swollen and bruised, and her hair was prickly. But Dane was right, and she'd seen versions of the shaved-back-braided look on several women of the clan already.

"I'm sorry," she said. "I look such a mess."

His eyes warmed. "You are the most beautiful creature I've ever seen. I just wanted to look at you in the firelight."

She smiled. "You're only saying that because Ilst is too far away to hear you."

A tiny shrug. "Well, you're not rainbow colored. But in a day or two that bruise will be very colorful, so..."

"Hmm," she replied. "I'll be colorful just like Ilst and the wild female dragons?" She took a step forward.

"You will." His voice was husky.

She dropped her pack and unbelted her tunic. "I have a lot more bruises. Maybe they'll turn colors, too."

He pulled the shirt from his body, revealing a wide chest crossed with new stitches, tied with her delicate knots. "You know what rainbow colors mean?"

She giggled. "That this time next year, I'll lay a dragon egg?"

His hands touched her waist, and she raised her arms as he pulled the tunic over her head. His pupils dilated as he looked at her bare skin, and she fought the urge to cover herself. "Not a dragon egg," he murmured. "But maybe a future dragonsworn."

The stitches on his chest tickled her skin as she stepped into his arms. Her hands traced their way gently up his ribs, up over his shoulders, and down his arms. His gentle touch caressed her bare back, fingers sliding up her neck to caress the shaved undercut of her hair.

His lips tasted just like she remembered from the first time they kissed. Spiced and warm. His tongue was soft, she met it with her own, heat flowing down from her lips to her neck, spreading across her breasts where they pressed into his bare chest.

He broke the kiss and laid his forehead against hers. "You don't belong to me anymore, Eryn. I have no claim to you. You're free dragonsworn."

She raised a finger to his lips, silencing him.

"I am Eryn Rowe, remember? I am no eindon. But I belong to you as long as you'll have me."

"And I belong to you forever."

He guided her to the flower-strewn bedroll and high above in the night sky over the torches, Ardos roared his joy as his maid of the mountains heartbonded to her dragonsworn.

***

Continue reading for an excerpt from Book 3
Crystal of Memory

BOOKS BY ALLISON ROOK

Stones of the Seven:

Stone of War
Dance of Dragons
Crystal of Memory

STONES OF THE SEVEN BOOK 3

CRYSTAL OF MEMORY

ALLISON ROOK

Chapter 1

Ashryn stood behind her cousin Carisa, both of them facing the mirror. It was Carisa's favorite luxury, the largest Ashryn had ever seen when she came to be fostered at her uncle's barony. She brushed Carisa's long red hair, peering over the seated girl's head.

"Maybe he'll be kind and handsome." Her fingers started the first of many plaits that would wind around Carisa's head for tonight's banquet.

"Maybe he'll be an impossible boor, and who cares if he's handsome?" Carisa scowled. "What does handsome matter in a husband I don't want?"

Ashryn sighed. She had learned so much since coming here four years ago as a girl of sixteen, more at home with twigs and leaves in her own brown hair than the elegant braids and jeweled combs Carisa favored. Hairstyles were one thing. Dresses were another. And the kind of arranged marriage that the daughter of a baron was expected to submit to— well, that was something she had never considered, and was glad her own father had never suggested. Better Carisa than her. Not that any men were clamoring for the half-elf niece of a city baron, but still.

"All we can do is hope for the best." She started another braid, gentle fingers in her beloved cousin's hair. "Your father said it's a good match. He's the head of the Duke's private guard, whatever that is. So at least you know he's trustworthy."

Carisa huffed. "I know he's good with a sword, and no more than that."

Their eyes met briefly in the mirror, as the unintended double entendre hit them both. Carisa covered her mouth for a delicate giggle, and Ashryn laughed out loud.

"There are worse things than a husband who's good with his sword." Ashryn waggled her eyebrows.

Carisa's personal maid bustled in carrying a mass of emerald fabric over her arms. Ashryn set the hairbrush on the dresser and helped Pima lay the heavy gown on Carisa's bed. The bodice was covered in a criss-cross pattern of tiny seed pearls, and the round, high neck was bordered in white lace. It had a train that would stretch out behind Carisa when she walked, and again, Ashryn thanked the gods that it was her cousin's proposal feast tonight, and not her own.

I'd trip over the train and sweat to death under the lace. She'd been practicing walking in long dresses so she didn't embarrass her foster family for this occasion, but was still far more at home in the brown suede trousers and soft boots she'd brought from home.

The thought gave her heart a squeeze. If her mother were still alive, Ashryn would never have had to come here and learn to pretend to be a lady. Merith Brinell was a full-blooded elf, and only her love for Ashryn's father had pulled her from the forest of her people. She had taught their only child how to move silently through the trees, how to climb, and shoot a bow, and throw a knife. There was no need for gowns and elaborate hairstyles with Mother. They were far too busy learning real skills. But Mother was gone now, and despite his love for both his wife and his half-breed daughter, Father thought it best that elven ways be put aside. So Ashryn came to the barony of her father's brother, to foster with the baron's youngest daughter and learn the skills that Carisa was born to.

Rain pelted the windows as they both looked at the dress.

Even Ashryn had to admit that the emerald gown was gorgeous. "It will set off your eyes so perfectly," she mused, running a hand down the soft fabric. *And weigh a ton, and squeeze your ribs so you can't breathe…*

"Yes," Carisa replied with a scowl. "I'll be a pretty little lamb on my way to slaughter."

Pima tutted, smoothing the dress on the bed. "We knew this day would come," she said quietly. "You have your duty, just like I have mine. And I'll be here when it's over."

Over? She meant the proposal dinner, not the marriage. Though Pima's devotion might well outlast a marriage to a guard captain. The duchy was wealthy, and a duke's guard must be willing to sacrifice himself for his lord. Maybe Carisa would be free of her groom in less time than she dared to hope.

Together, Pima and Ashryn finished Carisa's hair, adorning it with the emerald-studded comb that had arrived that morning, a gift from the duke himself. Despite her grumbling, Carisa's eyes had lit up when she realized the gems were real. They helped her into the heavy green gown and stood back to admire their work.

"You look spectacular," Ashryn said, and meant it honestly. Carisa filled out the top of a gown like Ashryn never would.

Carisa ran her fingernail over the beads on the bodice. "It's the most expensive dress I've ever owned. The duke of Stonebridge must really like this guy to help my father pay for all this."

The duke was helping pay? Ashryn had wondered where all the extravagance was coming from. The barony wasn't poor by any means, but this festivity far outstripped the wedding of Carisa's older sister a few years prior.

"You need to get ready too," Carisa said, and Ashryn nodded. "Pima, will you do her hair?"

She knows I'm hopeless with my own. Ashryn appreciated the help. She didn't want to embarrass her cousin on her big day.

Pima's fingers made quick work of a simple updo, and Ashryn peered into the mirror. She favored her mother, with the small, flat nose and wide eyes of her people. The hairstyle covered her tapered eartips, but Pima didn't mean it as an insult. Ashryn smiled up at her cousin's maid, just a few years her senior but polished in ways Ashryn would never accomplish. "Thanks, Pima. It looks perfect."

Carisa stood at her open wardrobe, pushing her own gowns aside, one after the other. "I think you should wear the blue one," she said, holding out the skirt of a dark-sea colored dress. "It will match your eyes. You can wear my sapphire bracelet with it." The sapphires weren't real, but they sparkled just the same.

"Sure. Whatever you like." Ashryn would support her cousin on this difficult night. She would wear a jester's costume if it made Carisa happy.

Pima helped her into the dress, lacing up the back until Ashryn couldn't draw a full breath. The gown was too long and dragged the ground, but no one would be outside tonight for it to get dirty. The great hall was decked with spring flowers, and the guests would already be arriving downstairs for the feast.

Tonight, Carisa would meet her groom, the captain of the duke's guard that her father had secured to be her husband. Everyone agreed it would be a good match. Carisa, with Pima in tow, would move to the duke's residence where she would be welcomed as an attendant to the duchess. It was an honor for the third daughter of a baron to enter a royal household, and any girl would be thrilled with such an ascent in status. But Carisa's eyes were full of tears when Ashryn stepped into the high heeled shoes that would keep most of her dress off the floor.

Ashryn wobbled over to her cousin and wrapped her arms around the girl, to the limit of the tightly laced dress. "Hey, it won't be that bad. Pima will be with you. And I'll come visit." She choked down the lump in her own throat. As much as she loathed the unstable shoes and the sweltering gowns, losing Carisa was a knife in her gut. *Don't say things like knife in the gut. Ladies don't talk about knives.* Tonight of all nights, she would try to remember all the things ladies didn't talk about.

A knock sounded at Carisa's door, and Pima hurried over to answer it. She spoke to someone, then shut the door and turned back, her own eyes full of tears as well. "It's time. The groom has arrived."

Tonight was the proposal ceremony, where the groom would formally request the bride's hand in marriage. Tradition required her to consider his proposal overnight, then respond in the morning in writing. The paper and quill were already set on Carisa's writing desk, as it was all a formality. Tomorrow night she and the man would become husband and wife, and Ashryn's best friend of the last four years would be whisked away to the duke's palace, leaving her here until… she wasn't honestly sure. Without Carisa, it hardly mattered.

As Carisa's first lady—Ashryn still giggled at the term— she was expected to precede her cousin into the great hall. With one final look, and a wipe of both of their cheeks, she left the safety of Carisa's room and tottered down the corridor.

Don't fall, don't fall, don't fall.

She paused at the top of the staircase. High heels and a long dress plus stairs could equal disaster.

You can do this. For Carisa.

With a hand clutching the banister, she took one small step at a time, planting her feet in the impossible shoes one by one. At the bottom she paused, taking as deep a breath as the dark blue gown allowed. Voices ahead led her to the entrance of the great hall. She heard her name announced.

"Lady Ashryn Brinell, daughter of Edwin and Merith Brinell, first lady to the intended bride."

She stepped forward into the hall.

Tables lined the wood-paneled space, each overflowing with fresh flowers in yellow earthenware vases. More flowers festooned the walls, cascading from the lit sconces. As Carisa's first lady, she would have to walk down the center aisle between the tables and take her place at the front of the hall where Carisa's father the baron would be waiting with the groom.

You can do this. Don't trip.

She held up the front of the gown just like Carisa and Pima had taught her. *Small steps. Shoulders back. Eyes forward. Smile.*

At the end of the aisle, the baron nodded encouragement. *Good old uncle Kerwin.*

And next to him stood a man in the maroon livery of Duke Domisor of Stonebridge. Broad shoulders in tunic embroidered with the duke's family crest. Soft brown hair that just curled over his ears and a close-trimmed beard. He wore a sword at his hip, a small ceremonial weapon in a black leather sheath.

He turned to look up the aisle, and Ashryn's heart flip-flopped in her chest.

Carisa's intended groom was the most attractive man Ashryn had ever seen.

***

For more information about Allison Rook's works, check out her website at <u>allisonrookromance.com.</u>